HARMONY'S Invasion

-THE WATER DWELLER KINGDOM-

TANYA STEVERDING

Harmony's Invasion

THE WATER DWELLING KINGDOM

TANYA STEVERDING

HARMONY'S INVASION

Content Trigger Warning

This Book is intended for adults only. Sensitive Readers may find content offensive. Please be mindful of your mental health. Read at your own discretion.

This book contains mature themes that may be triggering or distressing to some readers. It includes:

- **Graphic violence and war-related trauma**

- **Explicit sexual content, including BDSM elements**

- **Depictions of abduction and captivity**

- **Emotional distress, loss, and grief**

- **Alien and supernatural warfare**

- **Magical pregnancy and childbirth**

- **Themes of divine power, revenge, and cosmic destruction**

Reader discretion is strongly advised. This story is intended for a mature audience (18+).

Please take care of yourself while reading.

Contents

This Book is dedicated to all my readers.

With love, thank you for taking the journey of the Harmony series.

May magic and love follow you wherever you go.

Happy reading.

Blessings, Author Tanya Steverding

Chapter One: Last Moments On Earth

-Maddy-

My heartbeat thrummed in my ears as my nerves caused my anxiety to rise. Can I do this? Can I take this leap? I fiddled with the ring in my hand. I had borrowed my brother's boat and planned this romantic night. Finally, I was going to tell my best friend Billie how I truly felt. Will she feel the same? Or will this ruin everything between us?

I looked at Billie, her dark curly hair blowing in the breeze, the red glow of the sunset making her natural beauty radiate with wonder.

Damn, I loved her. "Maddy, this trip was so worth it!" Billie beamed, her dark eyes reflecting the golden ripples of sunset across the sea. A whale's tail breached the water, slicing through the air like a final salute to the day. It was the kind of moment that demanded silence.

We just sat there soaking in the magic. The moment was perfect in every way. I looked at her, lit by the fire of the dying sun. My Billie. Her laugh, warmth, and the gentle curve of her belly eight months along. Still, all I could think about was how much I loved her.

"You okay?" she asked, her voice pulling me back.

"You look pale." She shoved a water bottle in my face and started rummaging in her bag. I took a quick gulp to buy a second of calm.

"I'm not seasick," I said, forcing a laugh. "Just nervous."

"About what?" she asked, eyes sharp.

"Maddy, you know you can tell me anything."

That's just it, I wasn't sure I could. "Found it!" she said, holding up a pack of Dramamine.

"If it's not motion sickness, what is it?" she asked with a look of concern.

"I planned this trip to tell you something," I said carefully. "But maybe now isn't the best time." She caught my hand and pulled me down beside her onto the little nest of pillows I'd made.

"Maddy, tell me." Her smile was kind, almost too kind.

I inhaled slowly and finally uttered the words. "I love you and not just as a friend. I'm in love with you, Billie." Her eyes widened. "Maddy, I am..."

Before she could say another word. BOOM. The sailboat jerked violently sideways, sending the world into chaos. I was airborne and then I was underwater; the water was cold and sharp like a thousand knives. My boots and sweatshirt dragged me down. A flash of purple light exploded beneath me. I kicked hard and surfaced, gasping for air.

"Billie!" I screamed, coughing up seawater. "Billie!" The stern of the boat was gone, vanishing beneath the churning waves.

"No, no, no." In a panic, I spun around in the water.

"Billie! Where are you?!"

Pure terror seized my heart. Billie is pregnant, was she okay? What the hell just happened? I didn't know what to do. Frantically, I back-stroked to the surface, my clothes trying to pull me down to the depths. As I watched the bow of the boat sink underwater, I didn't see Billie anywhere.

"Billie!" I screamed just before a wave hit, pulling me underwater again.

Suddenly, something cold latched onto my ankle and yanked me further down, dragging me away from the air I so badly needed. There was no time to react.

A strong, unyielding arm encircled my waist in a firm grasp. "Stop struggling, I'm trying to save you both," a deep voice echoed inside my head.

What the hell? I should be taking seawater into my lungs and drowning. However, I was breathing underwater. Then I felt her hand.

"Billie!" I shouted, my voice muted in the dark. "Are you okay? The baby?"

"I'm not hurt," she said, dazed. "I'm actually warm." What is happening?"

"I have no idea." I reached for her again as if touching her would tether me to reality.

"We're alive, that's all that matters."

"Neither of you will be harmed." the voice in my head said again. "I vow it."

"You heard that, right?" Billie asked.

"Loud and clear."

"You two act like you've never seen a water dweller before." the voice chuckled.

I blinked and looked down. His lower body shimmered in the dark water and I could just barely make out he had fins. He did not have legs.

"Billie," I whispered. "He's a merman."

"No way, are you sure?"

"Touch his, uh, fin." She did. "Holy shit."

"My magic is fading. The oxygen in this bubble won't last. If magic worked fully here, I could have encased you both in a larger sphere of oxygen, but I need to surface soon."

"You're off the coast of California," I said, trying to be helpful.

"Earth, of course. The Dragoon Queens said this world lacked magic. I never imagined a world without magic."

We broke the surface, and cold air tore at us. The bubble popped, I gripped Billie's hand and helped her waddle ashore onto a deserted strip of sand.

"I think we're on one of the Channel Islands," I said through chattering teeth.

"Maybe San Nicolas." Billie stared out at the ocean, the moonlight was casting a silver glow over her.

"Is this even real?" she whispered. She rubbed her head and then ran her hands down to check her baby belly. Her panicked look had my heart racing at the thought she might be hurt after all.

"Did I hit my head or something, or am I dreaming?" Billie asked me.

"Oh Billie, you're okay honey. I don't understand any of this either, but I promise I will take care of you and the baby. I'm here no matter what."

At that moment we were interrupted by a moan of pain. Turning, we saw him collapse on the sand and start to shudder. "We have to help him," Billie said.

We rushed to his side. His skin was iridescent and sickly, eyes like polished obsidian. "Do you need water?" I asked, panicked.

"Can you get back in?" I had this undeniable need to help this man... uh, merman. The instinct to save him like my own life depended on it. An intense kind of panic overwhelmed me.

"My transformation is... painful here," he said, the words laced with agony.

Body spasming, his fins split with a wet snap, shooting blood across the sand and my shins. He screamed, a guttural growl of agony.

"God," I whispered.

"He's dying." Billie and I held onto him, trying to ease the pain any way we could.

"Breathe," I told him.

"Tell us how to help you through this," I asked softly.

"Just give me a moment," he painfully forced the words out.

All I wanted to do was help this gorgeous merman as his fins tore apart into a bloody mess as his human legs emerged. His dark black eyes closed, dark-skinned face scrunched in agony. Scary shark-like features morphed before my eyes.

Before I could release my breath, his face was fully human. He was the most alluring man I had ever seen was laying before us. When his eyes opened, I saw deep brown eyes locked onto mine.

Something sparked, a vibration in my soul instantly bonding me to this gorgeous male.

Billie moved his black long dreadlocks off his face. "Hang in there, big guy. We will help you."

Her words broke the spell. I tore off my wet shirt and tried to compress his bleeding legs. The ground shook, making me fall on the huge male.

"Earthquake?" Billie gasped.

No. It was faster than that. The sand opened up like a maw, and we dropped deep down into the dark. I thought I was going to surely suffocate now. In the dark, I must have fainted because I was in a dream-like state. I saw my brother, a flashback of when he helped me set up what was supposed to be the best night of my life.

Chapter Two:
Maddy's Flashback

-Maddy-

The dock was quiet at dusk, all silver water and soft creaking wood. Seagulls cried overhead, and the wind smelled like salt and old rope. I stood in a faded hoodie, one hand on my hip and the other in my pocket, fingers closing around the velvet ring box like a talisman.

I didn't hear him at first, not until the footsteps behind me stopped.

"I wasn't sure you'd come," I said without turning.

"I almost didn't," said a familiar voice, deep and cautious, my brother Ben.

I turned, breath catching a little. My big brother looked older, more tired around the eyes.

He still wore his church clothes like armor. Pressed khakis, button-up shirt, and wedding ring polished to a gleam.

"Hi, sis," he said simply.

"Hi," I whispered, the word trembling out of me. We stared at each other for a moment, the air thick with a thousand unspoken memories: bike rides, Sunday school, and whispered jokes during sermons. The night she left, and he hadn't said goodbye.

Finally, he took a step closer and looked down, his voice low. "I saw you in the paper, a local spotlight. The art fundraiser thing you and Billie did, you said you were building community for queer youth."

I shifted. "Yeah, that was us."

He let out a shaky breath. "Mads... I'm sorry."

I blinked. "For what?"

"For not calling, not standing up when you needed me, and letting them say all that stuff without saying a thing."

Her throat tightened. He looked up at her, voice cracking. "I'm not like Mom and Dad. I don't think you're broken, wrong, or going to hell. I don't care who you love. I just..."

He scrubbed his hand down his face. "My whole life is the church. My wife, my kids, and the community, it's all tied up in it. If they knew that I accepted you, they'd come for me too. I can't..." His voice caught. "I can't risk that."

I stepped back, pain blooming sharply in my chest.

"So, you're here to, what? Whisper your support in private but disappear again in public?"

"No," he said, eyes shining.

"I'm here because I heard Billie's pregnant. I thought, maybe I could do one small thing for you. Something real as an apology, of sorts."

I held his gaze. "I'm not ashamed of her baby or being bisexual if that's what you're thinking."

He shook his head quickly. "I don't care about your sexuality or if that kid's father was some rando or the second coming of Christ. That kid is important to you, and you're going to be one hell of a bonus mom. I figured maybe you could use this."

He reached into his jacket and held out a set of keys. I stared. "It's the boat," he said. "The Whistler. You remember her?"

My mouth parted. That old, worn little sailboat our grandpa used to take us out on. Ben had inherited it after he died. I hadn't seen it in years.

"You're giving me the boat?"

"Not giving," he said with a small, pained smile. "Just to borrow for one night. Maybe you and Billie could use it. A little birdy told me you are planning something special."

"Janet has a big mouth. I didn't realize she still attends church under the radar." I rolled my eyes.

My hand slowly reached out and took the keys. They felt cold and heavy in my palm.

"Billie doesn't know yet," I said softly. "About the proposal."

Ben gave a tight nod, emotion rising in his throat.

"Then maybe that boat can carry you into the next part of your life."

I stared at him. "Why now?"

"I had a dream last week," he whispered. "About us when we were kids, you were laughing, and I realized how long it's been since I heard you laugh like that. I just... I wanted to be your brother again, even if I have to do it in secret."

I looked at him, my expression fractured with sorrow and love.

"I want you to be in my life, I really do. But I won't go back to being your shameful secret."

"I know," he said. "I'm not asking you to. I...." He took a deep breath.

"Just promise me you won't tell anyone, about this. The boat, or me being here, please?"

I nodded, slowly. "Okay."

"If you ever need anything, really need it, and I can give it, call me at my office. I still love you even if it must be in the dark."

I stepped forward and wrapped my arms around him, the old familiar shape of my brother folding into me like it had when I scraped my knees as a kid. For a moment, it felt like forgiveness.

When I pulled back, I smiled, a little bittersweet.

"You'll always be my brother, Ben. Even if it's only behind closed doors; which I think is such a shame."

He blinked fast and nodded, a mix of guilt and sadness crossing his eyes. I turned back toward the bay, where the boat rocked softly against the dock. Billie was waiting at home, and the ring was still in my pocket. The baby inside Billie was gently growing, like a reminder of all the love still left in my life.

As Ben walked away, I whispered to myself, "It's not going to be the wedding I imagined, if Billie says yes, it will be the start of our amazing family. Now to surprise Billie. Turns out we were both in for a surprise."

Chapter Three: Hell, Seriously

-Maddy-

I hit my bottom hard, coughing and spitting up sand. "Billie?!" I choked out as visions from my past dissipated.

"I'm here," she croaked beside me. I turned, relieved to see her. Beyond her I saw him, the beautiful male with two legs no longer bleeding. But he was still suffering and not fully awake yet.

I took each one of their hands in mine, looked at them both and said, "I swear, no matter what I will protect you both with my life."

Billie looked around the strange, shadowy chamber. "What is this place? Are we dead?"

"No," I said quickly.

"You're not dead, you are amazing and perfect."

"We're queer, Maddy," she said, her voice trembling.

"Our families said that means we're going to hell." Her voice quivered with fear.

"Screw them. If love is a sin, then so be it. I'll burn with you and not regret a thing." I meant every word.

"Then why does the devil himself stand behind you, Maddy?" Billie asked.

I got a wave of goosebumps, a chill crawling up my spine as I slowly turned around.

Two figures stood before us, illuminated by flames. A woman, angelic, radiant and calm. Her companion was a towering male with eyes like a solar eclipse. His body radiated fury in waves. No doubt, Satan in flesh and blood.

We were no longer on the Earth we knew and our lives would never be the same again.

I watched the couple having what looked like an intense conversation but I heard nothing.

"Maybe we did end up in hell after all," I whispered in awe.

The mysterious woman gave a lazy wave of her hand, and suddenly we could hear.

I could feel the powerful, scary being even more intensely, making me fall to my knees in fear.

"Lucifer, darling, dial it down a notch. You're going full rage demon and scaring the guests."

Lucifer, aka Mr. Hellfire himself, snarled like a man monster, moments away from hurling bolts of hellfire.

"Guests? Lilith, these aren't guests. They're trespassers! If you weren't here batting your pretty lashes at me, I'd have turned them into goddamn ash piles. First Hecat sends that Vampire spawn here to kill you? I should be leveling realms right now. I'm not letting this slide. Hell no, I don't forgive, I incinerate."

Okay, full transparency. I was about two seconds away from peeing myself, I may have peed a little bit. We were definitely in Hell. Satan was very much, uh, not chill. We were not welcomed to hell. Great, I had been in Lucifer's presence for three minutes and he already hated me.

Lilith reached up and gently cupped Lucifer's face like she was calming a very pissed off pitbull. She gave him a sweet little kiss like they were in a romcom instead of literal damnation.

"My love, I'm fine, you're fine. We've got our infernal slice of paradise, the lava river and endless abyss. Every day here is one in paradise with you. These poor humans think they're in Hell for being naughty. If only they knew, we don't even do the whole 'torture evil souls' thing. Evil doesn't get reborn, it gets unmade. Poof, gone and done, no do-overs."

She shot us a soft smile that said, "Don't worry, sweeties," trying to be reassuring, yet the vibe could have also been, "Blink wrong and I'll set your eyebrows on fire."

Lucifer growled. "Do I look like I've got time for evil soul rehab? Screw that. I've got real problems. These Gods keep poking their noses where they don't belong.

"Kane! You, yes you! You omnipotent tool bag, you're screwing around with God Realms and portals like it's a party trick."

He stepped forward, eyes blazing, power emanating off of him like a supernatural nuke.

"You need to be listening to me now, Kane. Keep poking your greasy little fingers into my domain and I swear, I will drag your divine ass across the multiverse like toilet paper on a shoe. Even Lilith won't be able to stop me."

"Hear this, let it sink into your thick skull. The Goddess Harmony is off limits and you touch what's hers again, you'll be unmade so hard you'll wish you were just dead."

Yep, I was shaking, a full body tremble. I didn't trust my Kegels to save me from a wet disaster; it was going to be a close one.

Lilith sighed, smiling like a woman who's used to her husband threatening cosmic annihilation before breakfast as no big deal.

"Okay, love, that was very impressive and dramatic. Now, can we please send our guests home and get back to our lava bath?"

Lucifer finally looked at us. His gaze hit me like a freight train of dread. I grabbed Billie's hand like it was my lifeline.

"Water-Dweller Prince, take your mates. Go home."

He snapped his fingers, and then total darkness.

Chapter Four: The Night We Stopped Apologizing

-Maddy-

The neon sign buzzed faintly above the door. The Velvet Halo, its pink and blue glow washing over Billie and I as we stepped inside. It was a Friday night in LA, and the bar pulsed with low bass, clinking glasses, and feminine laughter that felt free.

Not the performative kind of happiness we were forced to wear in church pews or youth group lock-ins. This was the kind that made you breathe deeper.

I adjusted my denim jacket, the rainbow pin glinting under the club lights.

"You, okay?" I asked.

Billie nodded, but her hands trembled slightly. "First time being somewhere like this and not hiding."

"Yeah. Me too."

We smiled at each other, small and private, like a shared rebellion as we made our way to the bar.

We had not kissed, not even dating yet. This adventure wasn't about that, it was about being seen. Surrounded by others who didn't need permission to love who they wanted.

We were halfway through our first drink, something fruity and blue I had insisted on ordering, when Billie froze.

Across the room near the exit, a figure in a beige trench coat and tight frown stood wide-eyed. Mrs. Gretta Carlton, the choir director, church gossip queen, and mother of two teenage daughters from youth group. A prominent figure at The Bible Church of Christ. The one Billie and I had grown up in, the one where they met in teen club four years ago.

"Oh shit," Billie whispered. "Gretta's here. She saw us."

I didn't turn. "You sure?"

"She looked right at me. I think she took a photo."

I stiffened. "Well, fuck!"

We didn't run, maybe we should have. The moment was over in seconds. Gretta turned on her heel and vanished out the doorway, like a ghost made of air. The fallout came fast, by Sunday morning, we were summoned. Not kindly or quietly.

My parents were waiting in the living room with the pastor and two elders when I got home that night.

Billie got the same. Words like sin and perversion were hurled at us like stones. We were commanded to repent, and to "renounce the confusion." Mandated to stop seeing each other or any others that had the same urges. We were ordered to attend counseling with Sister Deborah.

Both of us were ordered to fast and pray and remember our true purpose as women under the Lord's gaze. To be mothers and wives and good women who serve God's will.

Billie's voice broke when she said, "I'm not confused."

I stood in aggravation. "This shit is for the birds."

The argument turned into shouting. My father pounded the wall next to my head. Billie's mother cried, her dad told her to pack her things that night. My mom just said, flatly, "you've chosen hell." Her voice filled with religious devotion. "No perverted sinner like you is welcome under my roof."

I didn't apologize, just packed my bag while drowning out the indignant hysterics and left the house without looking back. I went to find Billie, a defiant tear falling down my cheek.

Billie didn't beg; she was shoved out of her house with only the clothes she had on. I stormed up the street to hug her.

By the next day, Billie and I were staying in a cheap motel off Highway 10, everything I owned crammed into a backpack full of memories we weren't sure we were allowed to keep anymore.

We sat on opposite ends of the bed, still in our clothes from the night before, the silence stretching.

"They really meant it," Billie whispered.

"Yeah," I replied. "They did."

Then Billie laughed, bitter with tears. "All that talk about unconditional love, and Christ-like acceptance."

I rubbed my eyes. "Apparently it has conditions."

We didn't cry too much, not really until the next morning. I found an old photo in my bag of the church teen group, Billie and I in matching yellow T-shirts, holding hands and laughing like they'd never known shame. I passed it to Billie, who stared at it for a long time.

"We didn't do anything wrong," Billie said finally, voice hoarse.

"No," I said. "We just stopped pretending."

"Why would God create us this way if we aren't supposed to be this way?" Billie asked.

"Stop, that Billie, he wouldn't, don't let mere humans speak on behalf of God. You and me, we are good people. It's their loss not wanting us. I never understood why so-called people of God can be so cruel and judgmental."

The days turned into weeks. We couch surfed and found jobs. Billie was doing night shifts at a warehouse; I waited tables at a family restaurant. We saved what little money we had and eventually rented a basement studio in Pico Rivera. It came with peeling paint and a bed we had to share, but it was all ours. It was there I fell in love with Billie more every day.

We held each other through nightmares, through moments of wondering if we'd made the wrong choice. If being good girls again would bring our families back. Even in our lowest moments, we never tried to go back.

Instead, we found new families in chosen ones. A drag queen named Lola let us sleep on her futon for a week. A lesbian couple brought over home-cooked meals and told us that we were brave. A trans man named Jay offered Billie a better job at the manufacturing plant where he worked.

We went back to The Velvet Halo six months later, not as scared girls, but as survivors. On the six-month anniversary of the night we were seen, we made a promise.

Sitting on the steps of our apartment, the inner-city lights flickering, sirens in the background of the sound of traffic.

I said, "If I could go back and do it over, I'd still walk into that bar with you."

Billie nodded. "Me too, even knowing what we would lose."

"Look what we found." Billie finished.

We clinked our glasses together, filled with sparkling water and cheap wine. No more hiding or apologizing.

We weren't sisters by blood and not yet lovers, it was something else. We had a bond forged in fire, stronger than the lies we were raised on. We were bisexual, best friends, unapologetically alive and finally free.

Chapter Five: Triton's Trip To Earth

-Triton-

The water was my breath, pulse, and skin. It moved me like a second soul. I sliced through the water and turned towards the boundary's edge. The drop-off was sudden, like the world had been bitten into. Beyond lay the abyss, the true sea where the deep, unspoken creatures slept. Even the elders thought twice before crossing it.

I swam closer, checking the enchanted seals embedded along the stone wall, each pulsing gently with aquamarine light. They were the wards that kept the ancient beast Sea Gods below—Leviathans and Krakens. They alone had made our ancestors' kingdom flee into shallower sanctuaries.

I tapped a seal, murmuring the reinforcement chant to the rune. It glowed in response, steady and bright.

'Still holding,' I muttered.

'Thank the deep.' Something shifted in the magic vein of the sea. A hum, not from the seal.

No, it came from the water itself.

I straightened, my muscles coiling around me. The currents stilled, and the fish disappeared. The sea went silent, dreadful and heavy. A kind of silence that meant something was coming, and then it hit.

A crack of Magic, loud even underwater. Water bubbled around me suddenly, a tear opened in the fabric of the sea. It was a perfect circle of violet light; like a galaxy cloud here in the deep waters. A portal pulsing with unnatural energy, not of the sea but divinely made.

"Shit," I twisted to flee, but it was too late.

The pull was violent; my body was yanked like seaweed in a riptide. Pressure crumpled around me, ears ringing, Magic twisting as I was wrenched from its natural source. Blackness slammed into my vision.

Darkness, purple light, and murky saltwater followed an impact. I crashed through the ocean's surface and was flung up beneath the hull of a white boat. My back struck the metal edge with a sharp clang, and I felt myself sink.

Dazed, I felt the sting of the strange waters burning my eyes. Then came splashes and high voices, definitely feminine. Two figures teetered above me with arms flailing, then the sound of two distinct splashes.

Two women fell into the water beside me. I snapped back into focus, my heart convulsing, and chest tightening. Only one thought was clear to me with stunning clarity.

Mine.

The bond roared to life in my blood, louder than the displaced magic, stronger than the disorientation. I had never met them, but I knew them with my soul. Both of them were my true mates, and they were mine.

Two threads pulled taut in my chest, anchored, and destined for me.

And they were both drowning, I had to save them, it is my duty.

Chapter Six: From Hell To Hot water

-Maddy-

Darkness turned to sunshine, and we were suddenly out of hell. Now on a beach that boasted a Lisa Frank acid trip for a sky. Glittery clouds and purple dolphins doing synchronized flips. Definitely not Earth.

"Billie, are you okay?" I asked, still catching my breath.

"I'm fine. I'm more worried about Mr. Shark man over here."

Our sexy fish man was lying unconscious, but something wild was happening. His fins weren't gory wounds anymore. They were finally human legs. Dark, strong, glistening in the sunlight legs.

... Oh, lord... He was naked, and he was packing very anatomically generous equipment.

Am I in shock? I asked myself as I struggled internally with seeing all of his sexy glory before me.

"Okay, hormones, you can chill now," I muttered, trying to keep my eyes on his face. It didn't work.

"We need help," Billie said, practical as always.

"Yeah. Working on it." I looked around like a lost tourist in a fantasy brochure.

"Is that... a crystal cloud?" Billie pointed upward.

"Yup. Sure is. Those are purple dolphins too. So, either we're dead and this is Heaven, or we've been abducted into a Lisa Frank nightmare."

"No shit, Sherlock." Billie rolled her eyes.

"We've been to Hell. Must be Heaven and the merman dude is our angelic Uber."

"Still not buying the whole 'we're dead' theory. We're alive and we keep getting yanked into magical realms like discount adventurers. I will figure out why. Mark my words."

Then the water started bubbling like a horror movie. Shadows zipped toward the shore. I jumped up like my butt was on fire.

"What now?" At this point, I was prepared for anything in this strange world.

"Stay behind me." I braced myself for whatever monster was incoming.

Emerging from the shore were three aquatic beings. Brutal looking human-shark hybrids with murder in their eyes and spears in their hands.

"Step away from our Prince and live!" the lead one said in my head, baring her fangs like she flossed with razor wire.

"Oh, hell no. If you're not here to help, then take your sea spears and kindly fuck off!" I said, contemplating my chances of disarming her without dying a horrible painful death.

"Don't piss off the shark people," Billie whispered to me as I defiantly stared down the shark-like woman.

"I don't care if you're made of gills and murder, I don't let anyone threaten what's mine."

Mr. merman gasped behind me, and I didn't even look back. My eyes were fixed on Sharkzilla.

"Oh my god," Billie gasped. "You're awake!"

'My Prince,' the three said in unison, then dropped to their knees like they were in the presence of King Arthur himself.

"Uh... okay then." I slowly lowered my fists, still confused but slightly less ready to die by combat.

The merman wrapped his arms around my waist, and I turned and locked eyes with... damn, just damn. I forgot my own name looking at that face and hearing his voice.

"My fierce protector. Thank you, there's no need to fight, these three are our kin."

His eyes never left mine as he spoke. "Please meet my true mates."

Wait...mates?! My brain short circuited and my jaw dropped to the ground.

Spinning around, I was greeted by shark security starting to shift, like magically morphing into the two women and one man. All of them were stunning, unfairly attractive and so distractingly naked.

"I'm Rina. They are Coral and Jag," one of the women said like we were at a power brunch, and not an interdimensional crisis.

"Triton!" Coral beamed. "So glad you're alive, and with worthy mates!"

"Triton. Your name is Triton. Nice." I stood on my toes and kissed his cheek. What the hell was I doing?

"I'm just glad you three are not bad guys." I said, shaking my head. "I didn't really feel like fighting my way through Aquaman's extended family today."

"You're fierce," Rina said with a smirk. "A good match for my nephew."

"I'm Maddy. This is Billie Jo."

"Call me Billie," she said with a wave and then moaned suddenly and doubled over in pain.

"Oh no. Billie!" I caught her as she buckled.

"Get me a healer, now!" Triton barked, lifting Billie like she weighed nothing.

When Billie is not pregnant, she is full figured and curvy with her normal physique. To me, she is sexy no matter what. I can't imagine a human man being able to lift her with such power and ease.

Jag shifted into a black panther and vanished into the trees. Of course he did, why the hell not?

"I need Gemma, bring her to the East Beach now!" Rina's voice boomed in my skull.

"Jag is fetching the Dragoons, and Rina is spreading the word. Don't worry, Gemma is our healer, she's got this," Coral reassured me.

My soul felt like it was cracking open and tears stung my eyes. I couldn't lose Billie, not now or ever.

"I'm here, Billie. I'm staying right here."

"I love you, Maddy," Billie said through gritted teeth.

"I love you more than anything," I whispered, voice shaking.

"Ember is almost here," Coral said.

I looked up... And holy fire-breathing hell there was a giant blue dragon flying toward us.

"She's bringing Gemma," Rina confirmed.

The dragon landed gracefully, sharp lethal claws extended, as a tiny badass pixie woman with spiky blue hair hopped down like it was nothing.

"Hi. I'm Gemma. Let's work on easing her pain." She quickly got to work and was looking over the love of my life intently.

The dragon began to shift. Yep, into another naked woman, who casually got dressed from clothes in a bag she carried. Like it was normal, apparently it was a nudity-friendly world. I wasn't mad.

"Thanks, Ember. I owe you," Triton said, worry etched into his voice.

"May I touch your belly?" Gemma asked gently.

"Please make it stop, save my baby. It's too early," Billie begged.

Gemma went into full magic mode. Chanting, glowing and healing. Billie's face finally relaxed, as Gemma chanted and glowed using her healing powers.

Gemma had a spiky pixie haircut with black and blue highlights. Was that a white spotted feather poking out of her hair? I was too worried about Billie to ponder all this strangeness around me. My main focus was on her.

"Is she okay?" I asked, holding my breath.

"Your daughter is fine; your mate is well too. She just got scared from all the excitement, and I'll stay close to prevent early labor."

"A girl?" Billie blinked. "Can you really stop it?"

Gemma grinned. "Sweet Earthling, I'm more reliable than your entire healthcare system back on Earth. Just ask the Dragoon Queens, they were Earthlings once, too."

I didn't care how it worked. Right now, paramount to everything was that Billie and our baby girl were safe.

"I'm Maddy. Whatever I can do to thank you, just say it." I owed this tiny pixie being my life.

"Honestly? It's no biggie. Sacred healer and all that and it even comes with a sparkly crystal wand." She stood and brushed sand off her knees casually, as if this was just another Tuesday. The most epic Tuesday I ever had.

"Thanks, Gemma." I said with eternal gratefulness.

Triton spoke up, "I'm guessing the underwater water dwelling palace isn't an option for Billie?"

Gemma gave him the kind of look you give a toddler asking if chocolate cake was a vegetable. "Sweet Triton, the entire realm was freaking out looking for you. When you were here all snuggled up with your true mates; who I might add, did not walk through Harmony's blessed door. That alone is its own cosmic paperwork. We've got... a situation to sort."

She turned to Billie, softening. "Bonding will have to wait, darling. That island honeymoon dream? Not happening 'til after this baby girl pops out. Go to the Dragoon Castle, it is your best bet for now. I'll stay with you and make sure you and the little Sea Bean are safe and snug."

"My parents are en route with Jag," Ember chimed in like a plot twist. I tuned everyone out for a moment, and just cupped Billie's face like she was the only person that mattered, honestly she was.

"Billie, it's a girl. The magical glam healer says she'll keep you both safe. As long as you're okay, I don't care where we are. I've got you always."

Billie's eyes welled up. "Thank you, Maddy. I'm freaking out and can't do this without you."

She leaned into me and I kissed the top of her head.

"Good thing I'm not going anywhere then, huh? I love you, Billie."

A blue and a black dragon crash landing into the scene was just normal at this point, with the day we'd had so far. The black dragon shifted first, into a tall swaggering guy who strolled up to Coral and Rina like he'd just walked off a fantasy novel cover. The blue dragon became a breathtakingly perfect and beautiful Hispanic woman.

"These are my parents, Kayla and Talen," Ember said. Wait. What now?

The two very undragon and very attractive humans, that had just shape shifted, stepped up towards us. Kayla looked like a Latina goddess with big brown eyes. Talen was built like a gym ad and he was blessed with Ember's purple cat eyes.

"Excuse me, these are your parents? They look like they just finished college keg stands."

Kayla laughed, amused. "Yeah, the magic thing kind of cheats the whole aging system. You'll get used to it."

"Mom, meet Maddy and Billie," Ember said. "They're Triton's true mates."

Kayla tilted her head, looking at us. "Honey, I'm not sure they've had the crash course in 'true mate' instincts yet. Earthlings don't exactly run on divine love radar."

"Explaining will have to wait," Gemma cut in, all healer mode.

"These two have been through hell. Let's get them somewhere safe before this turns into another reality tv show that you're always going on about from your Earth years."

"Rina," Triton turned, all royal again, "Please let my father know I'm traveling with the Dragoons. Until we are bonded, I can't take them to my kingdom."

Talen nodded. "You and your family are welcome here as long as you need."

"All right." Gemma began delegating transportation.

"Kayla will take Gemma and Billie. Talen can carry Triton. Ember, you get Maddy," Kayla said, stripping casually as she turned into a dragon again. Being naked goddess gorgeous was no biggie around here.

"Wait, hold the phone. You want us to FLY in your CLAWS?!" I yelped, watching Talen shift into a skyscraper sized black dragon.

Triton looked like he was trying not to laugh. "I know this is a lot, you're safe I promise. Gemma's got Billie. Ember and I will keep you secure. Flying is the fastest way across the realm."

He kissed my forehead and somehow, all my nerve endings turned into jelly. Gently he picked up Billie, like she was spun sugar and carried her to Kayla's claw where Gemma waited.

"Billie, just close your eyes. We'll meet you at the castle. You will have a hot bath, a cozy bed and all the food you want." He winked at me before turning away.

"My very own prince charming," Billie whispered before Gemma zapped her into a sedated dreamland state.

"I've got her," Gemma smiled.

"Wait! I'm not letting her fly off without me!" I snapped, throwing some serious shade at all these magical people making choices like I wasn't standing right here.

"Maddy," Kayla's voice echoed in my head like a celestial phone call. "I apologize for taking over, being the Dragoon Queen tends to make me managerial. I just want to help, you both need rest and to get your bearings. You're not just passengers here, you're guests. I promise, Billie is in the best claws in the realm. Ride with Ember or Triton. It'll be safe, I swear it."

Ember offered her claw, patient and calm. Meanwhile, I was two breaths from a full meltdown. My brain, don't freak out, I tried to tell myself. My heart, freaking out anyway. Has it even been a full day since the boat sank?

Triton scooped me up before I could bolt, holding me like the answer to every panic attack. Gods, he smelled like sea wind and sin.

"My fierce protector, allow me to hold you as we fly," he murmured as he held me close.

"Let's just get this over with," I grumbled, letting him settle us in Ember's claw. He tucked me against him, and Ember curled her talons around us.

We lifted off, and my breath caught as we soared beside Kayla and Gemma. Billie was out cold, cuddled in Gemma's lap and I could've cried being away from her.

Then Gemma waved her wand at me and suddenly, it was like someone turned my anxiety off with a click.

The sky looked like something out of a dream, with floating crystal platforms and rainbow clouds. Disco balls of magic, I actually giggled.

"Looks like heaven," I whispered. Below, I noticed a massive purple blob swimming under us following like a shadow.

"Um... that's not a kraken, is it?"

"That's our Grand Guardian of the Seas," Triton said calmly. "She's a giant octopus and basically family."

"Of course she is," I said. "Sure, I'll add it to the list."

"She'll love you both," he said, kissing my cheek like it was no big deal.

As we crested the cliffs there it was, an actual waterfall palace. It was Alice in Wonderland on shrooms. A castle sat above the falls, shimmering with enchantments. We landed smoothly in a garden straight out of a fairy tale.

Ember opened her claw and I climbed out with my jaw practically unhinged.

"Thank you for the lift, Ember!" Triton called after her as she soared off again.

He scooped up Billie like she was breakable and my heart squeezed. I followed, nervous as hell. Walking into this castle felt like meeting royalty... oh wait, that's exactly what I was doing.

Gemma bounced along like a jittery golden retriever. "I hope you both get to relax here!"

"I appreciate how nice you all are, really," I said, side-eyeing the ornate doors, "I'm just waiting for the other shoe to drop. The one that squishes us." It was all so overwhelming mixed with excitement.

Inside, the doors opened, the Guards were smiling with welcome. What was this, The Good Place?

Kayla and Talen were back in clothes, thank goodness. They looked like elegant hosts.

"Welcome," Talen said. "We're honored to have you."

A man in a white toga appeared, all grace and warmth. "Welcome! I've prepared your wing. Stan, my mate, is cooking something special for you."

"Thanks, Richmon. You always think of everything," Kayla said with affection and pride. My mind was trying to keep up and process all of this.

"Wait. Mate? Like... Australian 'mate'? Or soulmate?" Kayla laughed. "More soulmate, life partners. A magical bonding, a marriage without the divorce."

"So, Richmon and Stan are married?" I asked. "Bonded, yes," Richmon said proudly.

My heart skipped a beat at what that meant. "So, there's no LGBTQ stigma here?"

"None," Kayla beamed. "This world runs on instinct and magic. You'll find nothing but celebration here. Love is love, always."

I almost teared up. "Billie and I, our families back home kicked us out. Cult level Christianity. No acceptance."

"Then it's time you found your home," Kayla said softly. "Here, every love is sacred."

"We celebrate all mating," she added. "Yours is probably being planned as we speak."

"Okay but hold up," I said, spinning to Triton. "You do know humans don't just consider themselves married because someone says we are, right?"

Triton, annoyingly confident, "We are a mate pod. Spawning or not, you and Billie are my bond mates."

"You might be hotter than a deep-fried jalapeño, but that does not equal marriage!"

Kayla tried to play diplomat. "It's instinct-based here. Your magic will awaken, and you'll understand. You'll become, well... let's say... less Earthling."

"I was born on Earth, so newsflash, I am an Earthling," I snapped. "And I'll decide who I marry when I say so."

"Fair enough," Kayla said with a condescending smirk that practically screamed, "You'll see."

Richmond opened the door to an ornate hallway, revealing a jaw-dropping gorgeous sight.

As I stepped inside my mind was spinning, heart pounding, and still not totally sure I wasn't hallucinating. Dragons, mates, babies, and a giant octopus Grand Guardian.

Welcome to Harmony, I guess.

It felt more like I fell down the rabbit hole, or a tornado took us over the rainbow.

Chapter Seven: What A Whirlwind

-Maddy-

"Welcome, royal guests. Please call for me if you need anything at all," Richmond said with a bow so low, I thought he might be proposing. He glided out like a hotel butler who moonlighted as a ballet dancer.

"This way, the bedroom's through here," Talen said, opening a door like he was unveiling a grand prize on a game show. Triton carried Billie like she was a glass slipper as Kayla started fussing with the unnecessarily luxurious bedding. It probably cost more than my entire rent history.

Triton laid Billie down like she was made of porcelain, tucking her in with all the care of a gentleman. Gemma plopped on a nearby couch and cracked open a book like she was settling in for an afternoon spa day.

"Is that an Elizabeth Briggs novel?" I asked, amazed that she had a book that was clearly written by an Earth author.

"Yes, blame Brooke and Kayla, they got me hooked on romance books. Thank the Goddess Harmony for that blue door."

"Well, I enjoyed that book myself. Wait until chapter fifteen, it will blow your mind," I said, as I turned my attention back toward Billie. Gemma's blue door comment confused me—what does that even mean?

"She'll need sleep," Gemma said without looking up. "I'll be right here if she needs anything."

"Great. Talen and I are off to update my sister," Kayla added, grabbing Talen's hand like they were eloping. "You two have fun chatting." With that ominous note, they were gone.

The second the door clicked shut, I felt it. Triton's gaze was all over me, like he was trying to telepathically melt my clothes. Here we go.

He stepped toward me, dark eyes stormy with want, and I swear the temperature jumped ten degrees. My cheeks flushed and my nipples decided now was the perfect time to go on high alert.

"I want to kiss you. I'm dying to taste your lips," he whispered, his hands cradling my face like I was made of moonlight and magic. And what did I do? I launched into his arms like a hormonal rocket. Tongues tangled and hearts racing. Dignity? Never heard of it.

Then he stopped cold. It was instant emotional whiplash. He pulled away like I'd burned him and just like that, total rejection.

"Sorry," I mumbled before dramatically fleeing into the en suite bathroom like a damsel in distress. Very original, Maddy.

"Maddy, wait!" he called, legs appearing in the doorway.

He followed me in, of course he did, and I backed up against the wall like I was being hunted.

"I didn't want to stop," Triton said, eyes wide with concern.

"If we keep going, I won't be able to stop."

"Oh great, now I'm a temptation you can't resist. What am I, a triple chocolate lava cake?" I sighed, feeling equal parts embarrassed and ridiculous.

"Look, I was gonna propose to Billie," I blurted. "With the ring, commitment, all the guts and glitter. Now? I've lost the damn ring!"

He blinked. "A proposal?"

Oh boy, I thought to myself, here we go.

I launched into the whole messy, complicated, emotionally exhausting saga. Our parents disowning us, and Billie's drunken attempt to prove she was "straight." Even though she is clearly bi. Followed by the pregnancy, our shared banishment, and how I had pawned the last nice thing I owned to buy her a ring that probably belonged in a Cracker Jack box.

Triton listened like he was watching a tragedy unfold on stage. Eyes full of gentle horror and the kind of sympathy that made it worse.

"We have jewelers too," he said, like that fixed everything. "They make the jewelry to find the right match."

"That's... wholesome. I can't ask you to buy me another ring." I was getting frustrated now.

"Buy?" he repeated, like I'd just coughed up a foreign word.

Oh right. No money here, just vibes and magic. Everyone works at what they love—no capitalism required, Kumbaya types.

"Honestly?" I should've been thrilled. Instead, I felt like someone had taken the world, flipped it upside down and handed it back with a "good luck."

As he ran me a bath he replied, "Yes, really."

He poured something floral and sparkly into the bath like he was the star for Fantasy Bachelor: Castle Edition. He handed me a dress and smiled that heart-melting smile.

"I'll take you to the jeweler. We'll find the right match."

My response? "This is some Twilight Zone level weirdness."

If a bisexual meter was a thing you could use to gauge it with, I would teeter more toward women than men. I am solidly attracted to both genders. My new attraction to Triton was very confusing. Earlier in the day I had just about confessed my love to Billie. Bi or not, I am monogamous, right?

I took the damn bath anyway. Let me tell you, magic water and silky gowns have a way of seducing even the most emotionally constipated lesbians. I only had minor anxiety after getting cleaned and dressed in a flowing gown.

Triton met me outside looking like a royal thirst trap in his tailored suit. We walked through manicured gardens full of statues, and honestly? I was trying not to spiral. My brain was clinging to sarcasm like a lifeline.

"My family was rich too, but not like this," I muttered. "This is the kind of rich where the statues probably have names after family, and favorite wines are served in honor of the royal kingdom."

The town looked like something out of a Hallmark movie. We reached a quaint little shop and inside was an overly enthusiastic man with a monocle and the energy of a caffeinated squirrel.

"GREETINGS!" he bellowed. "Looking for a match?"

"I'm here for a ring," I said, unsure if I should salute or bow.

"Try them all! They'll tell you who they belong to!" He said it like it was the most obvious thing in the world.

I humored him, poking at rings until, bam. One of them basically zapped me. Looking at the diamonds and pearls, Billie's face flashed in my head like a neon sign. This was the one.

"This is it," I whispered, heart in my throat. "This is her ring."

I should've known the universe wasn't done with me yet.

While the shopkeeper wrapped Billie's ring, Triton insisted I keep looking. Apparently, I had "more matches."

More? Like I'm a jewelry soulmate magnet?

I found three matching necklaces that practically sang to me, silver chains with platinum trident pendants. One for each of us: Billie, Triton, and me. I thought it was both cute and weird and potentially significant. Then it happened.

I touched a seahorse armband with fancy swirls, and zap! It vanished and reappeared on my upper arm like a tattoo with an attitude. Triton and Clark gasped. Clark hit the floor like he'd seen Beyoncé, as Triton exclaimed, "My Sea Queen."

"I'm sorry, your what?" I thought maybe the armband was cursed and tried pulling it off with no luck.

"You've been chosen," Triton said solemnly, like I'd just been knighted by Poseidon.

"The armband was created when our last Sea Queen was lost. It's been waiting for a new ruler. You are her." That was my cue to spiral.

"This isn't happening. I am not a Sea Queen. I'm a broke disaster with poor impulse control and a questionable relationship with hot baths!"

Triton was calm, annoyingly so. "You're not alone. I'm here. We'll figure it out."

The people around began to bow and kneel. "They are imprinting," Triton explained.

"Okay, this is not normal. This is Hunger Games level weird," I hissed as I stomped past everyone, thoroughly done.

That's when I saw her—Billie. She was awake, pale and shaky, so beautiful. She pointed to her upper arm and my heart stopped. She had the exact same armband as me.

"Holy...Shit!" I said, staring at her like she was an alien. "You too?"

Chapter Eight: Sea Queens And Fated Mates

-Maddy-

Triton dropped to his knees and bowed low before Billie.

"What is happening?!" Billie gasped, instinctively reaching for my hand, her voice trembling. "Why is everyone bowing?!"

"These fools think we're Sea Queens," I muttered, wrapping an arm around her.

"Triton says they're 'Imprinting.' Whatever that means."

"I... I was dreaming about having my baby girl," Billie said breathlessly.

Then a sharp sting in my arm woke me up. I didn't know where I was and thought I was still dreaming, until I saw Gemma hit the floor. Every room I went through there were people bowing. I'm so glad I found you, this is scaring the hell out of me."

"Same, Billie. I'm so sorry I wasn't there when you woke up, I meant to be." I tightened into the hug just as Triton seemed to snap out of his trance.

People's chatter rippled around us. The garden was brimming with magical beings and celestials, more crowded into the castle doorway.

"What do they all want?" I asked as Billie and I inched closer to Triton.

"They want to welcome you both as the new Sea Queens," he said, beaming with pride like it was the most normal thing in the world to announce.

"Shouldn't you need, I don't know, royal blood or something?" Billie asked, clearly unimpressed with being roped into alien royalty.

"If the Goddess Harmony sees fit to bless you, we rejoice," Triton replied reverently.

The crowd parted as dragons began landing with the grace of thunder. Kayla transformed in midair and walked up to us with a blonde girl at her side.

"This is my sister, Brooke," Kayla introduced.

"Welcome to the queen club." Brooke smirked and gestured to the dragon emblazoned cuff on her arm.

"Brooke, meet Maddy and Billie," Kayla added.

"I don't want to be a queen. I'm barely coping with being a pregnant human!" Billie exclaimed.

"We get it," Kayla said, shrugging.
"We weren't thrilled either. This world really supports mothers. You'll be an amazing mother and Queen."

"Kayla," Billie mumbled, "Can we please hide now?"

Triton gently stepped forward. "I'll take you to our guest suite."

"We'll send dinner to your room," Kayla called, already directing the crowd as Brooke proclaimed to the masses, "We have two new Sea Queens!"

Bless Brooke for taking over. The door to our suite shut and I finally exhaled.

Gemma stood, brushing herself off. "I'll give you three some space. I'm just across the hall if you need anything."

Billie and I sank into the plush couch like melting snow.

"I'll draw Billie a bath," Triton said, kissing the tops of our heads with such casual affection it made my heart hiccup.

"You're gonna feel like a new woman after that bath," I promised her.

"I can't wait. I've got sand in all the wrong places." She groaned, standing with my help.

She followed me to the bathroom and her eyes widened. "It smells so good in here."
She immediately darted toward the toilet. "I have to pee so badly."

I was still laughing when she realized Triton was still in the room too.

"Don't mind me. Pregnant ladies don't wait," he chuckled as he politely backed out.

"That man is way too sexy to be that sweet," Billie said, shimmying out of her pants.

"He's something. He gives Shemar Moore a run for his money in the looks department," I muttered, keeping my mouth shut about the whole 'we were both his wives' situation. One emotionally shocking revelation at a time.

"No kidding, that merman is tall, dark, and yummy," Billie agreed.

Once she was settled in the bath, I wandered back into the suite where Triton and Richmond were setting up dinner.

"That smells amazing," I said, my stomach audibly growling.

"I'll tell Stan you're excited about dinner, he'll be honored," Richmond replied before making himself scarce.

Richmond had set up an elaborate table covered in dark fabric with fine royal dinnerware. The utensils looked like they were made of extravagant silver and gems. Too fancy for cheeseburgers and fries. I would feel out of place eating in such a fancy way. However, I am starving and it is already hard for me to resist devouring my plate like a ravenous beast.

"I'll wait for Billie, I'm already drooling," I admitted.

"Here. Try this," Triton said, holding a french fry to my lips. I took it and groaned in delight.

"What is that? Wait a minute, I know that taste."

Triton grinned, teasing me with a second fry, this one from his fingers. I sucked on them without thinking, his eyes darkened and a low moan hissed from his throat.

"Behave, woman. I'm already, just barely able to contain my need for you."

He stepped back, clearly affected.

"This is just like a fast-food joint back on Earth. Is that an In-N-Out cheeseburger, animal style? How did Stan figure out how to make these?"

I tried to cool the sudden heat crawling up my spine by grabbing a glass of bubbly, fruity liquid.

"Wow, this stuff is dangerously good."

"It is for Kayla and Brooke. He makes them on their behalf because it's Kayla's favorite cheeseburger. Stan thought it might make you both feel more at home. Go easy on that drink," Triton warned. "It's potent."

"You don't say." I took another sip. "That was very cool of Stan, remind me to thank him later."

"It's not harmful. It's an aphrodisiac."

I nearly spat. "Oh, that's what this is? Nope, hard pass." I swapped it for water.

"Probably wise," Triton said. "You don't seem to need any help with arousal." However, his heated gaze was helping way too much.

"Who needs help with arousal?" Billie padded in with a towel wrapped around her hair.

I laughed. "Apparently, I do. This bubbly alien cocktail is basically liquid lust."

She snorted and joined us at the table, practically moaning at the food.

"I'm so glad you're both okay," Triton said between bites. "We have much to discuss."

"We're having a girl! Can you believe it?" Billie looked between us, glowing beautifully.

"I'm honored to have a daughter with you," Triton said with real and quiet awe.

He leaned in to kiss her, then teased, "You've got food on your teeth, beautiful."

"Oops." She took a big gulp of water and grinned. "Is it gone?"

Billie blushed. "This is nice and all, but kind of an overkill, don't you think?" Billie waved her hand to showcase the fancy table setup.

"My thoughts exactly," I said, as Triton gazed at the table looking confused.

I blinked at my beautiful lady, shaking my head as I wanted to establish what we were doing and if Billie was on the same page as I.

"Billie, Triton just called your baby his daughter. That doesn't seem weird to you?"

"Any child of either of yours is mine too," Triton snapped, then looked at me like I was the slow one.

"Wait, you're serious?" Billie asked.

"Why would I joke about this? You're my bonded mates, my family."

Billie turned to me, eyes wide. "Is he seriously serious?"

"Yup, he's been telling everyone we're his wives."

Triton tilted his head. "You said 'we have a girl.' I thought it was understood."

"I was talking to Maddy, she and I are obviously meant to be together and I've been waiting for her to propose!" Billie said bluntly.

"Sure, we both have the hots for you, that doesn't make us a ready made family. I'm open to exploring and building something with you, not jump right into an instant marriage with you as well."

"Hold up!" I threw up my hands. "You knew and you let me stress over it?"

I pulled Billie into a deep romantic kiss. It was everything I imagined, and more.

"I love you," I whispered. "I don't want to be without you. Will you marry me?"

I pulled out the ring I'd been carrying. Billie gasped, her eyes brimming.

"Yes. Of course, I will! It's about damn time!" she cried.

I slid the ring on and it was a perfect fit.

"This is a beautiful sight," Triton said softly.

"Babe," I turned to Billie.
"You missed a few things while you were napping."

I explained everything about the bond mate and instant marriage here.

"So, Triton's been telling everyone we're his wives this whole time?" Billie asked.

"Exactly, they're all thrilled and planning a spawning and everything. I think that means a wedding."

Triton nodded proudly. "See? We are a family."

Then to our utter shock, he dropped to both knees and pulled out two gleaming rings, holding them both up.

"Be my wives in the Earth way."

Billie and I just stared at him, our mouths open like twin fly traps. His smile faded, heartbreak clear on his face as he lowered his arms. He had a map of rejection written all over his expression.

"Triton, please," I said quickly. "We didn't expect this."

I cupped his face and kissed him softly and he finally wrapped his arms around me.

"Maddy, do you want to marry him too?" Billie asked gently.

I looked at her and then back to him. It had been a day of severely shocking events.

"I know it's fast and insane, but yes, I believe in this magical bond and I can feel it."

"I've never heard of mates who didn't want to bond," Triton said sadly, sliding the rings back into his pocket. He looked like an abandoned lost puppy dog with his sad pouty eyes.

"Is that why I want to climb him like a tree?" Billie asked.
"I thought it was just the hormones."

"Same," I said.
"I lost all thought when we kissed earlier. I should feel guilty, because I

am utterly devoted to you, Billie. You are all I ever wanted. This magic mate thing, it must be real for me to care this much about him. I don't feel guilt, I feel desire and need for both of you. I only feel more drawn to him every moment he is near."

"Maddy, I'd never shame you for your feelings," Billie said. "I've always been open to polyamory. You've been honest and that's all I care about."

She turned to Triton, pulling him down to her level.

"Oh, sweet prince," she said, smiling. "Come here."

She pulled him into a warm embrace, her belly between them.

"Kiss me?" she asked.

Just like that, we took the next step together, the three of us.

Chapter Nine: Kane's Wrath

-Kane-

The void of the God realm shimmered with an ominous brilliance, stars bending around Kane's will as if the cosmos itself feared to defy him. Clad in black and crimson armor forged from the shattered bones of forgotten worlds.

The God of war and chaos stood atop his obsidian dais. Below him, the swirling maelstrom of time and space bowed, pulsing with his dark intent.

Kane stared into the threads of fate, his jagged crown humming with ancient power. His shadow stretched across the realm like a living thing, curling around trembling acolytes who dared not breathe too loudly in his presence.

"Harmony," he sneered, the name like acid on his tongue.

"The Goddess Harmony, a meddler and coward."

With a flick of his wrist, he shattered a starlight mirror that displayed her realm. Glass and light scattered into the void like screams.

"She dares to love and protect them," Kane growled, pacing the length of his throne chamber. His every step cracked the fabric of reality beneath him.

"Love," he spat. "Such folly and weakness, who does this Goddess think she is?"

"She would have been a strong Goddess had she made masses of worlds. What a waste for a creator God. She dared to interfere in my business. I think it's a shame she is so weak, this will be too easy of a victory."

Kane turned to his war council, a circle of dark lesser Gods, their features hidden behind woven cloaks of the silence between galaxies. They flinched as he spoke.

"She defied my law to not cross into my territory, her beloved Hecat too. She defied me, I will burn her world until not even her name remains and then I will claim everything Hecat has created. These lesser Gods will pay for their insolence."

One of the cloaked Gods dared to whisper, "But my lord, Harmony is more than you believe she is, and not the timid spirit of old. She is forbidden to touch and protected, why do you think she is so unknown for a creator God?"

Kane's black eyes flared with a thousand dying suns. With a gesture, the God who had spoken erupted into ash, his scream echoing into eternity. He would be able to remake himself slowly and throughout a millennium of time. That's what the insolent God gets for speaking nonsense to me without an invitation to speak in my presence. It felt good to spank these fools when they dare to speak out of line.

"Let that be your last doubt. I am Kane, the storm that destroys, I will not be denied. Even the Great Creator himself cannot stop me."

A gasp of fear radiated amongst the lesser Gods. "He dares to speak of the Great Creator that way." A whisper echoed.

The veiled lesser Gods seemed to freeze, when they all felt the Great Creator, who was somewhere in a universe far away. The Great Creator turned his focus towards them and zeroed in on them all.

"Kane! You will mind your own, do not dare to defy me."

Every God and celestial there crumbled in pain from just that encounter, a painful warning in that swift gaze.

The lesser God that Kane had turned to ash was made whole again by the Great Creator and seated back in his place. Vanishing quickly and fleeing before Kane could strike again.

Kane recovered, laughing wickedly, "No matter, soon I will be strong enough to finally challenge the Great Creator, after I claim Hecat's universe. No God will match my power."

He turned back to the great viewing pool, a churning ocean of time. Within its depths he saw Harmony's world, still standing, bathed in the soft light of her healing magic.

He saw Maddy, touched by divine light, her soul crackling with blooming potential.

A Demi-Goddess. Maddy with her long curly blonde hair and her bright blue eyes, her sultry body.

One of the Great Creator's humans, so disgraceful to make those beings godlike. He saw Billie radiating strength and empathy, Triton loyal and fierce.

He saw the child growing in Billie, surrounded by a shield of light that even his gaze could not pierce. I make my beings small so they know their place. The lesser are just pawns and should never resemble celestials.

His sneer deepened. "The Goddess Harmony, she gathers her champions, rebuilding and hopeful." Disgusted that this Harmony would bless her creation so. He started to cast his powerful will out into the cosmos.

"Let it begin." Kane sneered.

The viewing pool flared red when he reached out his hand. Storms of chaos began to seep into the mortal realms.

"Let them build, I will destroy it all. One by one, their stars will fall. The child, all the heroes, even the Goddess herself, will bow before oblivion. It's like shoveling snow while it's a blizzard out. Their efforts, hope and fighting spirit I will break." Kane mused to himself.

The heavens answered when he raised his hand high and dark comets of annihilation shot through the celestial corridors. The Kanenites fleet stirred, war engines ignited, and dimensions cracked open to unleash an onslaught unlike any before.

"Send the signal," Kane commanded.

"We march on Harmony's realm, let the skies rain fire." He stepped forward, his voice ringing across the realms. As he opened his God portals to Harmony's precious planet.

"I will reduce her song to silence and turn her love into dust. When the Gods whisper in fear, they will know that I, Kane, Destroyer of Harmony, am the God killer."

A deep boom echoed as the God realms shook. Across the pantheons, divine beings paused, their eyes widening in dread.

War had begun, and Kane would settle for nothing less than complete and eternal ruin.

The Great Creator Stirred.

Chapter Ten: Seduction Between The Waves

-Maddy-

The sun was sinking behind the horizon, spreading molten gold and radiant purples deeper across the sky. I watched as the ocean started to glow. Tiny threads of turquoise shimmered beneath the waves, like the sea was exhaling starlight or maybe just breathing a little easier.

The salty air mixed with citrus and something sweeter, something alive, like the whole world was holding its breath. The magic was seeping into my soul.

I stood in the surf, the hem of my tunic soaked from the water, feeling the warmth of the day clinging to my sun-kissed skin. Behind me, Billie's soft laugh floated from the hammock that Triton had strung between two jeweled palms. They were similar to Earth's palm trees, but the color was more pastel green than the dark green canopy of them on Earth. Even glowing in a soft magical way.

Damn, that sound wrapped around me like silk. It was impossible to stay sharp, let alone paranoid, when Billie laughed like that. She always had this way of making everything seem lighter, even when my mind was tangled in knots.

Triton was sitting by a small fire he had built from driftwood. The flames shimmered blue, casting ghostly reflections in his dark brown eyes, eyes that always seemed to hold a secret storm. He looked up and caught my attention, the faintest smile playing on his lips.

"Hungry?" he asked. His voice deep and low, carrying softly over the surf.

I crossed my arms, raising an eyebrow.

"You fed us half the ocean already. I think we're good," I said as I waved at the seafood cart that we feasted on earlier. He pushed up smoothly, like a wave rolling to shore, and tilted his head.

"Then maybe it's not food you need." His eyes sharpened, teasing.

I rolled my eyes. "Are you suggesting something else, Triton?"

In one fluid motion, stepping closer until he was just close enough that the warmth of the fire met the cool breeze between us. "You're still waiting for me to prove something," he murmured, voice almost a whisper.

"Always," I shot back, trying to sound annoyed, but my voice was softer than I wanted.

He tilted his head and reached towards my face, slowly brushing a wet curl from my cheek, an intimate touch that burned hotter than the fire. I caught my breath.

"I don't trust easily, but our mate bond, this magic has me off kilter. Is it me that wants you this badly or is it just this magic?" I asked, a little breathless, trying to steady myself.

"I know Earth works differently. I just cannot imagine not having a mate bond and magic," Triton said quietly, almost reassuringly. "But you haven't run away yet."

The words cut through my defenses. I wanted to believe him, but my heart was still guarded. Billie's voice drifted over us, gentle and drowsy.

"You two look like you're daring the sea to swallow you up. I can feel the sexual tension from here."

Triton's gaze didn't leave mine. "It already has," he said softly.

Billie smiled, eyes half-lidded, and shook her head. "Then stop fighting it."

Night deepened around us. Two moons with shimmering rings hovered in the sky, framing stars that bloomed like tiny promises. I sat beside Billie, trying to stay calm but my heartbeat was doing a jittery dance against my ribs.

Triton sat on the sand across from us, elbows on his knees with the fire's glow painting his shoulders with gold and blue hues. His ebony muscled body showcased like an offering. I couldn't stop staring.

Billie reached out of her hammock and traced her fingertips along my arm.

"You're tense," she said quietly.

"I'm fine," I insisted, but my voice cracked.

"You're shaking," Billie whispered, voice softer now.

"You can relax here with us."

Her words hit me like a bomb, soothing, no game, just love pure and simple. I leaned into her, feeling her hand settle over my pounding heart.

"That male is too sexy for his own good. Umm, Umm!" Billie admired.

"I know, it should be a crime to be that good looking," I said breathlessly.

Triton watched the ocean quietly, eyes dark with reverence. The ocean responded, bioluminescent waves rolled closer, each crest pulsing with faint violet light. The fire flickered as if the air itself was leaning in to listen.

Then Triton finally spoke, almost as if to the water itself.

"This place was once sacred," he said, voice barely above a whisper.

"Before kingdoms and crowns, lovers new to the mate bond came here to vow to the tide and the ocean. If she answered, it meant their hearts would forever beat in the same current."

Billie brushed her fingers through my hair. "And what does the ocean say about us?"

Triton lifted his gaze, a shimmer dancing in his eyes.

"It's already singing. Listen..."

The waves hummed, deep and resonant, a low note that vibrated through my bones and heartbeat. It wasn't a sound exactly, more like a feeling that was warm, ancient, and alive. It felt like it was welcoming me home.

"Magic trick," I said, swallowing hard. I was trying to play it cool as my lust for them had me throbbing in all the right places.

Triton shook his head. "A blessing from the Goddess Harmony. She's listening."

That name hit my chest like a punch.

"The Goddess Harmony that carried us through war, loss, and now... hope. Her power is in every tide, every breath of creation. I am honored she has blessed me to be mated to each of you," Triton said in reverence.

"Maddy, my Sea Queen, my new daughter. Accept my blessing and enjoy your mating." An ethereal voice chimed inside my mind.

"Did I just hear my name?" I rubbed my arms that exploded in gooseflesh.

I felt my whole being react as magic infused within my soul. Looking at Billie swaying in her hammock, her skin was shades darker brown now after being in the sun today. She looked radiant, her eyes flashed brightly towards mine.

"Did you feel that too?" she asked, excitement written all over her like a spell.

The crystal platforms that were floating up among the clouds in the sky, they chimed and lit up in a magical dance of lights. The ocean glowed bright blue with purple light as far as the eye could see. The magic was divine, I could feel the Goddess as she and the sea accepted us as a trio of love.

I saw figures surface out in the sea. The water dwellers gathered, who knew how many waded out there. Their upper bodies bobbing like a thousand buoys dancing among the waves. Some of them blew into seashells, playing music that lent to the celebration of our blessing. After the music faded, the water dwellers sank below the surface of the sea. The sea slowly lost its intense glow and in the sky crystal platforms dimmed. Leaving me breathless and hungry. I was salivating with need.

I looked at Triton who stood up onto his feet, and he picked Billie up from her hammock. Both of them looking lustfully towards me.

"We need our bed, now!" I said, rushing past them. I slapped Triton's ass playfully. I picked up my pace to lead the way to the castle.

I made it to the cobblestone pathway that weaved itself up the cliff to the land kingdom above. The moon's glow showcased the giant Niagara Falls style waterfall that fell into the ocean below from the

Dragoon kingdom above. The rush of water was loud, I could still hear my Triton, as he spoke.

"As you wish, my Sea Queen," Triton's deep response, sending desire rushing down my spine.

Chapter Eleven: Feels Like The First Time

-Maddy-

My breath hitched as we entered the royal suite. The bed on display was waiting with a naughty invitation. My heart thrummed so hard I felt the drum of it pulsing in my ears, as if a wild bird was caught in my ribcage.

The opulence of the room was more than I could have even imagined when I dreamed of being intimate with Billie for the first time.

Now, I know she loves me in return as her lover too, more than just the friends we have always been. Our lifetime together is secure now, and now we had a sexy surprise merman thrown in the mix.

I see Billie radiant and beautiful as she scoots onto the bed while Triton slowly kisses her.

My desire to kiss her and taste both of them is heightening my arousal as I watch them. Liquid heat throbs down my thigh as my clit dances to the tune of my racing heart.

Triton undressed Billie, laying her naked on the bed. She was the most beautiful offering from the Gods themselves, perfect in every way.

I walked to Triton whose heated dark eyes captured all of my attention and need.

"That's my good girl."

When he kissed me, my knees buckled, and I moaned into his mouth as he began taking my dress off. I broke apart from his scorching kiss as he pulled my dress over my head.

He lifted me and placed me next to Billie on the bed so he could feast on me with his mouth.

"That was so fucking hot!" Billie whispered as our lips met for a sensual kiss.

Oh, my stars, her lips were soft, feminine, and sweet tasting. Our tongues danced together in uniform. I reached for her breast, and she gripped my hair. I knew then I was in Heaven.

"You both felt what this was from the start, now it's more than just desire. You're mine and I have claimed you in every way that matters. No one else will ever take what's mine."

Triton, in full naked splendor, was a sight to behold. Broad shoulders and a sculpted chest that seemed to ripple with every movement, the smooth, deep hue of his skin glowed under the soft crystal lighting.

Muscles spoke of strength and power, flexed as he stood tall, his presence commanding yet inviting. His dark eyes burned with intensity, locking onto mine with a look that promised more than just passion. It was an unspoken claim, a raw connection that made the air between us heavy with anticipation.

The way he moved towards me, slow and deliberate, exuded both confidence and tenderness. It was as if every inch of his body knew exactly what it was doing, and every step drew me closer to the undeniable heat between us.

He kissed me hard with an animalistic growl of arousal. "You respond so well to me, I can smell your need."

His hands mapped my body with his rough fingertips, Billie using her hands on the backside of me, both driving me mad with the softness of Billie and the hardness of Triton. The concoction was almost too intense all at once.

Triton pulled his fingers up to my heated core, teasing. I arched forward, wanting and needing him to fill me in every way possible.

"Please," I begged.

"Allow me to explore the sacred part of you, Maddy?"

"Don't hold back now. Take me!"

I smelled the sweet scent of Billie, jasmine and fresh air. I heard her hitch her breath and felt her lips on my shoulder as Triton played with my wet folds, expertly applying pressure and circling my sensitive bud.

"Oh, my fucking stars!" I was panting when he finally sunk his two center fingers inside me. I rode his hand, desperately building an arch, needing to crash over that edge with just his hand alone.

"Triton, don't stop!" I begged.

"Ride his finger, come for us," Billie urged.

I exploded, spraying all over his hand like a sinful waterfall.

"Fuck!" Triton hissed.

"I love how good you respond to my touch." He kissed me and then Billie. Licking his middle finger, he moaned.

"Sweeter than nectar from the Gods. Billie, taste our Maddy."

Triton took his other finger and placed it in Billie's mouth, moaning in delight as she eagerly sucked my taste from his finger. It was so fucking hot. All I wanted was to taste Billie. I crawled off the bed and gently touched her thigh, looking into her eyes, silently begging her for permission. She spread them wide for me.

Her velvet smooth pussy bloomed in wet folds like an opening flower. So beautiful and perfect. The scent of sweet wet feminine arousal, decadent and alluring, hung in the air around us.

"I need to taste you, Billie, may I?" I teased her, peppering kisses along her thigh, resisting the urge to taste her.

"Yes, Maddy, I need you so bad. Please let Triton take you first from behind so I can see both of you," Billie begged. I swear I saw her pussy pulse with need.

Triton kissed Billie hard and brought his big handsome body up to stand next to me. The size of his engorged cock had me slightly intimidated, but mostly eager for him to fill me. He kissed my lips, and I could taste myself.

His full lips worked on my ear and neck, working his way to my breast, replacing the fingers that were tweaking my nipples with his mouth. Triton stood, tall and sexier than any man should. His eyes hungry as he gently turned me towards Billie again.

He moved my hair off of my shoulder as he stood behind me and spoke in my ear, "Be a good Sea Queen and eat that perfect pussy that our Billie is offering you."

Goosebumps spread over my body, my mouth was eager. I gently kissed around Billie's folds, teasing her with my tongue. I took her rosebud in my mouth, sucking and licking, finding a rhythm she reacted well to. Her hips thrust and ground her heat into my face. I loved the taste of her, her softness, and the sweet little moans she gave.

Triton gripped my hips, grazing my entrance with his cock from behind. I tried to see Billie's face, her beautifully rounded ripe belly blocked my view.

Closing my eyes, it felt like I had found my soul. My body stretched with a delicious ache as Triton slowly entered me.

His grip tightened on my hips. "You are so perfectly tight, Maddy, you were made for me." He said with a strained voice as he held back.

"Right there, Maddy, just like that, don't stop." I heard Billie beg.

"I have to move now, Maddy, I can't resist any longer."

I arched back and moaned from tasting Billie and Triton claiming my body from behind.

Billie screamed in pleasure. "Maddy, oh, my God, Maddy, you're so fucking good!" Her wetness slathered my face with her orgasm, and it was the hottest thing I had ever experienced.

I lifted my head to see Billie, eyes hooded in the aftermath of her release. She moved to bring her face close to mine and kissed me, tasting herself on my lips.

"He looks so fine, fucking you. Do you like how he feels, Maddy?"

"Yes, he's so big, so good." Then I felt fuller than I thought I could possibly stretch. I felt his hardness vibrating. That's new. Oh, that is amazing.

I felt her grab my hair at the base of my skull. She pulled with the perfect amount of pain and pleasure.

"Then show both of us how you can take it like a good girl, Maddy," Billie said in my ear.

A wave of liquid heat lubricated Triton's large vibrating cock. I felt him smack my ass, the sound a lustful clap in the room. He pounded my wetness from behind, our bodies and our moans filled the space in sync.

Billie moaned in my ear and hearing her say, "Yes! Fuck her good."

Her enthusiasm made each of his vibrating strokes fill me with more pleasure. Time was lost on me. The only sensation was the love growing between us. I was wrapped up in bliss.

The sight of Billie's face was the final push that made me crash over the crescendo. My heart pounded, my orgasmic release had been soul deep. Panting, we all ended up on the bed, our limbs entangled, reveling in our entwined love.

The bed held us as if it was satisfied that we were sated, as a triad, together eternally.

Chapter Twelve: Too Good To Be True

-Maddy-

By the time the sun began to dip behind the glittering spires of the Dragoon Castle, the dining den echoed with laughter, clinking glasses, and the occasional dramatic groan over a bad card draw. The golden light filtered through the stained-glass windows, painting the table in shifting mosaics of blue, violet, and gold. The sweet, spiced aroma of berry cider lingered in the air, mingling with the salty tang drifting in from the coast.

Billie tossed her last hand onto the table and pouted, lips forming a perfect, exaggerated frown. "Seriously? Again? Ugh, that's like, five times in a row." She slumped in her seat, throwing her hands up in mock despair.

Talen, ever the showman, smirked and leaned into Kayla's side, his arm draping over her shoulders. "You keep betting against me and you'll never defeat the royal family's undefeated poker God." He stuck his tongue out at me behind Kayla's back, his index fingers pressing into imaginary dimples on his cheeks.

Kayla nudged him. "You're only undefeated because you cheat, Talen."

He gasped in mock offense. "I'd never! My hands are clean."

"Show them, Maddy, show them how a real card shark plays," Billie insisted.

I grinned, swirling my cider. "I don't reveal my secrets for free."

Fang, not bothering to look up from his carved horn of cider, said flatly, "You've won twice, Talen. Don't get cocky."

Brooke, reclining into her lover's arm, flashed a slow and knowing grin. "Twice too many, if you ask me." She drew a lazy circle on the table with her fingertip, her eyes glinting with quiet amusement.

Billie looked up at me, her eyes wide and pleading, and huffed dramatically. "Help me! Defend my honor, Maddy! I can't keep losing to these sharks."

Triton, beside me, bare-chested and still smelling faintly of salt, leaned forward, his eyes gleaming with mischief. "If we're teaming up, it's not going to be fair. The rest of you might as well fold now."

Billie clapped her hands together in mock prayer. "I accept these terms. Maddy, you're my only hope."

I gave her a sly look. "Only if you promise to let me sleep in tomorrow morning."

She grinned. "Deal and breakfast in bed, if you help me win."

Talen groaned. "You're all cheaters, every last one of you."

Kayla winked at me. "That's why we love her."

The card game became a battle of wits and flirtation, full of whispered secrets and lingering touches. Fingers brushed against fingers beneath the table, knees knocked together, and laughter spilled over like wine. Every so often, someone would lose a hand and demand a forfeit, a story, or a kiss on the cheek.

Brooke, typically the most composed of us, arched a brow when Triton casually stroked a line down my back while answering a question about oceanic sonic communication. "Not fair, using your magic touch to distract the competition," she teased.

Triton grinned. "I make no apologies. Maddy's my lucky charm."

Billie, slightly flushed from her pregnancy or maybe from the company, leaned in between us and whispered, "I think they all know."

I tilted my head, amused. "Know what, love?"

"That we're going to disappear and do unspeakably delicious things once this game ends."

Triton chuckled, the sound low and rich as the sea's waves. "Then let's make sure the game ends on a high note."

Fang raised his glass. "To high notes and hedonistic thoughts."

"Here, here!" Talen and Kayla chorused and we all laughed, the warmth in the room growing deeper.

Just then, a sudden, odd flash of light illuminated the room, casting stark shadows across our faces. The laughter faltered.

"Was that lightning?" Billie asked, her voice uncertain.

Before anyone could answer, a thunderous crack echoed from outside. The tower's walls shuddered faintly, followed by a rumble like stones sliding down a mountainside.

Suddenly, a scream pierced the air. Talen was on his feet in an instant, his chair clattering to the floor. "That came from the cliff."

We all ran toward the open doors to view outside. The wind whipped through the skybridges as our group bolted toward the watchtower, hearts pounding, adrenaline surging. The castle's cold stone floors chilled my bare feet as we raced past tapestries and flickering torches.

Fang muttered, "Please let it not be what I think it is."

A bear shifter, a massive guardian named Bodrick, loyal since the old days of the throne, had been stationed there to monitor the coast for dangers. We arrived just in time to see his large, furry form, half shifted, slip off the crumbling edge of the cliff.

"Shit!" Fang shouted, voice raw with panic.

My heart leapt into my throat. I reached for Billie, steadying her as she stumbled.

"It's okay, I've got you," I whispered.

But Triton was already gone, a streak of shadow, leaping over the edge with unnatural grace, diving straight into the roaring sea below.

Kayla gasped. "He's insane!"

Talen peered over the edge. "He is the prince of the water dwellers. He will be just fine."

The fall would have broken a human apart. Even a shifter wouldn't survive long in those waters, churned wild by the stormy winds. Bodrick thrashed as rocks scraped his limbs, the surf dragging him under again and again.

I found myself clutching Billie's hand, both of us silent, eyes wide.

But Triton hit the waves like a torpedo, the ocean bowing to his command. Underwater, he moved with effortless power, muscles surging as he caught the limp bear shifter and kicked hard for the surface. The sea, once dangerous, bent itself around him in a swirling shield of current and foam. The water was his to command.

We watched breathless, as he emerged holding Bodrick in his arms, half drenched in light, as if the Gods themselves had drawn a spotlight down just for him.

When they reached shore, Gemma was already kneeling on the slick rock. She pressed her glowing hands to Bodrick's bruised chest. "I've got him," she murmured after a long pause.

Bodrick coughed up seawater, his eyes wild and confused, before collapsing into a healing sleep.

The group let out a collective breath. Gemma brushed damp hair off her face, exhaling. "He'll live. He'll be sore as hell, but he'll live."

Kayla grinned shakily. "Remind me to never complain about guard duty again."

Talen clapped Triton on the back as he trudged up the path, water streaming off him. "That was one hell of a dive. You alright?"

Triton nodded, breathing hard. "I'm fine. Bodrick's heavy, but I've handled worse."

Billie squeezed my hand. "You did it. He's okay."

I nodded, my throat tight. "Yeah. He's okay."

Talen's voice was all business now. "You'll have to excuse us. We need to investigate this collapse. The rest of you, get inside and stay warm."

The card game was forgotten, replaced by the urgency of the moment.

It all happened so fast. My anxiety spiked, worried for Triton as he had jumped off the cliff to the sea below. No human could survive a dive like that. These beings moved fast and in impossible ways. But he returned, running back up the path to us again, water streaming from his skin, his chest rising and falling in deep, steady breaths.

Triton stood there, water cascading down his bare skin, as he turned toward Billie and me. In that moment, something invisible shifted. It was in the way Billie looked at him, mouth slightly parted, and the way I gazed at him, lingering on his chest, shoulders, the curve of his mouth, and the darkness of his eyes. Just like that, my anxiety twisted into another type of need.

We held hands and went to our room.

Back in our shared chamber, the fire roared high, casting flickering shadows across the stone walls. I pressed a towel to Triton's wet chest, scowling with affection. "You could've died."

He caught my wrist, his eyes deep and dark, searching over my face. "There was never a danger of me dying. The water is my home. Fear not, Maddy."

I shook my head, voice trembling. "You say that, but I watched you go over the edge and I couldn't breathe until you came back."

Billie's fingers brushed down my back, gentle and reassuring. "He saved a life tonight, Maddy. He'd do it again."

Triton looked at her, then at me. "I'd do it a thousand times for either of you."

"Yes, he did. Our own sea hero," I said, my voice gone soft, almost reverent.

He stepped closer, his presence filling the room. "You were scared for me."

I tried to laugh, but it came out shaky. "I'm not used to being scared over a man."

He traced a line along my jaw, his touch feather light. "You don't have to be. I'll always come back to you."

Billie slipped between us, her arms circling both our waists. "Can we just... stay here? The three of us. No more cliffs or storms. Just this?"

Triton's lips curved into a slow and wicked smile. "That's the only kind of danger I want tonight."

I leaned into him, feeling the heat of his skin, the steady beat of his heart. "You're reckless," I whispered, my forehead pressed to his chest.

He tilted my chin up, his thumb brushing my cheek. "For you? Always."

Billie's laughter was soft, breathless. "Gods, you two. You make me feel like I'm caught in a riptide."

Triton's gaze flicked to her, hungry and adoring. "Then let me pull you under."

He kissed her first, slow and deep, his hands framing her face. I watched, while my heart was pounding, desire curling low in my belly. When he turned to me, I didn't hesitate. I met him halfway, our mouths colliding in a kiss that tasted of salt and longing.

We tumbled onto the bed in a tangle of limbs, laughter and moans mingling with the crackle of the fire. Billie's hands found mine, our fingers lacing together as Triton's lips traced a path down my neck.

"I thought I'd lost you," I murmured, my voice barely a whisper.

He stilled, his forehead pressed to my shoulder. "You never will. Not while there's breath in my body."

Billie pressed kisses to my shoulder, her voice soft. "We're safe now. We're together."

I let out a shaky breath. "I think I love you both a little more every time we survive something like this."

Triton laughed, pressing his lips to my forehead. "Then let's keep surviving, so you'll keep loving us."

Billie grinned, her cheeks flushed. "Deal, but only if you promise never to scare us like that again."

He raised his hand in mock solemnity. "I'll try, but no promises. Trouble tends to find me."

The storm outside faded into a distant memory, replaced by the warmth of the fire, the softness of their skin against mine, the steady rhythm of our hearts beating in time.

Later, as we lay tangled together, Triton traced lazy circles on my back. "Tell me what you're thinking."

I smiled, eyes drifting closed. "I'm thinking I've never felt more alive."

Billie snuggled closer, her breath warm against my ear. "I'm thinking we should never play cards with Talen again."

We laughed, the sound bright and free. For the first time in a long time, I felt whole.

Triton kissed my temple; his voice made a promise. "Whatever storms come, we'll face them together."

Billie squeezed my hand. "Together. Always." At that moment, I believed them both.

Chapter Thirteen: The Devil's Warning

-Lucifer-

The sanctuary of Hell is a pocket of stillness, a secret folded into the creases of forgotten time, deep beneath the layers of Heaven and the mortal world. It is my sanctuary, exile, throne, cage, and kingdom. Crimson light spills across the obsidian stone floors, slanting through cracks in the ceiling where the bones of ancient angels are mortared into the rock. Vines wrapped with living fire slither up the walls, hissing and whispering secrets only I understand. They are my companions, my reminders.

In the center of the chamber, a single pool steams with molten gold, its surface rippling to the rhythm of my breath. I sit on a throne made of shattered halos, one boot resting lazily on a demon's skull, arms draped across the carved bone. After eons of war, betrayal, exile, and blood, I finally have peace. I have Lilith, or so I thought. There is always something threatening to unravel the fragile fabric of my contentment.

She stalks across the room like a black flame, her presence more shadow than flesh, her lips stained with wine and defiance. I know that look. I know the storm gathering behind her eyes.

"You're really not going to do anything?" she hisses, the firelight catching in her gaze, making her irises burn like coals. "While Kane moves against Harmony?"

I don't open my eyes. I've learned that sometimes, the best way to win an argument with Lilith is to pretend not to notice it's happening. "The last time I got involved with divine drama, I fell from grace and landed in fire."

She scoffs, a sound sharp as broken glass. "You built the fire, Lucifer. Don't pretend you're just a victim of circumstance. Do something! Harmony is my best friend."

I sigh, letting my head fall back against the throne. "I like the fire," I say, my voice smooth as oil. "It keeps the others out. It keeps the world at bay."

She circles me, bare feet slapping the stone, her anger a living thing. "She's like a sister to me."

I crack an eye open, watching her pace. "She's the Great Creator's child. A godling made of creation, destruction, and love. A power none of us truly understand. She was never mine to protect."

Lilith stops in front of me, her silhouette a cutout of darkness against the gold-lit pool. She steps between my legs, grabs my face in both hands, and forces me to look at her. Her fingers are cool, but her will is fire.

"She's mine to protect then. Whether you like it or not, her essence echoes through me, your favorite fire. If you let Kane consume her, there won't be a sanctuary left for either of us."

Her words are a blade, but I have been cut before. "Then maybe they should all burn," I said, my voice low and dangerous. "The whole damned pantheon deserves to fall."

She doesn't flinch. "Then help her light the match," Lilith growls. "Don't you dare sit on your throne and pretend you're not still a God."

I rise slowly and deliberately, letting my power coil around my limbs, old and raw. When I look at her, my eyes blaze red gold. "I'm not a God," I say. "I'm what he made when he tossed me out. I will do as you wish, and I will try, my dear Lilith. But don't mistake me for a savior."

She leans forward, pressing her forehead to mine. "I don't want a savior. I want you. I want the Devil who made the angels tremble. I want the man who loved me before the world had a name."

I close my eyes, letting her words sink into the cracks in my armor. "Then you shall have him," I whisper. "For you, I would burn the stars themselves."

I do not walk, I arrived. The sky split like paper, and I stepped through, smoke rolling off my coat. My horns curved from my temples like molten iron. Black wings flared behind me, the edges bleeding starlight.

Kane stands on a floating citadel of obsidian, surrounded by followers cloaked in silver veils. Below them, entire star systems crack beneath the weight of his ambition. The veiled disciples fall to their knees, wailing and blinded by my presence. I ignore them, they are nothing.

Kane turns, his face impassive, but I see the flicker of fear in his eyes. Good.

"You've gotten comfortable playing king, Kane," I say, my voice echoing across the planes. "You're still just a spoiled boy with too much power and not enough purpose."

He narrows his eyes. "I didn't summon you."

"You didn't have to," I growl. "I smelled the rot from my sanctuary."

He smirks, but it's brittle. "You're afraid. The gods bow and the mortals pray, while you hide in your pit with your queen. Harmony threatens your isolation, that's the only reason you're here."

I bare my teeth in a grin, terrible and sharp. "I care because you're too stupid to know what you're waking. Harmony is not your conquest and definitely not another throne to break, or soul to defile. She is beyond you."

He steps closer, radiating cold, crackling divine force. "Then why hasn't she destroyed me? Why hasn't her so called power revealed itself?"

I let my face darken, my true voice rising, a force older than the stars. "She still hopes and loves and hasn't tapped into her full power. It's not wise for you to bang on that door."

Kane laughs, the sound brittle as glass. "You're protecting her. How quaint, does your queen know you still play at being Heaven's warden?"

I let my anger show, letting it curl around my words like smoke. "I am no warden. I am the fire at the end of all things. I am the last word the universe will ever speak."

He sneers. "You're a relic, Lucifer. A warning story for children. I am the future, the gods are dying and you're too afraid to let go."

I step closer, letting my shadow swallow his. "You don't know what fear is, Kane, but you will."

He lifts his chin, defiant. "Try me."

The Devil in me rises. I let my true voice loose. It isn't sound, it's fire infused with infernal will. The scream of a thousand fallen stars, the raging judgment of a God cast out and risen again.

"Back off!"

The force of the warning shatters nearby moons. Kane staggers, a line of blood dripping from one ear. I vanish in a blink, leaving nothing but scorched stone and silence.

I return to my sanctuary and find Lilith waiting. She sits on the edge of the pool, her feet dangling in the molten gold, her eyes distant.

"Well?" she asks, not looking at me.

"He's persistent," I admit, dropping into my throne. "But he's not as clever as he thinks."

She glances at me, arching an eyebrow. "Did you threaten him?"

I smirk. "I gave him a taste of what happens when you poke the Devil."

She laughed, low and dangerous. "You always did have a flair for the dramatic."

I lean forward, elbows on my knees. "He wants Harmony. He wants what he can't have. It has always been his weakness."

Lilith sighs. "It's everyone's weakness, isn't it? Wanting what we can't have."

I watch her, the way the firelight dances on her skin. "Is that why you stay with me?"

She meets my gaze, unflinching. "I stay because I choose to. Not because I can't have you, but because I do."

I reach for her, pulling her into my lap. She fits against me like she was made for this place, for this moment. "Then let's make sure we keep what's ours."

She kissed me, fierce and unyielding. "Promise me you'll protect her."

I sigh, resting my forehead against hers. "I promise I'll try. But you know how these things go. Gods make promises and the universe laughs."

She smiles, sad and sweet. "Then let's make the universe weep."

I remember the first time I fell. The shock of cold air, the burning atmosphere, the way the stars spun above me as I tumbled through creation. I remember the taste of ash, the sound of angels weeping, the weight of my own regret. I remember thinking, this is the end.

But it wasn't, it was only the beginning.

Now, I sit on my throne of bones and broken halos, Lilith curled at my feet, and wonder if I am doomed to repeat my own history. To watch as the things I love are torn from me, one by one.

No, not this time. I am not defying the Great Creator this time. I will aid him and fight for Harmony.

I rise, power thrumming through me, and call the shadows to me. If Kane wants a war, he will have one. But he will learn, just as Heaven did and just as I did, that some fires cannot be quenched.

I will protect Harmony. For Lilith and myself, and the sanctuary we've carved out of the ruins of our past.

And if the universe burns, so be it.

"You always say you're powerless, but you're not. You're just afraid of what you'll become if you care again." Lilith pouts.

"I am not afraid of caring. I am afraid of what caring costs. The last time I cared, I lost everything."

"You didn't lose me." Lilith said.

"Not yet."

"So fight, for me, Harmony, and yourself."

"You ask for war."

"No, I ask for love. Sometimes, they're the same thing."

I have been many things, a son, soldier, angel, monster, king, and a fool. But above all, I am a survivor. I have survived Heaven's wrath, Hell's hunger, the slow erosion of hope. I have survived myself.

Lilith is right. I cannot sit idle while Kane threatens the fragile peace we've built. I cannot let Harmony fall. Not for her sake, but for mine. Because if I let her die, I will lose Lilith and myself.

So, I will fight and if the universes must end, let it end in fire.

Chapter fourteen: The Womb Of All The Gods

-The Great Mother-

I stand alone in the Garden Between Stars, a sanctuary older than memory, where time does not pass and love first bloomed. Here the universe is quiet. The air is thick with the scent of celestial blossoms, their petals shimmering with dew spun from the first dawn. The ground beneath my bare feet pulses with the heartbeat of creation. This is my place, carved from longing before even the Great Creator awoke.

There is no one here but me. Not even the Great Creator can enter unless I will it, for I shaped this place from my own heart, never have I surrendered its keys. I made it as a refuge, a secret place where I could be more than a Goddess, where I could simply be.

Crimson light spills across the stone paths, winding between trees whose branches cradle galaxies. Vines of living fire curl lazily up cracked pillars, their warmth a comfort and a warning. In the center of the garden, a pool steams with mist and blue waters, its surface rippling to the rhythm of my breath, reflecting the infinite stars above and the sorrows within me.

I press my hand to my chest and close my eyes. Across the countless galaxies, I feel her, my daughter Harmony. Her presence is a tremor in my soul, a song threaded with both hope and dread. She is so close now to breaking.

I whisper to the silence, "You're trembling, little one. I can feel it."

A petal falls from a nearby celestial tree. As it touches the ground, it becomes a nebula, spinning outward in slow luminous spirals. I smile faintly, the ache in my heart both sharp and sweet. This is the nature of love to create, destroy, and change.

"She was never meant to be known," I say softly, my voice carrying to the void, the stars, and the secret places within myself.

"Unlike the others made from thought, word, or decree, she was made from our desire."

The wind answers with memories. I remember the loneliness of the first light, wandering eons without companionship. I was worshipped, yes, but never known. The ache grew unbearable, a wound that would not heal.

So, I did what I had never dared before. I made my mate. The Great Creator, so powerful and brilliant, my answer to the void within me. I sculpted him from every curve of my loneliness, forged him in the fire of my longing.

He was not made from the dust of stars, nor bone or wind, but from want. When he opened his eyes, he saw me truly before creation, ego, and all else.

He worshipped me and in his worship, he created everything else. The stars, time, other Gods, and the realms of light and shadow. None of them knew my secret, how I had made him and why. The most powerful of all, able to shape universes with a word, breathe Gods into existence, and yet even he bowed to my love. He always knew I was the source.

I kneel by the crystal clear pool, the place where I once lay in divine labor. My voice is soft and reverent, a prayer to the memory of pain and joy.

"We had a daughter," I whisper.

"She was not like the others. She didn't come from thought, or a spark. She is of our flesh and bones, screams and blood. I carried her within me, not in spirit, but in truth. She broke me open with her birth, and she set me free."

The trees around me weep tears of golden sap, their branches bowing in empathy. "She is not light, or shadow. She is the Void, the unmaking."

I run my hand over the pool's surface, and it shows me a vision of Harmony as a child, laughing and glowing, flowers blooming beneath her bare feet. I remember the day she first learned to shape reality with her laughter, how the cosmos itself bent to her joy.

I remembered her childhood as if it were yesterday.

She was radiant, even as a child, her skin aglow, her hair a river of moonlight. She would chase stardust through the garden, giggling as nebulae blossomed in her wake. When she was happy, the universe brightened. When she cried, comets would streak across the sky, drawn by her sorrow.

There was a day when she found a wounded starling in the grass. She cupped it in her hands, her eyes wide with worry.

"Mama, it hurts," she whispered. I watched in awe as she breathed on it, and the bird's wings mended, feathers shimmering with new constellations. She set it free and it became a cluster of stars singing her name.

But there were darker moments, too. Once, in a fit of childish rage, she screamed at the sky, and a planet shattered in the distance. She stared at her hands, horrified, and ran to me sobbing. I held her close, smoothing her hair, whispering lullabies of love and forgiveness.

"You are not destruction, sweet one," I told her, though I feared it was not true.

The other Gods watched her warily. They whispered that she was too much, too powerful and unpredictable. Some wanted to hide her away, others wanted to use her. Only her father and I saw the innocence in her heart and the desperate need to belong.

She would climb into my lap and ask, "Why am I different?" I would answer, "Because you are made of love and longing, of everything that makes the universe ache for more."

I remember the day I realized her power was growing beyond anything we could guide or contain. She was barely more than a child, yet galaxies trembled when she dreamed. I saw fear in her father's eyes, the fear in my own.

That was when we made the choice.

We could not destroy her, nor could we let her become the end of all things. Together, her father and I wove a spell, a tapestry of love and memory, designed to anchor her in gentleness. To keep her from awakening the fullness of her power. We removed any memory of her from all Gods and celestial beings.

We waited until she slept, her breath soft and even, her dreams a swirl of creation and light. I brushed her hair from her brow, kissing her forehead. My tears fell on her cheeks, shimmering into tiny jewels.

The Great Creator stood beside me, his hands trembling. "Are you certain?" he asked, voice rough.

"No," I whispered, "but it is all we have."

We began with a song, a lullaby older than the stars, the same melody I sang to her as she grew within me. Our voices merged, weaving threads of love and hope, memory and forgetting. We called on every kindness, every moment of joy she had known. We wrapped her in a cocoon of beauty and warmth.

As we sang, I poured my own essence into the spell. I gave her my patience, compassion, and yearning for peace. Her father gave her his strength, wisdom, and longing for order. We braided our souls together, binding her to the memory of laughter and the promise of love.

I shaped the spell to mask her true nature, to make her believe she was only what she chose to be, a creator and lover, bringer of light. I hid the void within her, tucking it away behind layers of memory and tenderness. I left a path back, should she ever need to find herself, but I prayed she never would.

The spell shimmered around her, a gentle veil. She sighed in her sleep, curling closer to me. I pressed my lips to her ear and whispered, "You are loved, Harmony, and you are safe."

When the spell was done I collapsed beside her, empty and full all at once. The Great Creator gathered us both in his arms, and together we wept.

For years, the spell held. Harmony grew, believing herself to be only what we allowed her to remember. Her power flickered at the edges, but she did not see it. She loved fiercely, creating a world just for herself of beauty, balance, and magic. The universe flourished.

But the void cannot be denied forever. I feel it now, stirring in her heart, calling her to awaken. The spell is unraveling. I fear what will happen when she remembers.

The Great Creator appears beside me, his presence both a balm and a wound.

"We cannot save her," he says softly. "Not if she chooses destruction."

I nod, tears slipping down my cheeks. "But we can give her a reason to choose otherwise."

He kneels beside me, his hand covering mine. "How?"

I close my eyes, searching for an answer. "We remind her of who she is. Not a weapon or Goddess, but our daughter. We remind her that she is loved, not for her power, but for her heart."

He leans his forehead against mine, his breath warm against my skin. "Then let us begin."

We weave a second spell, not to bind, but to call her home. We pour our memories into the garden, into the fabric of the universe itself. We sing of her birth, laughter, and the love that made her. We sing of the pain and fear, the hope that she might find her way back.

The garden responds, blooming brighter, the air thick with the scent of promise. The pool glows, showing Harmony as she was, is, and could be.

I send my voice across the cosmos, a whisper only she can hear. "You are not alone, Harmony, you are loved. Come home."

I know the danger. If Harmony unleashes her full power, she will become destruction itself. The Gods will fall, worlds will burn, and even the Great Creator and I may not survive. But I cannot choose the universe over my child. I cannot choose safety over love.

I am the Mother Goddess of Love. I am the source, the beginning and the end. I am the reason the Great Creator exists. I am the reason Harmony exists. I will not abandon them.

If the universe must fall, let it fall. But let it fall knowing that it was loved.

The Great Creator stands beside me, his hand in mine. "Whatever happens, we face it together."

I nodded, my heart breaking and mending all at once. "Together always."

We watch the stars, waiting for the end, or the beginning.

Chapter Fifteen: The Other Shoe Dropped.

-Maddy-

Triton swooped Billie up in his arms and carried her to the sleek black couch. He sat with her cradled in his lap and kissed her like he had been starving for it.

Watching them turned me on instantly. Billie adjusted to straddle him, robe falling open as she deepened the kiss. I was willing to bet he was one very happy male.

He broke away from her lips to explore her breasts. Her robe had fallen open, her full chest on display, with nipples peaked and begging for attention.

Fuck, she was sexy.

Billie moaned as she ground her core against his lap, and he sucked a nipple into his mouth. Her gaze found mine, hot and heavy, and she crooked a finger, beckoning me closer.

She didn't have to ask me twice.

I slid in beside them and kissed her. She moaned into my mouth, the towel slipping from her hair, her robe pooling at her hips. She grabbed the back of my head and gently pushed me toward Triton, offering me to him like a gift.

His kiss devoured me.

"You two are so fucking hot," Billie murmured, voice rough with lust.

She slowly moved off Triton's lap, giving us space. I was already lost in need. His hand kneaded my breast, and he sucked in a shocked breath.

I broke away long enough to see Billie on her knees, working her magic as she sucked Triton's colossal cock. The sight made my head spin.

Billie pulled off with a wet pop and licked her lips. "He tastes so fucking good. You have to try this."

I eagerly joined her, taking him into my mouth. Billie's hands roamed over my breasts, teasing and squeezing, making it hard to focus on anything but the overload of sensation.

"You look so fucking hot, Maddy. Suck that huge cock," Billie whispered in my ear, her voice all smoke and sin.

"Fuck! You two are killing me," Triton groaned, pulling me off his vibrating, impossibly hard cock.

"We need the bed," he insisted, already stripping his pants as he stalked toward the massive bed, leaving a trail of clothes behind him.

I tore my clothes off, my skin buzzing, as Billie wrapped her arms around me from behind. I turned and kissed her, finally touching her the way I had craved for so long.

"His vibrating cock is incredible. Definitely not a human guy," Billie whispered between kisses.

"He's all ours now," I breathed. "Billie, this is all so perfect."

Triton came up behind her, pressing his chest to her back. He kissed the curve of her neck.

"I think we should lay Billie down and eat her sweet pussy. I want to take you both. I won't risk your pregnancy, Billie, I'll wait to fuck you the way I truly want to claim you, gods, I want to complete our bond. But I promise I'll give you orgasm after orgasm with my mouth."

"Don't tease me with a good time," Billie said, lying back on the bed and spreading herself like an offering.

Triton and I both moaned at the sight. Confidence looked so damn good on her.

"Fuck me, she's so damn sexy," I sighed.

"Devour me," Billie begged.

Triton moved before the last word left her mouth, latching onto her glistening pussy like a starving man.

"Oh my God, you are good at that," Billie moaned, her dark thighs wrapping over his shoulders.

I joined her, giving her a brief kiss before leaning down to suck one of her pebbled nipples into my mouth. Her hand fisted in my hair, sending a wild thrill through me. Her tits felt even better than I had ever imagined.

Billie writhed as her first orgasm crashed over her, a sharp, beautiful sound tearing from her throat.

I heard Triton moan against her, the sound of pure and satisfied triumph.

I pulled back for a moment just to take them in. Triton slowly lifted his mouth from between her thighs, his face slick with her wetness, his eyes dark and hungry as he stared up at her. They held each other's gaze, wrapped up in the moment, and it was so fucking sexy I almost forgot how to breathe.

"You came so well for me," he praised. "That's my good girl. Billie, you taste so sweet I didn't want to stop."

Then his gaze slid to me, hooded and blazing.

The heat between us could have melted castle walls.

He kissed me like the world was ending. It was brutal, wild, and claiming. My back hit the cold stone wall and I moaned into him, every nerve lit up. His hands roamed like he needed to memorize every curve.

Billie slipped off the bed and pressed herself against his back, her body molding to his. Her breath fanned hot over his neck. "Why should Maddy have all the fun?" she teased, voice pure velvet.

Triton growled and dragged us both toward the bed like a man possessed. He tossed me onto the silk sheets and pulled Billie with him. She straddled my thighs, her skin warm and smooth, her lips crashing into mine as Triton positioned himself behind her.

"You both drive me insane," he rasped.

Billie moaned when his cock pressed against her ass, her fingers tangling in my hair.

"Then lose control," I whispered.

He did, curses and gasps tangling in the air. Billie's mouth explored every inch of me while Triton claimed her from behind, groaning as he slowly thrust into her.

Her cries vibrated against my skin as she licked and sucked, as I arched beneath her, overwhelmed by the intensity. We moved together like a storm, wet, chaotic, and perfect.

"Lie down and let me taste you now, my fierce protector," Triton growled.

He pulled my legs until I was at the edge of the bed. The moment he settled my thighs over his shoulders.

The castle rattled with a bang and a boom.

Then the other shoe dropped.

BOOM.

The tower shook. Heat and pressure slammed into us as the air erupted with a blast of unnatural fire and debris. I bolted upright as dust rained from the ceiling. The scent of sex still clung to my skin, but adrenaline hit like a punch.

"What the fuck?" Billie gasped, scrambling for her leggings.

Triton was already shifting, his body flickering with bioluminescence, skin turning iridescent as his oceanic magic surged. In a breath, he was in his land battle form. An evil-looking shark beast, all teeth and power.

A second blast rocked the tower. The wall behind the fireplace cracked, flames bursting free.

"Who is attacking us?" Triton's voice boomed in my head.

The door slammed open. A man with crimson dreadlocks and obsidian armor stormed in, double axes humming with arcane energy. "We are breached!" he roared.

"Get the royals to the safe zone!" Gemma appeared behind him, her robe torn, with blood flowing freely from her right shoulder.

"Invaders," she panted, "with a full sky fleet of cloaked ships. They knew exactly where to hit us. Ember said she has battled them before, on her sister-in-law's planet."

My gut dropped. "How?"

Gemma didn't answer. Her gaze locked on mine. "You need to run."

Triton moved like lightning, scooping up Billie's satchel, the enchanted jewelry inside singing with protective energy.

"To the sea. Now." His command thundered through my mind.

We sprinted into a hidden corridor, the stone floor cold under our bare feet. Billie clutched my hand, her breath ragged.

"What are these invaders?" I panted.

"Alien mercenaries from another universe," Gemma growled, running ahead. "Ember said they don't just kill. They harvest."

Billie went pale. "Like... harvest us?"

"Yes. Every resource on the planet."

Triton's voice rumbled in my head. "They came for us. Now we must risk taking Billie to the safety of the water-dwelling kingdom."

"They came from the sky in metal flying things," Gemma said as she yanked open a hidden door at the bottom of the stairs. "They have weapons that blast and destroy with beams of light. It's a swarm. They are not from our world."

"Hold up," Billie said, breathless. "We're being invaded by UFOs?"

"Figures," I muttered.

Chapter Sixteen: The Escape

"Of course, we find ourselves in love in a magical world, a utopia. Sure, war has to rain hell on us the moment we arrive. Just my luck."

"Do earthlings have knowledge of these invaders, too?" Gemma asked.

"No, on Earth we call them unidentified flying objects that some suspect as aliens from outer space monitoring us. There are a few reported sightings. Most earthlings don't believe in them. Some say there are conspiracy theories that believe we will be invaded one day." I tried to explain.

"Well, I'd say these UFOs are real and we are definitely being invaded," Gemma says as we walk down a white hall towards a guard who is holding the door for us.

"This used to be where we kept our females and children safe when the vampire was among us. Now Star has turned it into a library. She does story time and crafts with our children. We are blessed with so many now," Gemma explains.

"I will fight these invaders. They will discover Harmony's Eden will not be an easy defeat," Triton declares, his anger thrumming in our heads.

"Agreed." The big man booms behind us.

"Balthazar, Triton, you both are worthy warriors. I know you want to join the battle, but I need you here to help me save the children," Gemma says.

The castle shook as we were in the bowels of the building. I would imagine this area as dungeons if we were on Earth, but it was bright and welcoming.

Gemma opens a door to a library full of kids. A woman was singing a soothing melody to them.

"Star, we are here," Gemma says, interrupting the lady's song.

A beautiful ebony black woman with aqua green eyes so bright they almost glowed faced us, concern filled her stunning features.

"Billie, Maddy, this is Star. She is a witch, and she runs the children's library," Gemma introduces us.

Star gives us a sad nod of acknowledgment.

"Have you heard word of Hudson, my mate?" she asked, clearly worried.

"I haven't heard much, just that we are being invaded and the enemy has weapons we have not seen before," Gemma replied.

Another series of booms and explosions shook the castle, more cracks appeared down the walls, and a line of bookcases fell. The kids started crying.

"How can we help?" Billie asked as she walked towards the children.

"Hi, I am Billie, would you like me to sing you a song that I like to sing when I feel a bit scared?"

"Yes please," a small voice said.

Billie started singing the soundtrack to "Frozen" from an animation movie she loves.

The kids seemed to love it and calmed down a bit.

"Kit is making them tea that will help them stay calm," Star said, as she looked at Billie singing to the children.

"She is naturally good with children," Star acknowledged.

Ember came into the room looking disarrayed with debris in her disheveled hair, the wildness in her eyes had me instantly terrified.

"It is the Kanenites. I fought them before with my sister-in-law in Hecat's universe. They came in masses. The castle will not stand long. We need to retreat to the water-dwelling kingdom if we stand a chance."

"Come now," Ember demanded. She opened another secret door under a throw rug that was hiding in the floor. This was a slide that her mate Balthazar went down first.

"This leads to the base of the mountain with a cave full of sea water. King Trent is waiting with water-dwelling warriors to escort you to his kingdom," Ember explains quickly as she settles Billie on the rim.

"I want to help the children first," Billie says as she tries to get off the slide.

"Be there to help catch them and keep them calm," Ember says as she pushes Billie.

"Wait!" she yelled. I numbly watched her disappear down the slide.

"Go, you're next," Ember said to me.

"Nope, the children now," I demand as I crossed my arms in defiance.

Star starts ushering a line of kids to the slide.

"You are going on a fun ride. Your new friend Billie will greet you at the end of this ride."

I can feel a spell of comfort in Star's words as I help each child to the slide.

"We did not have time to give the children calming tea. My spell will only last moments. Have your mate Billie sing to comfort them," Star says as she strains like she is struggling to stand.

"What is happening, are you injured?" I asked.

Star was struggling to stand and did not respond. The guard that manned the door reached to hold Star steady. The huge red-headed female ran to hold Star's hand.

"Thank you, Kit," Star struggled to say.

"I am here, Star," Kit said, gripping Star's hand.

"Take what you need from me as I give it to you freely," the red-headed lady offered.

Star stood stronger, as if she was the support beam that held the castle up all on her own power. Books rattled on the shelves, the sound of stone cracking filled my ears. I barely heard Star.

"I... am... sorry... Hudson..." Star strained to say.

Triton grabbed me and took me to the slide. "Go now!" he said. "Ember, you too, go!" Triton demanded as he pushed me. My stomach dropped like I was on a roller coaster. A subtle light surrounded my body, following me as I slid the spiral slide downward.

With just moments of being on the slide, I dropped into the arms of a strange man. He handed me off to another male who helped me stand next to Billie.

"What is this?" I asked as I saw we were standing on water but not getting wet.

"Beats me, water magic I guess," Billie says as she starts to sing to the children who are all sitting cross-legged in front of her.

Gemma and her mate were standing behind the children. She had her wand in hand, glowing brightly as she chanted softly over and over.

My heart started pounding in fear for Triton when we all heard a thunderous crash echo from the slide.

Seconds later I saw Triton, with Ember in his arms as he fell on the huge white male with bleach blonde hair and light blue eyes. Something about him just screamed fuck around and find out. The man caught them with ease.

"I told you I needed to save Star!" Ember cries out at Triton.

"She was holding the castle up for us to escape, it took all she had, Ember. I tried to save her, to save them all. I would have saved them if I could, but she put that shield up to block me. I am sorry, Ember. I will make these Kanenites pay for this devastation. I vow it," Triton said as he held Ember in a hug while she sobbed in grief.

The male that caught Triton and Ember ushered them to our water magic transport.

"We must retreat now, son," he said, gripping Triton's shoulder. He changed into his battle form and jumped into the water with the other water-dwellers.

A magical transparent bubble held us safely as we descended into the water below.

Chapter Seventeen: Wings of Fire and Ships from the Stars

-The Dragoons-

Smoke curled in spirals above the castle, thick and bitter; laced with the scent of ozone and dragon fire. The air vibrated with the tension of a coming storm. A storm not born of nature but of war and something wholly unnatural. Brooke landed hard on the high battlement, her talons scraping stone, wings folding with a metallic hiss. Kayla was already there, blue scales humming with magic, her eyes scanning the horizon where the sky boiled with the shimmer of incoming Kanenite ships.

Brooke's heart pounded, each beat echoing in her chest like the tolling of a funeral bell. Below her, six children clustered together, small and vulnerable; scales barely hardened, their eyes wide with confusion and fear. She wanted to gather them up, to shield them with her wings, but there was no time. The invasion had come faster than even the oldest dragons could have imagined.

"We need to send them away," Brooke rasped, her voice rough with worry, eyes never leaving her children. She felt the ancient instinct to protect and hide her brood beneath her body. This was no ordinary threat. This was annihilation from the stars.

Kayla crouched beside the human warriors Sam, Dean, and Blaze, who had sworn blood oaths to the Dragoon family.

"You three are blood-sworn to protect them. Get them underground, and don't stop until the tunnels collapse or you've reached the wildwood forest. Understood?"

Dean's jaw clenched, his eyes shining with a mix of fear and determination. "You have our word, mother."

Brooke knelt beside her youngest, brushing scaled fingers over his black curls, memorizing the softness and warmth of him.

"You are the fire in my heart, all of you. Go now!" Her voice cracked, but she would not let them see her break.

Blaze pulled the children close, nodding to her cousins. They disappeared into the winding stairwell, shadows swallowing their silhouettes, as the first shriek of Kanenite engines shattered the sky.

On the ramparts below, Talen and Fang prowled in their human forms, sharp-eyed and tense. Brooke could smell their anxiety and the bitter tang of adrenaline. The castle seemed to hold its breath as the sky above warped, the blue turning black, violet, then the sickly green of Kanenite energy fields.

Talen's spine cracked, black scales bursting from his skin in a violent, beautiful transformation. His roar echoed across the cliffside, shaking stones and sky alike. Fang began to shift with him, his bones lengthening, body contorting into the obsidian form that had once made the world tremble. Two dragons, ancient and proud, both rose into the air on wings that blotted out the sun.

Brooke rose next, her crimson wings spread wide, molten heat pouring from her nostrils. She felt the power of her ancestors burning in her veins, the promise that the Dragoon throne would never fall quietly. Kayla followed, glowing azure as lightning danced along her spine, her roar was a song of defiance and hope.

They launched into the sky together, four dragons with fury and flame, heart and hope. The wind screamed past them and the castle shrank below, the world falling away until there was only the battle, enemy, and the desperate need to survive.

As if the Kanenites kicked a hornet's nest, all the grey dragons swarmed the skies to fight the Kanenites and follow the royals to defend the Dragoon kingdom.

"Does anyone know where my phoenix is?" Brooke called, her voice nearly lost in the roar of the wind.

Kayla's voice crackled over their mental bond. "I believe he went with Jason through the portal door, to work with Terrek on something."

Brooke's heart twisted. "Thanks, Kayla. I just want all my kids to be safe."

"Same," Kayla replied, her tone grim.

"Let's kick some alien ass now. We have to trust the Goddess to keep our kids safe for now."

Behind them, the grey-winged legion of dragons rose, their scales glinting in the unnatural light. It was a sight to inspire awe, a tide of dragons sweeping upward against the obsidian void of spacefaring invaders. For a heartbeat, Brooke felt hope. They were the Dragoon throne, ancient and indomitable.

But the Kanenites were beyond anything she had ever faced. Their ships were monstrous, black and gleaming, covered in runes that pulsed with alien power. They moved with impossible precision, weaving through the sky like predators. Brooke could feel the wrongness of them, the way their presence twisted the very air and how the world seemed to shrink in their shadow.

Talen let loose a breath of pure fire, raking it across a gunship's hull until it screamed and spiraled down. Fang took a steep dive beside him, flames curling around his body like a meteor from the Gods. Brooke soared higher, her heart breaking and beating all at once, hurling fire at the fleet. Kayla howled beside her, bolts of blue lightning arcing from her maw, crackling through the clouds and electrocuting the metal wings of a Kanenite craft until it exploded in midair.

For a fleeting moment, they were winning. The sky blazed with dragon fire, the enemy ships faltering under the assault. Brooke felt the ancient pride of her kind swelling in her chest with the certainty that they would prevail.

Then the sky blinked. A flash of white, blinding and absolute, that sent a silence so heavy it felt like death itself had exhaled. Brooke's wings faltered and her senses were reeling. She saw the beam, impossibly cold and bright, cutting across the horizon.

It struck Fang first. He froze mid-flight, his obsidian form encased in a shell of ice that shimmered with alien energy. Brooke screamed, the sound torn from her throat, raw and desperate. Talen veered to protect his brother, only for the second beam to slam into him, freezing him in place.

Their bodies flashed to human mid-air, naked and suspended, their faces frozen in a roar of defiance. Brooke's heart shattered. She reached for them, but the cold found her next. It was not the cold of winter, not the cold of death. It was something deeper, a void that devoured hope and everything else.

As her fire went out, her wings vanishing, limbs shrinking, her scales falling away. The last thing she saw was Kayla's hand reaching for hers. Both of them had been swallowed into stasis bubbles as they hung like marionettes.

The sky cracked open and a ship descended, monstrous and humming with victory. Claw-like arms reached down and scooped the stasis bubbles up like trophies. Brooke felt herself lifted, weightless and powerless, her world narrowing into a prison of light and silence. Then everything faded to darkness.

Below, the castle crumbled, collapsing into the sea with a howl of broken stone and shattered legacy. The remaining greys watched as the home they had fought to protect was swallowed by the waves, taking the memory of the Dragoon Kingdom into the abyss.

The Kanenite ships turned back toward the stars, pulling the frozen forms of the Dragoon throne behind them like prey caught in a net. The once mighty dragons were plucked like berries from a ripe tree, unable to escape their prisons.

They had lost the world and legacy they had built. One guarded for generations was gone. The dragons were defeated and their fire snuffed out by an enemy they could barely comprehend.

Far below, in the shadows of ancient roots and hidden tunnels, six dragon children still breathed. The fire had not gone out completely, yet. As the Kanenite fleet vanished into the void carrying the last defenders of the Dragoon throne away, hope flickered and nearly died.

The world was changed and broken. The age of dragons was ending. And no one could see what would come next.

Chapter Eighteen: Descent into the Deep

-Maddy-

We sank below the waves like a haunted vessel, the sea swallowing us whole and the light fractured into a kaleidoscope of fading color. Soon the darkness would close around our protective sphere. The only light was the faint glow of Gemma's wand, lighting the faces around us in a trembling circle of grief and uncertainty.

Billie and I sat close, shoulder to shoulder, our knees brushing the children in front of us. As if it was holding its breath, the air was tense.

"I'm going to move near Triton and Ember," I whispered to Billie, pressing a kiss to her cheek.

"They need us."

Billie nodded solemnly, her eyes lingered on them. Ember wept silently in Triton's arms, her sorrow an echo of the chaos we'd left behind. Billie's expression said it all, she wanted to wrap them both in her arms.

She turned to the children instead and began to sing a soft lullaby that barely rose above the quiet hum of magic. Crawling to Triton, I wrapped my arm around his back, while resting my hand gently on Ember's spine, offering what little warmth I could.

Outside the shimmering dome, the shadows swam fluidly, silent and watching. Something massive moved through the gloom. I gasped as a colossal tentacle wrapped around our sphere, jarring us slightly.

"Do not be afraid," Triton's voice brushed through my mind like a whisper across water. "Our Grand Guardian Octopus only means to escort us swiftly to the safety of the Kingdom."

Still, the sense of something vast and ancient lingered, and the ocean around us was no longer just water. It became a presence; it was aware and watching.

Ember stirred. "I'm sorry," she murmured to Triton. "I know you did your best. I don't blame you for what happened."

"You have every right to your anger," he replied, holding her tighter. "I should have saved them all."

"Are we not going to get decompression sickness descending this fast?" Billie asked suddenly, a hint of panic in her voice.

"My magic shields your bodies from harm," Gemma reassured her, though her grip on her wand was tighter than before.

"I wish I could have brought you home under brighter skies," Triton said through his mind link, sounding hollow.

I tightened my arms around him. "Home is where you are. We're lucky to still be breathing."

A glow bloomed below us, a luminous aura expanding in the black sea. It revealed a vast dome of light, suspended like a pearl inside a shell of darkness. The Water-Dwelling Kingdom.

An army of Mer-warriors circled the dome in tight formation. Their sleek armor shimmered with bioluminescence and their weapons pulsed with power.

A voice thundered through our minds, sharp and commanding. "Triton, settle the guests, I must return to the surface to face the intruders."

A fleet of warriors peeled off and ascended into the dark sea like bolts of silver lightning.

"Yes, Father. I'll join you soon," Triton responded.

"No!" Billie and I cried together.

Triton turned to us, shifting out of his battle form. The tension in his shoulders remained, but his face softened. He knelt and drew the rings from his coat.

"Billie, Maddy... my loves and heart. Keep these rings safe for me. I must fight for you, our daughter, and all of us." After he slid the rings onto our fingers, he kissed us both and rose.

"Is that huge white male your actual father or is son a term that every male calls the younger males? Why should what he says matter?" Billie asked in desperation.

"Yes, my love, he is Trent the king of the water-dwelling kingdom and he is my father."

"Don't you dare die," Billie whispered, crying now.

"I'll beat your ass if you do," I added, voice thick with unshed tears.

He nodded, turned, and vanished through the dome's wall. As he phased, his clothes ripped away and his tail unfurled, in a flash of silver as he surged into the depths.

A new wave of warriors took our sphere, guiding it gently to a crystalline dock attached to the dome.

We emerged, the air tasting faintly of salt and magic. A woman stood at the dock, tall and graceful, with aquamarine hair that flowed like seaweed.

"I am Blue," she said solemnly. "Welcome to our Kingdom. I wish it were under kind waves."

"Little ones, we have a special gathering for children your age," she added, addressing the children.

Billie and I lingered at the rear. As we stepped out, Blue dropped to one knee.

Blue had a presence that was as quiet and mesmerizing as the moonrise over the open sea. In her humanoid form, she moved with an effortless grace, every step on the dock as fluid as a tide. Her skin shimmered a delicate blue, the color of deep water at midnight, kissed by hints of silver that caught the light with every subtle gesture.

Her hair fell in long rippling waves, a luminous blend of indigo and sea-glass green, threaded with tiny pearls and the faintest trace of salt. Eyes the color of sunlit lagoons, clear and unblinking. Ancient. They seemed to hold the memory of every ocean current and storm. When she smiled, it was like a hush before dawn, soft and secret; promising wonder.

Around her, the air felt charged, as if the world itself paused to watch her pass. Even the wind grew gentler, swirling with the faint scent of brine and wild lilies. Blue's beauty was not merely seen but felt, the kind that lingered in the heart like a remembered song, both haunting and impossibly lovely.

She was ethereal, otherworldly yet undeniably real. A living embodiment of the sea's mysteries; Blue left the impression of something powerful and fragile. It was as if she were both the calm and the storm;

all at once longing and homecoming. Her magic was a reminder of stories back on Earth that told of sirens leading seamen into the depths of the seas.

"My Sea Queens," she whispered in reverence.

"Please, don't bow," I murmured awkwardly. It was ironic that this mystical woman was kneeling for Billie and me. Yeah, imposter syndrome is real here.

"We're just grateful to be here," I said.

"I don't think I'll ever get used to this," Billie muttered, rubbing her belly.

"Me either."

Balthazar, Gemma's mate, silently handed me Triton's pack and I clutched it to my chest. The weight was more than just supplies; it was the burden of survival.

"Thank the Goddess you are here with me, my love!" Gemma squealed, jumping into his giant massively muscled arms.

"He has to come back," Billie whispered to me, voice laced with dread.

"He has to," I whispered and followed Blue into the Kingdom.

Chapter Nineteen: The Water Dwelling Kingdom

-Maddy-

What a spectacular kingdom it was. The castle rose from the heart of the land like a vision from another world. Spires twisting skyward, sheathed in iridescent mother-of-pearl with veins of living coral. The surface shimmered with opal hues, rose gold, seafoam green, and luminous lavender, shifting with every breath of the wind. Beneath the dome, the air was thick and warm, perfumed with the scent of alien blossoms and the salt tang of distant oceans.

The dome itself arched high above the kingdom, a marvel of ancient magic and lost technology. It was clear as crystal and strong as diamonds. Its curves over the city held back the crushing depths of the seas.

Diffused by the swirling clouds above, magical sunlight bathed the land in a perpetual gentle twilight. The dome's inner surface was etched with intricate patterns, runes, and swirling designs. They glowed faintly, casting the kingdom in dreamlike radiance.

Pathways wound between towering shell-like structures, the palaces carved from coral stone. Their walls adorned with living vines and flowers that bloomed in impossible colors. Groves of silver-leafed trees swayed in the warm breeze, their roots dipping into pools of crystal water.

Rivers of pure sapphire-blue water cut through the city, fed by hidden springs and the distant sea. These rivers wound around plazas and under bridges of polished abalone, their currents slow and inviting. Along their banks, water pods and large glimmering spheres filled with seawater pulsed with gentle light. They served as gateways, portals allowing merfolk to slip through the membrane and glide instantly from land to sea, or return to the air-filled kingdom at will.

The mermaids moved with effortless grace both on land and in the water. On the docks, they walked with the lithe beauty of dancers; their skin shimmering with the colors of the sea. Others swam through the rivers, their worry ringing out as they dove in and out of the water pods. The children that played in shallow lagoons were told to retreat to the castle. Their tails flashed as they leapt onto the grass to follow their guide to the castle.

The kingdom was alive with urgency and movement. Vendors from the marketplaces that bustled with the trade of pearls, rare stones, and fruits grown in the rich underwater soils frantically packed up their merchandise. Lanterns made of translucent shells hung from the branches of towering flora, casting iridescent patterns on the ground.

Statues of legendary queens and guardians stood at every crossroads with features both serene and fierce.

At the city's heart, the castle gates stood open, guarded by warriors clad in armor woven from the scales of ancient sea creatures. The grand halls inside were lined with mosaics depicting the history of the merfolk. There were scenes of migration from the sea and peace forged beneath the dome, and of the harmony between land and water.

The throne room rose like a shell from a floor of sparkling sand, its dais surrounded by streams that fed into a great central pool. It was here the Queen could slip into the water and disappear into the network of rivers at a moment's notice.

This was a kingdom of wonder and balance. Where the air was sweet and the water always near, merfolk had the freedom of land or the embrace of the sea. Beneath the protective embrace of the dome in a world both lush and wild, the water-dwellers flourished. A people of two realms united by the magic of their homes. They had the endless possibilities of both land and sea.

Blue gave us a quick tour as we followed, captivated, like fish to a lure.

"I've never seen anything like this," I whispered.

"It's like Venice if the canals were alive," Billie said.

Blue smiled gently. "Some dwell in the sea; however, this is the heart of our Kingdom."

Massive doors parted for us, revealing a center glowing with warm light. Inside, laughter and whispers both struggled to mask the under-current of fear. A little girl clung to Billie.

"Can I stay with you?" she whispered.

"What's your name, sweetheart?" Billie asked, kneeling.

"Lisa. I'm five," she said, showing tiny fingers.

Billie smiled. "You can stay with me. You're safe with me."

Ember appeared beside me with purple eyes blazing.

"I need to reach Harmony's Hall. And from there, I can take the portal door to the planet Laverian and call the Galactic Empire Space Force."

Blue nodded. "We'll escort you, but first let the children rest."

Billie settled Lisa on something similar to a bean bag and tried to find comfort. However, the weight of it all was hard to overcome.

"She needs real rest," I told Blue, and without hesitation, the guards prepared a bed fit for royalty.

"I'm going to help Ember," I told Billie.

She nodded. "I'm not moving."

Blue led me outside where water pulsed beyond the dome.

"You age?" I asked suddenly when I saw an elderly woman.

"We can choose when we want to return our magic to the world and become elders. It is a sacred thing."

Ember stepped forward. "Time is short."

"Then we'll use the fastest route," Blue said.

"Sea Queen Maddy must escort you."

I laughed. "I'm not your Queen."

"You are, you and Billie both. The sea has chosen and you wear its power."

"That's ridiculous."

"Command the lights to dim," Blue challenged.

I rolled my eyes. "Fine. Water-Dwelling Kingdom, dim the lights."

The world obeyed. As the darkness settled, we saw them: whales, sharks, dolphins, and schools of fish swimming in protective formation around the dome.

"They guard you and await your command," Blue said.

I turned to Ember, stunned. "This can't be real."

"You must ask them to open a path."

I hesitated, then snapped, "Fine. Open a path for the rescue of our people!"

The sea obeyed again, and a sphere broke through the sea. Blood stained the dock, as a transport sphere opened to a water-dweller carrying a man missing a leg. More people with injuries were carried out.

"Get Gemma!" Ember screamed.

When the Kingdom of the Sea trembled beneath our feet, I knew with growing fear that everything had changed.

Chapter Twenty: King Trent & Triton

-Triton-

Black fingers of smoke curled around the broken spires of the land fortress, blotting out the morning sun. The world had turned to ash and shadow. King Trent stood amidst the wreckage, his dark crown cracked and askew. Green alien blood dripped from his jawline; however, his trident was a blur of steel and lightning in his calloused hands. The earth beneath his feet was slick with plasma and scorched by the aftermath of relentless assault.

The Kanenites infantry swarmed like a plague. They were child-like in size but moved with tech-enhanced speed that defied the eye. Their eyes glowed with cold blue light and the weapons they carried were alien. Plasma guns implanted into their wrists fired rapid sizzling bursts. They were surrounded by insectoid war pets that scuttled and leapt, their exoskeletons pulsing with blue energy and mandibles snapping in eager anticipation of the kill.

Trent's chest heaved as each breath was a ragged growl. His cloak was half burned away, exposing skin laced with fresh plasma burns and old scars. His skin was a map of a thousand battles. He barely flinched, he was a water-dweller, King of the deep and battle hardened beyond mortal reckoning. He was also Triton's father. Today, he was the last wall between the Kanenites and everything he loved.

"Come on, you tiny buffoons!" he roared, voice like a storm breaking against mountains. "Come see what a real King can do!"

A Kanenite leapt at him, plasma blade extended. Trent impaled it on his trident, wrenching the body free and swinging it in a wide arc, smashing three more aside with a single brutal motion. Bones cracked and blue blood sprayed as the king pressed forward, heedless of the pain.

A shriek rang out over the carnage, one of the insectoid pets lunged at him, legs a blur. Trent spun, catching it midair with the shaft of his trident and then hurled it into a knot of Kanenite soldiers. The impact sent bodies flying as more poured in, relentless and undeterred.

Suddenly, a familiar voice cut through the chaos. Urgent and furious, impossible to mistake. "Dammit! If it was this bad you should have brought me with you!"

A burst of water magic erupted above and Triton dropped down in a swirl of mist, sliding across the blood-slick stones. He landed beside his father, twin coral blades gleaming in his fists, his eyes wild with battle light.

"And miss the fun?" Trent sneered, blocking a plasma bolt with a flick of his trident.

"I'm old, not dead."

"Old and reckless," Triton growled, slicing clean through a Kanenite's tech-pack with a single fluid motion. The enemy's gear exploded in a shower of sparks, taking two more with it.

"Your army's scattered! You should be in the medical bay, not charging into a trap!"

"You sound like your mother," Trent muttered, parrying a Kanenite blade and driving his trident through the attacker's chest. "Goddess help me."

"I sound like a warrior who knows your ass isn't immortal. You may look twenty-five but I know better!" Triton spun, ducking under a plasma bolt. He drove his blade upward, severing a Kanenite's arm at the elbow.

As the fight raged on, father and son moved in perfect brutal tandem. Trent swept his trident in wide arcs, knocking aside attackers; every movement was an echo of the tides, unstoppable and relentless. Triton darted and weaved, his blades flashing, water magic swirling around him like a living shield. They fought back-to-back, reading each other's movements, covering every angle.

"What about Maddy and Billie?" Trent barked, his voice a thunderclap between parried strikes. "You have mates now, no time to play life and death games, son."

"They're in the underwater kingdom, alone, without you!" Trent shouted, kicking a Kanenite into a wall hard enough to crack stone.

"I should be there protecting my mates!" Triton's voice broke with worry, his focus wavering as he glanced toward the horizon.

Trent's eyes flicked to his son, something like pain buried behind his sarcasm.

"Then go," he snapped, spinning his trident in a defensive whirl. "Run home and cradle your lovers, let your old man handle this fight."

"You are bleeding!" Triton hissed, slashing at another Kanenite, green blood spattering his arms.

"You think I don't see how this war is breaking you? You can't hide that from me, Father!"

For a moment Trent didn't answer, his face hardened and the King's mask slid back into place.

"I've bled before. I'll bleed again. But I'll never run."

The Kanenites pressed in tighter, their war pets shrieking, the air thick with plasma fire and the stench of burning flesh. Trent and Triton moved as one, a living storm of steel and magic, but there were too many. A Kanenite stealth unit shimmered into view behind Trent, its weapon raised, its eyes cold and merciless.

"Look out!" Triton roared.

He lunged, intercepting the blast meant for his father. The plasma bolt carved into Triton's side, deep and brutal, searing flesh and bone. He staggered, dropping to one knee, blood pouring between his fingers.

"No! Triton!" Trent's scream tore through the battle.

He caught his son as he fell, the rage blazing in his eyes. With a roar that shook the ruins, he drove his trident through the attacker and turned on the rest, raining vengeance with every blow. He was a tempest, a god of war incarnate; for a moment, the Kanenites faltered before his fury.

But the damage was done, Triton's breathing grew shallow and his face paled. The Kanenites regrouped, circling with weapons raised and war pets hissing and snapping.

Above them, a dark shadow swept down; the collector ship, its hull black as the void, its pincher-like claws unfurling with mechanical hunger. Trent looked up, both despair and defiance warring in his gaze.

"You will not take my son," he growled, voice cracking under the weight of fury and grief.

The Kanenites net closed in. Trent was hit square in the chest by a plasma burst and the impact drove him to his knees. Still, he held Triton close, shielding him with his battered body. They were surrounded and outgunned.

Trent pressed his forehead to Triton's, his voice a broken whisper.

"I'm sorry I couldn't keep you safe, son."

A beam of stasis light lanced down, encasing them in a shimmering frost. Time slowed as muscles locked and eyes froze open. Father and son touching and together, still breathing, just not free.

In the glowing stasis pods towed behind the Kanenite ship, they were reduced to trophies, fading into the black void of space, as the world behind them burned. Their final effort, love and fury, would live on only in memory. Until someone, somewhere, found the strength to fight again.

Chapter Twenty-One: The Sea Queen Awakens

-Maddy-

As they shoved people out of the sphere, I walked into a waking nightmare. The world was a blur of shrieks and crimson. Blood spattered the dock, slick and sticky beneath my knees, mixing with seawater and the acrid stench of burning flesh. My lungs seized, every breath tasted of salt, copper, and smoke, thick enough to choke on. I gagged, bile burning the back of my throat, but there was no time to be sick.

Bodies were everywhere. Some were sprawled and unmoving, limbs twisted at impossible angles, eyes wide and glassy. Others writhed, clutching wounds and howling for help. The air vibrated with screams, animal and desperate. I wanted to cover my ears to shut it out, but my hands were already slick with someone else's blood.

A man was laid at my feet, his body so mangled I almost didn't know him. The stump of his leg oozed blood, bone jutting like a jagged spear through shredded flesh. The skin of his thigh was charred and blackened. The smell... oh God, the smell, was like burnt meat and rotting fish. His face was a mask of agony, teeth bared, his lips peeled back in a silent snarl. Blood and dust clung to him, like a grotesque second skin.

I dropped to my knees, hands shaking so hard I could barely press them to his wound. My fingers slipped, sticky and hot.

"Hold on," I whispered, voice thin and useless.

"The doctors are coming." Was I lying? I didn't know.

His hand shot out, clamping my wrist with a strength born of terror. His fingers dug into my skin, his nails leaving crescent moons.

"Stan," he gasped, his voice wet and broken.

"Have you seen Stan?" Recognition hit me like a fist.

"Richmond..." His name was a prayer, a plea.

"He's looking for you. You have to hang on. Stan needs you." My throat ached with the lie.

Balthazar appeared out of the smoke, a mountain of calm in the chaos. The dock trembled with his footsteps, the air hushed around him. He gathered Richmond up, cradling him like a child.

"I've got you," he said, voice deep as thunder, but soft with grief. "Let your pain rest."

Gemma's wand blazed white, the scent of ozone cutting through the blood and char.

"He needs blood. Now!" Her power sizzled in the air, sealing flesh but the wound smoked and hissed, the smell of burnt skin rising.

Around us, the dock was a hellscape. The slap of wet feet, the metallic tang of blood, the sharp bark of orders. Shouts overlapped with sobs, the air vibrating with panic. My vision blurred as I tried to focus, the world was tilting and spinning.

Above, the glass dome caught the magic light, casting fractured rainbows over the carnage. Fish glided past, serene and oblivious. Their scales glinting in a cruel, beautiful reminder that life continued, even as ours unraveled.

The noise faded, replaced by a roaring in my ears. My knees buckled. Darkness crashed over me, cold and absolute.

I woke to silence. The sheets beneath me were too soft, the pillow too cool. My skin tingled, every nerve singing with something alien. I dragged myself to the bathroom, feet heavy as anchors. The mirror showed a stranger; skin shimmering faintly, eyes too bright, lips pale. I pressed trembling fingers to my cheek. Was this still me?

"Damn," I whispered. "It wasn't just a nightmare."

A voice, soft but urgent, "Maddy?" Billie's silhouette filled the doorway, eyes red-rimmed and hopeful.

"Just... looking for my toothbrush," I lied, my voice brittle.

She smiled, dipping an odd brush into a jar of powder. "Try this. Sea mint and pearl. It's better than anything on Earth."

The taste exploded, icy sharp, almost electric. It scraped away the taste of blood and smoke; however, not the memory.

She watched me, worry etched into every line of her face. "You've been asleep for three days."

My heart stuttered. "What?"

"Gemma said the Sea needed time to finish bonding with you. The magic of this planet, Maddy, you're the chosen one. It didn't give me as much power. And... I'm pregnant."

The news crashed over me and I clung to her, desperate for warmth, for proof I was still real. "I love you," I whispered, voice raw.

When we parted, I forced the question out: "What happened? The war? Triton?"

Billie's eyes filled with tears. "Let's get you some food first."

The dining hall was a hive of whispered dread. The air was thick with the scent of broth and fear. Billie pressed a mug into my hands.

"Sea mushroom brew. It helps." The taste was earthy and grounding, though I could still taste the copper of blood on my tongue.

"Stan made it here. He's alive... barely. Cooking like a man possessed. Triton..." She faltered, voice cracking. "Gemma didn't want to stress you. The aliens took him. He's on one of their ships. We don't know how to get him back."

My heart twisted, a hot, pulsing ache. "No..."

"Ember was escorted to the shore; she has gone to Laverian for help."

I couldn't stay still. Rage surged through me, sharp and cold. I stood, the mug rattling in my hands. "I need answers. Now!"

The dock was slick with blood, the boards stained dark. My footsteps echoed, brittle and sharp. "Blue! Gemma! I need to speak to whoever's in charge!" Blue skidded to a halt, breathless and wide-eyed.

"My Sea Queen, you are in charge. The invaders have captured every other leader."

Trent's mate and Triton's mother, Queen Delany, has gone into deeper waters to bring the rural isolated water-dwellers back to the kingdom for safety measures.

Her words cracked something inside me. The dome above trembled, fish scattering in sudden panic. My scream ripped through the air, wild and shattering.

I dove into the water, surrendering to the pull. My body shifted, bones lengthening, skin tingling; senses sharpening until every heartbeat and every current was mine. The sea wrapped around me, cold and alive. I belonged to it now.

Below, the invader's ship pulsed, a foreign wound in the ocean's flesh. Sharks circled, their eyes dark and ancient. I bared my fangs at the ship.

Mine. These waters were mine.

The purple guardian octopus rose, massive and silent, wrapping the ship in her arms.

"Not yet," I told her, my thoughts were sharp as knives. "Breach it, I want what's inside."

She breached the ship, metal screeching and buckling. When a laser sliced through one of my sharks, something inside me snapped. Fury flooded me, electric and overwhelming. I sent the wounded shark to healers and called the Sea itself. A waterspout exploded from the surface, hurling the ship toward the shore.

I rode the current, shifting as I hit the sand, claws, teeth, and rage. Smoke blackened the sky as grey dragons battled above, their roars shaking the earth. I ripped through the ship's hull, metal shrieking beneath my hands. Alien soldiers screamed, their blood hot and strange on my skin. One pointed, trembling, to a sealed door where stasis pods held my people and sea creatures entrapped. They lay in bubbles, a pale cluster of faces floating, frozen inside their transparent prison.

"Release them!" I roared, voice inhuman.

The alien hesitated. I snapped his neck, grabbed his device, and dragged every pod into the Sea's arms. Alien ships dove after us, dozens of them. Power and rage consumed me, it was like I was a vessel and not operating in my own human nature.

I summoned storms, waterspouts tore through the surface, flinging the invader ships in my waters skyward, throwing those bastards back in orbit and out of my waters. The ocean obeyed my every thought.

My strength faltered. The sea caught me, cradling me as darkness closed in. In the black, I saw her, a woman of light and sorrow, a Goddess weeping. Her tears fell into the void, each one a silent plea. I reached out, trembling.

"Don't cry, I'm here. Tell me what you need." This Goddess is in pain; it is as if my own mother were before me and all I want is to help her. Ease her sorrow and kick the ass of anyone that would dare offend her.

But this time, I didn't wait for an answer. I knew now what it meant to have power. A power wild, terrifying, and mine.

When I woke, Billie was by my side, her eyes wide with fear and hope.

Chapter Twenty-Two: Embers Escape

-Ember-

The Wildwood burned, ancient trees that had stood for centuries. Licked by flames, their once majestic canopies were collapsing into ash. The air was thick with smoke and the sharp tang of burning sap. My wings, once strong and proud, were torn and scorched. They barely carried me above the treetops. Every push through the hot, choked air sent agony pulsing through my body, but I couldn't stop. Not now.

Above, alien ships hovered with hulls black and gleaming, sending out weapon drones to scan the burning forest below. The Kanenites were relentless, their technology a blight on this world. They searched for survivors, or any spark of resistance they could snuff out. I could not be discovered. I had to reach the grand hall and the Goddess Harmony's ancient sanctuary. It was the only place left untouched by the invasion, or so I hoped.

A sudden burst of energy exploded nearby, the force knocking me sideways. I spiraled, helplessly crashing through brittle branches and landing hard on the forest floor. Pain shot through my leg, white-hot and blinding.

I gasped, trying to move, but the limb wouldn't bear my weight. Broken. Shifting into my human form, I gritted my teeth against the agony.

"I don't have time for this pain," I hissed, voice trembling.

"I won't die here."

Dragging myself forward, I clawed through the underbrush, every inch a battle. The world narrowed to the pounding of my heart and the distant roar of the fire. The grand hall loomed ahead, hidden on a hillside. I made it into the hall with its blue portal door shimmering with energy. It was so close. I could feel the hum of ancient magic and the promise of safety, just beyond reach.

With the finish line this close, I forced myself onward. Every step was too slow and every breath a struggle. I reached out, fingers brushing the warm surface of the portal door. A surge of power enveloped me, washing away the worst of the pain. I fumbled for the ancient book that hung at my side, flipping it open with shaking hands. I scrawled a few desperate words, Laverian portal passage.

Knocking three times, I seized the crystal doorknob. The door swung open and I was pulled through the dark void beyond. For a few blissful moments, I floated in the darkness, weightless, all pain forgotten.

Then I fell, tumbling through the red door that hung attached to a forest tree on planet Laverian. I landed in a heap, the air was cool and clean, a stark contrast to the smoke and chaos I'd left behind. Before I could even catch my breath, Candy pounced on me, licking my face and chuffing, the huge cheetat beast's golden eyes bright with concern and joy.

"It's good to see you too, boy," I whimpered, clinging to his thick fur.

"I need your help. Take me to your parents, please."

Candy let me use him as support, his powerful body steadying me as I limped through the forest. Each step was agony, but I focused on Candy's warmth and the promise of safety ahead. We reached the Laverian Chief's cabin, a beautiful structure of polished wood and living vines, nestled among ancient trees. I collapsed onto the floor, my breath coming in ragged gasps.

The air inside was cool, filled with the scent of herbs and earth. It felt like stepping into another world. Looking up, I saw my brother-in-law, Emperor Terrek, standing over me. His black eyes were wide with concern.

"Ember," he said, kneeling beside me. "You're safe now."

Moments later, Empress Darah and Empress Flame rushed in. Darah's blonde hair was pulled back, her blue eyes scanning my injuries with clinical precision. Flame's red eyes glowed, her military training evident in every movement. Their faces were etched with worry but also with resolve.

"We need to get her to the Med Bay," Darah said, already moving to lift me.

"NOW!" Flame barked, her voice sharp as a blade. The two of them moved with practiced efficiency, supporting me between them.

Candy padded over, his barbed tail twitching anxiously. He nuzzled Darah's hand, earning a gentle pat.

"It's okay, Candy. Ember will be okay," Darah soothed, her voice steady. Candy chuffed, walking by my side as we made our way to the infirmary.

The pain was so intense I couldn't speak. Every jolt and movement sent fresh waves of agony through my leg. The Med Bay was a marvel of Laverian technology, sterile and bright, filled with the hum of machinery and the scent of antiseptic. The cyborg doctor, all gleaming metal and cold logic, treated my injuries with its usual indifference for bedside manner. I winced as it set the bone and sealed the wound; finally, blessed relief flooded me as the pain ebbed away.

Jason, my mate, burst into the room, his presence a blaze of comfort and fury. His hair seemed to flicker with fire, his eyes burning with worry and anger.

"Who do I need to burn?" he growled, taking my hand in his.

"Exactly my thoughts too, brother," Terrek said, his voice grim. He stood at the foot of my bed, with arms crossed, every inch the emperor.

Flame's fingers began to glow, tiny flames licking at her fingertips as she morphed into her battle form.

"The Kanenites are harvesting planet Harmony," I said, tears slipping down my cheeks.

"Fuck!" Terrek spat, his posture radiating fury.

Jason pulled me into his arms. "Oh baby, I am so sorry, darlin'."

Darah paced, her fists clenched.

"I am going to open a can of whoop-ass on them so hard. I'm gonna knock their teeth out so hard we won't know if they be spittin' or shittin'. When I'm done, I'll let Candy turn them into a puddle of acid."

Candy hissed in agreement, his tail lashing the floor.

Terrek managed a grim laugh. "These fools, I've seen my ladies take them on in battle before. They'll fall again facing us."

"We'll get Galactic Enforcement," Flame rumbled in her monster voice. "Immediately."

"We have to save Harmony's planet," Jason demanded, still holding me close.

My strength was returning, fueled by their love and determination. "I'll fight," I said, voice steady. "I won't let them win."

Terrek placed a hand on my shoulder. "Together, we'll stop them."

As the family prepared for battle, Laverian children watched from the doorway, their eyes wide with a mix of fear and determination. Candy sat beside them, ever vigilant, a silent promise of protection.

Darah was already moving, gathering supplies and barking orders. "We need to coordinate with the other houses. Get the portal network ready for the Enforcer ships. If there's a way to Harmony, we'll find it."

Flame nodded, her eyes still burning. "I'll alert the guards and prep the war room. We can't afford to be caught off guard again."

Jason squeezed my hand. "Rest, Ember. We will need you strong."

I nodded, exhaustion washing over me.

"I will drink too, so I can meet with the Goddess Harmony," Darah spoke.

"I need to sleep, to see if the Goddess Harmony can help us find a path through space to get to her planet. We need a portal for our Enforcer ships."

Darah handed me a sleeping tonic, her touch gentle.

"We'll watch over you both. Let the Goddess guide your dreams, my love," Flame encouraged Darah.

I drank the tonic, the bitter liquid sliding down my throat. The world blurred at the edges, the pain fading into a distant memory. As I drifted into sleep, I heard the voices of my family, strong, determined, and unyielding. The fight for Harmony's world had begun. We would not back down, not now, not ever.

Darah took Ember with her to visit the Goddess Harmony, in the way of her dreams.

I dreamed of the Wildwood, whole and green, the trees unburned, the sky clear. I saw the Goddess Harmony standing among the ancient oaks, her hair shimmering with starlight, her eyes filled with sorrow and hope.

The Goddess addressed them, "Darah, Ember," her tone calm and composed, like the wind through leaves.

"You are not alone. The fire in both your hearts is the fire of the world. Protect it and you will find your way."

I reached for her but she faded, replaced by visions of battle. With dragons soaring above burning forests; merfolk rising from the seas and warriors rallying beneath the banners of Laverian and Harmony alike. I saw my family standing together, unbroken, a wall against the darkness.

When I woke, the cabin was quiet. The pain in my leg was a dull ache. Jason sat beside me, his hand warm in mine. "Did you dream?" he asked softly.

I nodded. "The Goddess spoke to us. She said we are not alone."

I think she gave Darah a way to open a God portal large enough for the Galactic fleet.

He smiled, fiercely and proud. "Then we fight, for Harmony, for all of us."

Outside, the sun was rising over Laverian, painting the world in gold and promise. The battle was coming, but so was hope.

Darah

While stars shimmered like shards of glass in a black velvet sea, the twinkling was far beyond the veil of Darah's consciousness. Standing barefoot in a field of lavender mist, the petals brushing her toes. The air was warm and silent, eerily still. The stillness was unnatural, hinting that this place was not real. She turned around slowly.

The Goddess stepped forward from the mist, tall and radiant, draped in robes that shimmered with galaxies. Her hair was made of stardust and her eyes were the color of the cosmos.

"Harmony," Darah whispered.

"My darling Darah," the Goddess said softly. Her voice echoed with the notes of ancient songs, flowing through Darah's bones like the hum of celestial winds.

Darah nodded. "I remember we would always meet in clouds. What is this place?"

"A little hideaway I made between worlds," Harmony replied, "where dreams are more than memories, they are bridges."

The mist parted around us, revealing a view of Darah's home world from orbit. Laverian framed in all its green beauty spanning outward; far beyond all of it was Harmony's own endangered planet. The purple sphere shimmered with rings of iridescent dust, encircling its twin moons like the delicate halo of a Goddess.

This must be the God's way of viewing us, it was beyond anything I have ever seen before.

"My world is dying, Darah."

My breath caught. "We know. Ember had escaped Harmony's planet through the portal door. The Kanenites are invading your world right now."

"The Kanenites and the God Kane are worse than you know." Harmony stepped closer, her eyes flashed with divine pain and raw hope.

"I need your help to open the gateway, not a portal for a few ships, we need a rift across space vast enough to pull our entire fleet through.

My Goddess Harmony, we need your help to open a portal," Darah pleaded.

Harmony immediately replied, "As you wish, consider it done."

"That's why I came to you in dream form," Harmony said, placing a glowing hand over my heart.

"I've marked you. You are my bridge. Go now dear, I am trying not to explode and let loose my full power. I will be extremely dangerous should I break any further."

A burst of energy surged through my chest, my eyes glowed blue as celestial runes were seared into my skin. They lined my arms like divine circuitry.

"Wake now and build the bridge."

Behind her, the Galactic Enforcer fleet began pouring through the portal like a silver river. There were dozens of ships varying in size and function. The fighters, tactical destroyers, and medical crafts all aligned in coordinated formation. A beautiful brutal ballet of war. The space battle had begun.

Flame expertly barrel-rolled past the first Kanenites fighter, slicing its hull open with a concentrated plasma beam.

"This one's clear," she barked.

"No prisoners. Light it up!"

Explosions bloomed all over the vacuum like supernovas. The Enforcers locked non-lethal capture beams on the prison ships with green rays of light that sent them to stasis. They disabled weapons and propulsion without causing harm to the prisoners within.

The rest of the Kanenites fleet retaliated hard, launching waves of drone pods. They sent them weaving toward the Enforcer vessels in suicidal spirals. A few made contact, shields flared and systems screamed. The fleet formation didn't falter.

Flame's fingers were a blur on her console as she maneuvered the ship like it was an extension of her body. She wove with precision through both the debris fields and lethal enemy fire.

"Two more ships with prisoners," she yelled.

"I need three fighters to create a buffer zone while the extraction drones board them!"

"On it, Flame," came the familiar voice of Ember, who was now piloting a borrowed strike fighter, her voice was laced with vengeance.

A blue and red blur zipped past Flame's viewport, as Ember lit up a Kanenites destroyer roaring, "That's for Harmony's children, you bastards!"

The purple planet glowed in fragile beauty. From orbit, Flame could see the long silver lines of the enemy's weapon installations on the surface, they looked like scars across sacred earth. The rings of the twin moons caught the light from the nearby sun, casting long dreamlike shadows across the battlefield.

It was then that the portal pulsed again. My voice rang across the fleetwide comms. "Reinforcements incoming, hold the skies. Planetary support status... en-route."

Back at command, I stood with Harmony whispering in my head, together we wielded the forces that bent space, creating a portal.

Terrek placed a hand on my shoulder. "You did it," he murmured with pride in his voice.

Flame's ship rocked as she took a hit, but she didn't slow. She locked onto the largest Kanenites warship, now trying to escape with two prison-pods in tow.

"No," Flame whispered, her voice like steel. "You don't get to run."

She launched a wave of disabling pulses, all of them landing on target. The prison-pods were detached and let loose in space, a desperate attempt to distract Flame's advances so they could escape. The pods were immediately secured by Enforcer ships. Now, it was the warship she focused on. Flame flipped her ship and twisted backward while shooting lethal lasers through the enemy's shield, detonating its core.

The explosion lit up the system like a miniature sun. The battle raged for another hour before the last of the Kanenites fleet had fled or were captured. The skies above Harmony's planet were quiet again and stars returned.

Inside her cockpit, Flame leaned back, blood roaring in her ears, a faint smile touching her lips.

"They'll think twice before trying this again."

From the surface below, Brooke's children looked up at the sky and saw glowing arcs of red, blue, and gold across the moons. To them it was not war; it was magic. A sign that they were not alone.

Harmony's world was still in danger, but hope had returned; in the form of fire, light, and a family of warriors from beyond the stars.

Chapter Twenty-Three: Gods And Their Secrets

-Maddy-

"Oh, my fierce little Sea Queen," Harmony began, her voice silky with divinity and more than a dash of dramatic flair.

"I am positively livid that the God Kane dares to lay a single finger on my beloved Harmony." Oh great, another God with a personal vendetta and a flair for monologues.

"I am the Goddess Harmony," she declared, as if the title alone should send shivers down my spine.

"Kane is the god of war and chaos, his hobby is devastation, his love language is conquest; his favorite pastime is ruining everything beautiful. He's targeting my planet because I dared to help rescue the beings he stole from Hecat's universe. Hecat is my true mate and I had every right to intervene."

She was glowing, all Goddess-like while sending off waves both ethereal and furious; her sadness reaching out and wrapping around my chest like a weighted net.

"I can feel you," I whispered. "Your pain is deep and overwhelming."

"Oh, Maddy, I'm so sorry. I will shield you from the full blast of my divine emotional hurricane."

The pressure eased in my chest, and I was able to breathe normally again, thank Goddess. Harmony conjured two elegant chairs, apparently even Gods vent better with furniture, and gestured for me to sit.

"I'll let you in on a secret Maddy, one that no other mortal or God knows. I'm not just another Goddess, I'M THE GODDESS. My father is The Great Creator, and my mother is The Goddess of Love and True Mates. I wasn't conjured into existence like every other celestial ego up there. I was born in the human way from my mother's womb, with contractions and screaming, the whole divine delivery package."

I blinked to try to understand what her point was, she was serious and mildly smug.

"My birth was hidden, Gods just don't do envy well. My existence alone would spark a cosmic hissy fit. I was born with power that could make suns blush. However, Daddy dearest suppressed most of it away and Mommy kept the rest under divine lock and key."

She smiled at me then, not warmly, it was the kind of smile that read more like I could end you.

"I'm working on my temper."

"Are you okay with that, your parents taking your power away?" I asked, trying not to flinch.

"At first yes, I loved Harmony, it was my world, and my creation. Until Hecat yanked me into his world like some cosmic kidnapper. I forgave him, of course, true mate and all. Then Kane happened." Her eyes darkened, galaxies swirling in them.

"Now I wonder if I'm capable of being the very monster I fear, the end of all things."

"That's... a lot," I said eloquently. "How can I help?"

"You already are," she said, and her voice turned warm.

"Maddy, you and Billie arrived here through Kane's reckless meddling. Portals torn through realities, scattering my people and others like confetti on New Year's Eve. Before you landed here, my mother saw your soul. She fated you to Triton, this world and to me. Mom knows things before they even happen." The Goddess smiled sweetly with a mother's gaze.

"I've given you the power of the sea, closer to a Divine. You are now my daughter, my mother bonded us together. I have turned you into a Demigod, if you must define it."

I stared at her. "Wait. What?! I don't want to be a God, it sounds like a you problem."

She laughed, softly, almost bitterly. "Welcome to the club, darling. No one asked me either."

"Why make me your daughter if you're just going to ghost me mid-crisis?" I shot back, my panic rising.

"I'm trying not to destroy the universe in a grief-fueled meltdown, sweetie," Harmony replied dryly.

"This is me being responsible."

Before I could throw another existential fit, she faded. Just vanished in a typical Deity move.

"No! I still have a thousand questions!" I shouted into the Void.

The Void didn't answer.

I woke up in the arms of Rina, Triton's aunt and the most fearsome sea warrior this side of the universe. She was dragging me through the water toward the kingdom.

"Have you heard anything about Triton?" I asked, my chest aching.

"He's still missing," Rina said, her voice dipped in poison.

"Stolen by Kane's scum."

"I swear I'll get him back," I vowed, all vengeance and zero mercy.

"I'll help," she said, as casually as offering to pick up groceries.

We swam hard and as we entered the underwater dome, every sea dweller froze in place, staring intently on full mute. If I didn't know better, I'd say they were terrified.

"What is this?" I asked, scanning the silent crowd.

Rina shrugged. "You've made the Sea do things no one's ever seen, your power is beyond planetary magic. They don't know what you are and they fear what they can't categorize. It's easier to fear you than worship you."

"Please don't call me Sea Queen. Just Maddy. We're family now."

"Sure thing, Maddy, let's not pretend you're not terrifying. It's a good thing that I like terrifying females. I am proud to call you family, Maddy." Rina announced.

Billie barreled into me with kisses and frantic words.

"I'm so glad you're okay, first Triton disappeared and then you vanished, then the seas dropped so low we could see the sky. THE SKY, MADDY!!! Blue practically had a panic attack and then a goddamn octopus dropped off an injured shark with a bunch of weird magic bubbles. Maddy, it's been wild."

I grabbed her and kissed her, comforting myself in the only real thing I had left. "I missed you too, my love."

Gemma and Balthazar stood a respectful distance away, probably giving us five minutes before they asked for battle plans and divine miracles.

"Can we go somewhere else?" Billie asked, voice soft.

"I like the way you think, besides I hate scaring everyone." Beings from the land and the water dwelling kingdom, stared at me like I knew all the answers. It's all too much!

"I'm trying to help, okay? Maybe stop looking at me like I'm the final boss." I snapped, annoyed before catching myself.

My energy was giving divinely gifted rage, it was probably leaking out and spooking the locals. Give a girl a break, I had never been a Demigod mermaid queen in charge of a magical planet at war with invading evil aliens before; I needed a minute to process.

Billie raised an eyebrow. "Pretty sure that girl over there just peed herself."

Right. Demigod here with big emotions and overwhelming aura. Fuck! I focused on intentionally sending out a calming pulse. The tension in the air cracked and everyone exhaled, movements resumed.

"Thank you," Billie whispered, rubbing her belly.

"Let's go home." Home to our shared space, a little corner of sanity.

The crystal shower was divine; I moaned as hot water jetted from all directions and Billie's hands sliding all over me like silk.

"I love this shower," she said, soaping me up.

"I love you," I replied, watching suds trail down her breasts.

Taking the sponge from her and returning the favor, unable to resist the soft moans she made under my touch. The way she reacted to me was intoxicating. Dropping to my knees and kissing her lush fertile belly, my fingers teasing her folds at the apex between her thighs, my mouth following in hot worship.

"That's it, babe, right there," Billie moaned.

She was heaven. Then she came undone for me, trembling and wet. Billie was mine. She pulled me up and kissed me, then turned the water off with impressive dexterity. We stumbled to the bed.

"My turn," she said, eyes gleaming.

Oh, gods. "Yes, fuck yes!"

I cried as she devoured me, her fingers and mouth pushing me to the edge and over it. I came hard, gasping her name, clutching at her like she was the last good thing in this chaotic cosmos.

"I love you," I breathed.

"I love you too," she whispered, just as someone pounded at the door.

"You've gotta be fucking kidding me!" I groaned.

Chapter Twenty-Four: The Gods That Started It All

-The Great Creator & His Bride-

The Gods that started it all, in the space beyond the cosmos, where the threads of reality were woven by thought and breath. No sun, moon, or stars, only the radiant presence of two beings whose power transcended all known laws of creation.

They did not sit upon thrones; such things were beneath them. Instead, they walked barefoot along an endless stretch of stardust sands, their footsteps creating galaxies with each step. The Great Creator, tall and silver-eyed, with a voice that could form planets or collapse stars, turned his gaze toward the only being who had ever truly silenced him. His mate, the Goddess of Love, The Great Mother.

She shimmered like opal light, her presence fluid, her form shifting between beauty and wrath, softness and infinite force. When she smiled, time danced. When she wept, the universe mourned. Today, she was quiet.

The Creator's fingers trailed through the cosmic dust as he walked, his thoughts louder than any spoken word.

"She's waking," he said at last, his voice low, as though the very truth of it might spark a storm in the divine ether.

The Goddess of Love nodded. "Harmony has always been awake. We just suppressed her power and our chains are about to snap."

"They will all know of her now," he murmured.

She stopped walking, turning to him with sorrow etched across her infinite face.

"She is the one thing they cannot control. They will try to figure out what she is, bind her and even try to destroy her if they think it will save their power structures."

He looked away. "They will fail."

"Not before they hurt her."

Silence fell between them, deep, shivering around them, galaxies spiraled in slow mourning.

"I fear her wrath," he admitted finally.

"Not because she is dangerous, because it would be justified and she would become the destroyer of all."

The Goddess stepped closer, brushing a hand across his cheek, a gesture so intimately given the stars bowed in reverence. "You designed the framework and I built the thread of love into every soul. Harmony, she is the balance. When love is violated and innocence is destroyed, she becomes the consequence."

"She could unmake me," he whispered, not in fear, but in awe.

"She could unmake all of us."

"Still," the Goddess said softly, "you love her."

He looked at her, eyes glinting like collapsing suns. "How could I not? She is the child of us both, our flaws and perfection, the combination of our fury and grace. She is what comes after creation."

"That, my dear," the Goddess of Love said, "is what terrifies them."

They walked again, and stars danced behind their wake.

"She was never meant to be born like the others," he said after a while.

"That's why we hid her birth and cloaked her origin in stories and myth to keep her hidden. If they had known..."

"They would have shaped her," the Goddess interrupted.

"Instead of love she'd be destruction already."

"But Harmony is beyond what those Gods can understand."

"She is the truth," the Goddess said. "Truth is always dangerous."

When they moved again, a ripple passed through the fabric of the cosmos, an echo of something breaking.

The Creator frowned. "Did you feel that?"

She nodded. "Kane is moving."

His hands clenched at his sides, not in anger, from pain. "He thinks he can undo what we've made."

"He doesn't understand that Harmony is not a piece of creation and the most powerful among us. Remove her suppression and the God of the void, the destroyer will rise."

"We cannot interfere directly," he said reluctantly.

"No," she agreed. "We can prepare her and speak to her through dreams, with what she loves."

"She listens to Hecat and her beloved creations, her people. As long as she feels their love, we may be able to stop her from transcending."

"They don't try to define her," the Goddess said. "They love her and that is the only thing that keeps her rage from destroying everything."

The Creator nodded, then looked at her with a flicker of uncertainty, something no being had ever seen from him.

"Do you think she will forgive us?"

The Goddess of Love didn't answer right away. She reached for his hand, entwining their fingers, the act caused a supernova in the far reaches of a newborn galaxy.

"She already has," she said. "She may never forget."

He closed his eyes, the weight of eternity on his shoulders.

"When the time comes," she whispered, "She will not need our power, she will be the power."

"She will still be our daughter."

The Creator looked up at the starlit nothing. "I will still love her, even if she unmakes us all."

Around them, the universe sighed in relief, as the two Gods relaxed into each other's embrace.

Chapter Twenty-Five: Boys will be Boys

-Maddy-

"I can't catch a break!" I snapped, dragging a damp shirt over my head, the sting of salt still in my eyes. Billie was already scrambling for her boots; her brow furrowed in silent alarm.

The pounding on our door wasn't just frantic, it was desperate. A war-drum beat of chaos on the rise.

"It's probably important," Billie said, trying for calm. But her fingers trembled.

"Yeah? Then it better be another damn invasion," I muttered, storming to the door. The second it creaked open, the fire in my chest sputtered out.

A child with wide violet eyes and barefoot, blood on his knuckles and terror smeared across his face. His skin was damp with sweat, his bottom lip trembling like a leaf in a storm.

"Hey, hey... breathe," I said, kneeling, rage dissolving in an instant. "You're safe here. You came to the right place."

Billie appeared beside me, her voice a soothing balm. "No one's mad, sweetheart. Tell us what happened."

The boy looked up, gulping air like it might vanish. "I... I did something bad, really bad."

"Okay," I said slowly. "Start from the beginning. What's your name?"

"Onix."

"Alright Onix, you're not in trouble. What happened?"

He clenched his fists. "Neo's dead and it's my fault."

Billie gasped. I froze.

Onix pressed on, breath hitching. "We were playing 'Dweller Warrior.' We always do. I was hiding in the old command room, under a desk. Neo didn't know I was there."

He paused, eyes wild. "Rina and Gemma came in. They were talking about some artifact that fell out of your armor after they pulled you from the water. They didn't see me and one of them left the thing on the table."

My heart dropped into my stomach. "The alien interface," I said under my breath.

Onix nodded. "It looked broken. So, I pressed buttons, I didn't think it could do anything! Then Neo found me, jumped out and I hit something. A button. He froze. Just... froze."

Billie crouched beside him. "He's not dead, baby. He's just trapped. These invader tools, they don't kill, not usually. They only freeze."

He started sobbing. "I didn't mean to! I just wanted to scare him, not..."

"You did the right thing coming here," I said firmly. "Now take me to him."

The command room was cold, really cold.

The walls still held the echo of old battles, with peeling paint and scratch marks from boots and claws. This had once been a center of power, the map room, a war council chamber from Harmony's peak during the Vampire days. Now it was a dusty tomb.

In the center of it floated a stasis bubble, with soft light humming around it like a heartbeat.

Inside Neo hung suspended, limbs curled like he'd fallen asleep mid-game.

The device that caused it lay nearby, humming faintly, responding to my presence.

I picked it up. The alien language across its surface shimmered, then bent to my understanding.

Harmony's coding modified and personalized. She'd left her signature in my newfound powers.

"I can free him," I told Onix. "But you need to understand, you didn't just push buttons. This thing is connected to alien technology and if configured wrong it is dangerous. You're lucky it only froze him."

Onix blinked, barely comprehending. Billie squeezed his shoulder.

"Ready?" I spoke. "Watch." With a press of my thumb the device obeyed me. The bubble popped like soap. Neo fell gasping but alive.

"Neo!" Onix sobbed, hugging him. "You're okay!"

Neo blinked. "You scared me!"

"Boys," I said, standing. "This room is forbidden and if I ever catch you in here again without a guard, I will assign you latrine duty for life."

"Yes, Queen Maddy," Neo chorused.

"Sea Queen," Neo corrected Onix. "She's the Sea Queen now."

I rolled my eyes. "Out. Blue's waiting." They scrambled away. I turned to Billie.

"They could've died. If I hadn't unlocked the language..." She nodded. "We're going to need a vault to lock these devices away and a team to study this tech."

Rina met us in the hallway, pale. "I didn't know," she said. "About the device, I thought it was junk."

"It's not," I said. "Now I need to see the stasis captives."

Gemma arrived with a Water-Dweller female I had yet to have met. "Follow me to the lower levels..." Gemma spoke then she noticed us. "Oh, hi, My Sea Queens, I was just about to show Triton's mother Queen Amelia, the recovered stasis bubbles.

Standing taller than Gemma, was a mermaid water-dweller that looked as if she just left battle. And somehow, she stood regal and alluring with her pale eyes and pink skin tone. I could see Triton in her facial features.

"The alien prisoners?" Billie asked.

"Not just aliens. You've got Harmony's best warriors locked up down here, waiting for me."

"Billie, this is Triton's mother." I pointed out.

"Oh, my, you must be my son's newly formed mate pod. I am so blessed for my son's happiness and my early retirement as the Sea has chosen her sacred Sea Queen."

Amelia pulled us in her strong arms and hugged us tight for a moment.

"I wish we could have met without the war and so much loss."

"Triton and Trent have been taken by the Kanenites, we don't know how to find them yet." I said.

Amelia was stoic and resumed walking. "I know, I trust the Goddess to guide them home somehow. In the meantime, we do what we must to keep fighting."

We entered the room where, now we were calling the cryo vault. The walls pulsed with crystalline light. Countless pods stacked to the ceiling, from what recovery we've managed. Half held those I recognized by their energy of Harmony's mark left on them. The others? Unfamiliar and strange things. A few emanated powers so cold it felt like being submerged in deep space.

"We split them," Gemma explained. "We couldn't risk mixing unknown species with our kind."

"Smart," I said. "It's time we opened the first half." My fingers brushed the interface.

The alien script burned gold. Each pod was a soul, silent, waiting and ancient. I opened the first. A woman fell into my arms with bronze skin and tattoos like circuitry. She opened her eyes and smiled.

"Queen of Waves," she said. "You finally came."

I blinked. "You know me?"

She nodded. "We dreamed of you."

Others followed. One by one, I freed them. The vault became a temple of waking power.

Harmony's lost warriors. They bowed to me, and I knew we were no longer just survivors.

I waited on freeing the alien unknowns, I just wanted to be safe, give myself time to examine each one with my new Demigod senses.

We were a rising army. That night in the private dining chamber, I found Billie holding Lisa in her lap, surrounded by laughing children.

My heart swelled.

"Maddy!" Billie waved. "You're just in time. We were about to eat without you."

"I'd never let that happen," I grinned, sitting beside her.

The meal was chaos and warmth. Stan had outdone himself, roasted sea fish, candied sea grapes, and something that tasted suspiciously like cheesecake. The children sang and danced; they forgot the world outside the dome. Afterwards, we bathed them, followed by pajamas and bedtime stories. Lullabies were sung in two languages. Billie stood in the doorway, watching Lisa sleep.

"She's mine now," she whispered. "If her parents are gone. I'll raise her."

"You won't do it alone," I said, wrapping her in my arms.

She turned to me. "Let's make a home, Maddy, for them and us."

"We will," I promised.

We drifted to bed, skin warm from the bath, hearts full... Until Billie gasped and clutched her belly.

"Maddy!"

"What? What is it?" Her eyes widened, stunned and gleaming.

"My water just broke." The storm had come again.

Chapter Twenty-Six:
The Birthing Pools

-Maddy-

Billie's scream shattered the crystal hush of the palace, ricocheting down the corridors like a war horn. I was out of bed before my mind caught up, heart hammering as if it would burst from my chest. "I need help now!" I called out my doorway.

The world narrowed to the sound of her agony; they were sharp, animalistic, and primal cries. My bare feet slapped the cool, iridescent floor as I sprinted toward her.

She was doubled over, hands clutching her belly. Her eyes, usually soft and honey-warm, were wild, with pupils blown wide in terror and pain. I slid to the floor beside her, gathering her into my arms, my hand instinctively cradling the back of her neck. She was trembling so hard I thought she might break apart.

"My water broke," Billie whispered, voice splintering. Her breath was ragged and her skin was clammy beneath my touch.

For a heartbeat, I froze, panic and awe both warring inside me. The moment felt impossibly huge, sacred and terrifying all at once. Then Blue appeared in the doorway, face pale, eyes bright with fear.

"The child... it's coming early." Blue's voice was tight, barely above a whisper, but the words felt like a thunderclap.

From behind Blue, Amelia burst into view, her pink hair wild, cheeks flushed with urgency. "The pools," she gasped, already moving toward us. "We must get her to the sacred birthing pools. Now."

Billie screamed again, her body convulsing. For a moment, her form shimmered. Her skin flickered with iridescent scales that chased each other down her neck, catching the fractured light of the corridor. Her eyes glowed bioluminescent teal, as if the sea itself was looking out through her.

The baby's magic was calling to her, awakening the dormant mermaid blood in her veins. I'd seen hints of it before, when she laughed in the surf, or when we made love in the showers, but never like this. Never so raw, so utterly total.

Before I could process it, Balthazar swept into the room, his massive arms gentle as he lifted Billie. She clung to him, gasping, tears streaming down her face. Gemma, our healer, was already at his side, chanting in a language older than the tides, her crystal wand pulsing with blue-white light.

"Go!" I barked, voice hoarse. "Don't wait for me!"

The castle itself seemed to sense our desperation. The walls veined with living crystals that lit up, casting shifting rainbows over our path. The corridor behind the throne chamber yawned open, the crystal archway humming with ancient power. Each step we took, the castle responded, guiding us deeper; the air thickening with the scent of salt and ozone.

We descended a spiral staircase, the sound of Billie's breathing echoing off the walls, each gasp a knife to my heart. The corridor opened into the Sanctum and there, a chamber unlike any I'd ever seen, even in my dreams.

Crystalline stalagmites hung from the vaulted ceiling, dripping luminous droplets into a pool so vast it seemed to hold the night sky itself. Stars and constellations from both our land and sea twinkled on the mirrored surface. The water glowed from within, alive with Harmony's essence. The air here was heavy, sacred, and thick with the memories of every birth that had ever happened in this place. It hummed in my bones, a lullaby and a warning.

Balthazar knelt at the pool's edge, lowering Billie into the water. The moment her skin touched the surface it shimmered, her legs fusing and her fin unfurling like a lotus in bloom. She gasped, arching as the water embraced her, her body relaxing and surrendering to ancient magic.

A barrier of light shimmered up from the pool, encasing her in a womb of pure energy. I could see her through it, peaceful now, her belly round and glowing as her curly hair fanned out like seaweed. The water cradled her, holding her and the child in perfect safety.

"She's safe," Blue whispered, voice reverent, almost afraid to break the spell.

Gemma nodded, her face streaked with sweat and tears. "She and the child are protected now. The pool will act like an external womb; her baby is safe. The magic of this pool will help the baby develop faster."

Amelia pressed her hand to the barrier, eyes shining. "The pool will incubate them both until the child is ready. The water mothers are with her."

I knelt at the edge, pressing my palm to the barrier. The magic tingled against my skin, cool and alive, humming with the pulse of the sea. I leaned in, lips brushing the surface, and whispered, "Stay safe, my love. I'll protect what's ours."

Billie's eyelids fluttered, her voice barely audible in my head. "Maddy..."

I wanted to stay, all I wanted was to crawl into that pool and hold her, to shield her from every pain and fear. But the world was shifting, the danger pressing in.

A low, unnatural rumble split the air, vibrating through the crystal. The pool's surface trembled. Then the alarms shrieked high, metallic and urgent, the sound of doom.

A warrior's voice crackled over the comms, harsh and panicked. "Multiple breaches across the outer dome! Kanenites are punching through every defense line. There's... something else, something bigger..."

My heart seized as the world spun. I pressed my lips to the barrier one last time, tasting salt and light. "I'll come back," I promised. "I swear it."

Amelia stepped forward, her private guards fanning out around the pool, weapons drawn and eyes hard. "Go, Maddy. I will protect Billie and the baby. You must lead."

I hesitated, torn in two, every step I took away from Billie felt like a betrayal. My chest ached and my breath came in ragged gasps. But I forced myself to move, to trust Amelia and the Goddess Harmony. I ran.

The corridors blurred around me, crystal walls flickering with warning sigils. The air was thick with fear, panic radiating from every surface and every living thing. I could feel the castle's heartbeat, both frantic and wild, echoing with my own.

As I burst through the upper doors, the world beyond was chaos. The once calm blue dome was now marred by spiderweb cracks spreading across its surface. Through the gaps, I saw the Kanenites ships; black, angular, and bristling with weapons. They moved like sharks, circling, waiting to strike.

On the ground, warriors rushed to their posts, weapons drawn, armor gleaming in the fractured light. The air was thick with the scent of ozone and fear. Somewhere, a child was crying. Somewhere else, a dragon roared, the sound shaking the ground beneath my feet.

I sprinted toward the warrior's center, my mind racing. Every instinct screamed at me to turn back, to run to Billie and protect her with tooth and claw. But I was the Sea Queen now. The fate of everyone here rested on my shoulders.

Inside, the command center was chaos. Blue was there, issuing orders, her face grim. A male warrior stood like a statue, his eyes cold, his hands flexing restlessly.

"They're targeting the Water-dweller Kingdom in masses," Blue said, her voice barely steady. "They know where all the stasis bubbles are."

A cold wave of terror washed over me. "They can't get through the barrier, can they?"

Gemma's voice crackled. "Not unless they bring something that can shatter Harmony itself, but the dome is damaged, so they have something."

A shudder ran through the floor, dust sifting down from the crystal ceiling. The sound of battle was everywhere now, blasters whining and swords clashing. All around was the roar of beasts and the screams of the dying.

I squared my shoulders, forcing the fear down. "We hold the dome at all costs. Nothing gets through."

Blue nodded, her eyes meeting mine. "You lead us, Sea Queen."

I swallowed hard, feeling the weight of every life in this place pressing down on me. I thought of Billie, floating in the pool, her body glowing with new life. I thought of the child, the future and hope waiting to be born.

Outside, the world was ending. But inside, in the heart of the castle, life was just beginning. I clung to that and let it anchor me.

I turned to the warriors, my voice ringing out, stronger than I felt. "Defend the pools. Defend each other and this kingdom. We are the tide, and we do not break."

The fear was still there, sharp and cold, gnawing at my insides but I let it drive me. I was Maddy, The Sea Queen, protector of this world, and I would not let it fall.

As I charged, I dove into the sea to battle, the memory of Billie's hand in mine, her whispered "Maddy..." echoed in my mind, the image of Triton and Billie's faces flashed in my head. My love and my family, my reason to fight.

I swam toward the storm, ready to face the darkness and whatever it brought with it.

Chapter Twenty-Seven: The Reckoning Skies

-Friends From The Stars-

Their ships shimmered like obsidian daggers cloaked in aurora light.

At the head of the fleet, the warship led the charge, its spearhead tip emblazoned with the crimson sigil of Gias, the militant female war-planet. Empress Flame sat rigid in the captain's throne, her red predator eyes glowing with calculated rage. Her sleek red hair was bound back like a blade. Beside her, her wife Empress Darah tapped into the targeting systems.

"Lock onto the ships carrying the stasis chambers. Prioritize the Dragoon signatures. We get them back or we die trying," Flame commanded.

Her voice cut through the bridge like a plasma blade. The holograms pulsed before them, red for enemies and green for captured allies. The map bloomed like war flowers, hundreds of Kanenites vessels spread across the Dragoon Kingdom's broken orbit. Terrek, looming like a giant horned purple God behind his wives, cracked his neck and tapped into the intercom.

"All units, this is your Emperor speaking," Terrek said in his deep, gravelly voice. "Show 'em what Laverian fury looks like. Also, someone bring me a Kanenites skull for my bookshelf."

Ember, still singed and bruised from her escape through Wildwood, sat in the co-pilot seat of another ship. Her scales were dull from the burns, her eyes bloodshot. Her will? Unbroken. Her mate's absence drove her, made her fangs clench with each breath.

"Jason better be safe in this battle," she growled, her claws flexing. "Or I'll burn every last one to stardust."

The portal behind them surged with light, sending wave after wave of Galactic Enforcer ships into the Dragoon system. Below, the once-glorious Dragoon kingdom was a broken husk of ash and rubble swallowed by shadow. Mountains cratered, rivers boiled, and the moons above wept dust into the starless sky.

The Kanenites ships opened fire, plasma beams lighting up the blackness. The Laverian fleet responded in kind, return fire cutting through the silence with relentless precision. Flame dove like a phoenix reborn, its belly opening to release ten smaller fighter crafts. Darah directed them with graceful precision.

"Flame! The five ships on our right are holding stasis chambers. Trent, Triton, Kayla, Tallen, Brooke, Fang, Jag, Coral, those signals are clear," Darah called out, eyes glowing with neural-link overlays.

"Copy. Weapons lock. Let's bring our friends home," Flame replied.

The first burst of the capture beam hit a Kanenites vessel holding stasis bubbles. A whining shriek rang through the ether, as the Laverian tech overrode the alien systems, disabling the tractor fields and disengaging stasis locks.

Inside the captured vessel, the bubbles trembled. Kayla blinked. The light came back. She gasped for air.

"Tallen, Fang, wake up!" She choked, pounding on her own transparent prison as it began to melt away.

On another ship, Jag groaned in pain. Blood had dried into his panther fur. Coral floated nearby, unconscious in their stasis prisons, fingers barely brushing his.

He bared his fangs, snarling through the pain, "You took my pride, my sea pod... now you die."

On the Laverian flagship, Terrek's fists clenched as the holograms showed the stasis bubbles were disengaging.

"Bring them in! Lock on and teleport now!"

The Laverian ship teleport bays surged with starlight as bodies dropped from the void. Kayla landed first, crumpling onto the bay floor with a cry. Tallen dropped next and Kayla caught him in her arms.

"Kayla!" he choked. "You're alive?"

"You idiot," she whispered, clinging to him. "You weren't allowed to die first."

"I did not die, my heart, I just got caught first."

Brooke and Fang hit the floor hard, gasping and coughing.

"Fang, your arm, it's..."

"Don't care," Fang grunted, lifting her up by her waist and pulling her to him. "You're breathing. That's enough."

Coral came in last, followed by Jag's bloodied body. He collapsed between them.

"My love, are you okay?" he asked, voice ragged.

"Jag," Coral sobbed, grabbing his hand.

"I thought we lost you," Coral whispered.

"I don't die easy," he chuckled darkly.

Ember's screen blinked.

The map blinked, a Kanenites mothership farthest from the planet. The largest ship command center.

"Darah, permission to burn that ship into a memory?"

"Granted," Darah said instantly.

The three royal ships dove like war gods into the final confrontation. The Laverian vessel hit the enemy ship first, Ember's shots tearing through the shielding like divine vengeance. Her precision piercing it, ripping metal as if it were flesh. She roared, and the ship shook.

Darah initiated a rescue pulse, detaching stasis chambers from the hull and pulling them through a portal beam.

Jason in his phoenix form blinked into safety, gasping, wings flaring wide in defiance.

"Ember!" He called.

She turned, barely registering his voice over the blast in her ears.

"Jason!" She sobbed, diving into his arms.

Behind them, Flame directed the final barrage.

"No survivors. End them."

With a focused beam of atomic fusion, she blew the Kanenites mothership into fragments. The explosion scattered into the Dragoon sky like broken stars.

As silence fell, the fleet gathered in orbit.

Below, the Dragoon Kingdom smoldered, but now fires of hope burned in the wreckage. Jason flashed Ember and himself to the surface to help with the fight there.

Later in the Grand Hall, the reunited warriors stood together. Bloodied, exhausted, and scared but alive.

Kayla and Tallen held hands, fingers twined tightly.

Brooke leaned against Fang's scaled chest, her tears soaking his skin, worry for her children evident.

Jag stood beside his wives, holding them close.

Ember and Jason clung to each other, breathing in the scent of safety.

"Phoenix?" Brooke asked Jason with worry.

"He's on Laverian just in case Kane attacked there too."

Relief flooded her face, knowing her oldest son was safe.

Terrek clapped a hand on Fang's shoulder.

"Not bad for a royal lumberjack, eh?"

Flame rolled her eyes. "You're lucky you're pretty."

The stars watched as new hope rose from ashes. The war... was far from over.

But this, this was the turning point.

Chapter Twenty-Eight: We Took A Hit

-Maddy-

The world was ending, and I was at its center.

The dome's crystal corridors pulsed with panicked light; alarms blared like the heartbeat of a dying beast. The burnt air and salt stung my tongue, mixing with the metallic tang of fear. My bare feet slapped the cold stone floor, echoing through the chaos as I raced away from the sacred birthing pools, where Billie lay cocooned in magic and water.

Outside, the sky was a bruise, streaked with black and violet. Ships blotted out the sun, Kanenites warcrafts descending like a swarm of hornets, their hulls glinting with hellfire. The air vibrated with the shriek of blasters, the thunder of explosions, and the guttural roar of Harmony's defenders. Every breath I took was ragged, every step a battle against the dread clawing at my chest.

That's when I felt it; a surge of energy so vast it nearly knocked me to my knees. Kane. The God's power pressed against my mind, cold and ancient and filled with hate. His flagship hovered above the dome, a monstrous shadow. A beam of red-gold light shot from its belly, striking the dome with a sound like the world cracking in half.

I watched helpless as a fissure zigzagged across the protected dome, spider webbing outward, growing and widening. The dome groaned, its song turning to a scream. Panic threatened to swallow me whole, but Harmony's magic surged within me, warm, wild, and alive. I felt my Demigod strength unfurl, ancient and unstoppable.

I screamed and the sound wasn't human. Power pulsed outward from my core, a tidal wave of force that sent the Kanenites ships spinning and tumbling up toward the surface. The Sea itself answered my call, the currents lashing and waves rising in fury.

But in that moment, I felt something else; a seal breaking deep beneath the sea, a presence older than memory stirring awake. It was seeking me, hungry and cold. Fear slithered down my spine. I didn't have time to worry about that showdown. The Kanenites were here and my people needed me.

Warriors swam beside me, their bodies shifting into battle form. Scales gleaming and claws extended, their shark-like eyes burning with resolve. We raced through the water, chasing the ships as they fled to the surface, our tails slicing the currents like blades.

Then the sea shuddered, a thunderous, volcanic eruption that sent a sonic cry through every water-dweller. The sound was monstrous, shaking the marrow in my bones.

"Freedom," crackled a voice ancient and terrible, reverberating in my skull.

My blood ran cold. The Kraken, the Sea's greatest terror, the ancient beast, had broken free. I could feel its mind brushing mine, vast and alien; imprinting on me, marking me as its queen. The fear of every warrior echoed in my head, a chorus of dread.

"Great," I muttered, teeth clenched. "Another nightmare to add to the list. Fuck my luck."

The Kraken's presence was suffocating, but I seized it and bent it to my will. I felt its massive tentacles coil beneath the waves, ready to strike.

"Keep the ships out of my sea," I commanded, my voice a whip of power.

The Kraken surged upward, its shadow blotting out the light as it wrapped itself around the invading vessels. It crushed them like toys and hurled the wreckage toward the surface.

Outside, Harmony's skies had split. A rift yawned open above the dome, a bleeding wound in the heavens from which black-purple lightning danced. Out of the maw surged the Galactic Empire's forces, sleek dark ships riding the storm, their hulls reflecting the lightning.

Ships swirled overhead, a swarm of hornets descending for the kill.

"The Galactic Empire has come." Ember's voice thundered in my mind, a psychic shout that rattled my teeth.

The Kanenites returned, more brutal than ever, their ships upgraded, hulking tank-sized monsters glowing with infernal energy. They weren't raiders now. They were conquerors. The sky erupted in battle, a storm of fire and steel. This wasn't a skirmish. This was annihilation.

"Then we hold the line!" I snarled, yanking Harmony's trident from the holster at my back. A gift from Amelia. The weapon thrummed with living energy, its tips sparking with blue-white lightning. I waded into the current, feeling the pulse of the ocean in my veins.

A Kanenites ship fired at the crystal cloud above, sending a hail of razor-sharp shards crashing toward us. I flung up a water shield, magic coalescing in an instant, bouncing the shrapnel away with a hiss and a flash of steam.

Blue and Rena flanked me, armored in light-forged scales, their faces set and grim. The warriors I'd freed earlier stood shoulder to shoulder with our defenders, forming a living wall of scales and steel. On the shore behind us, others guarded the land.

"We die before we let them touch the water," I vowed, my voice echoing across the battlefield.

Then the world exploded.

The Harmony Keepers formed a shining phalanx, their staffs channeling pure energy that lashed through the air like solar whips. The Kanenites moved faster than before, warped by a God's dark tech; teleporting in flickering bursts, punching through our defenses with lasers and smoke.

I glimpsed Onix and Neo, just children, hiding behind the warriors, hurling glowing orbs into a knot of Kanenites. Brave little fools. My heart twisted.

"Blue!" I shouted, hurling a Kanenites ship through a crystalline cloud. "Get the kids back to the kingdom!"

"I've already called the Great Guardian," she replied, voice taut. "But Maddy... Ember is coming to you."

Through the smoke and ruin, I saw her, Ember, gliding in as a blue dragon, flanked by a fire phoenix, its wings crackling with ethereal flame. She landed in silence, the battlefield pausing around her.

"Maddy," Ember purred, her dragon form melting away as she approached. "The Laverians and Galactic Enforcers have come to assist us."

I hefted my trident, ready for anything. "Good. We need all the help we can get. Let's kick some Kanenites ass."

"The Goddess Harmony opened a portal so the Galactic forces could come. We've tracked the ships holding the harvested, and we're saving them now. But Kane's furious; he wants this planet destroyed," Ember said.

She turned to a tall, dark-haired warrior at her side. "Maddy, meet Jason, my mate."

Jason grinned, eyes glinting. "Hi, Maddy. Looking forward to getting to know you. But first, what do you say we fry up some alien assholes?"

I laughed, raw and wild. "I like the way you think. Let's get to work."

A Kanenites ship spiraled down from orbit, laser cannons blazing, targeting us. I met it mid-strike, channeling Harmony's power through my trident. Lightning and shadow collided, the blast shattering the towers and sending both armies reeling in stunned silence. For a moment, we were titans, rewriting the sky with every blow.

Still, they kept coming. My arms ached, blood—both mine and others—slicked my skin. My allies staggered, pushed back inch by inch toward the underwater Dweller-Kingdom. Rina collapsed, Blue holding the line with a dozen desperate warriors. The shield around the sacred waters flickered, thin as hope.

Then I heard it, a cry, not with my ears but in my soul. Billie, calling for me in pain.

A vision flashed before my eyes; Billie cradling our child, the baby shining like a living star. The air shimmered thick with energy.

With a voice like ocean thunder, Billie roared, her words echoing in every mind: "You will not touch our child. You will not take this world!"

The waters surged from the sea, racing across the battlefield in giant, serpentine tendrils. Every ally they touched was healed, wounds closing and strength returning. Every enemy they touched screamed and withered, burned by the power of a mother and her baby.

The tides turned. The Kanenites tried to retreat, but the divine surge destroyed them—no mercy, no escape.

I dove into the sea, going deep, drawn by a force stronger than fear. I saw our dome, with no cracks, healed and pulsing strong. I found Billie in the heart of the birthing pool, her eyes glowing, her arms wrapped around our child. I took her hand, our fingers locking, magic weaving together.

"Let's end this," I said, voice trembling with exhaustion and hope.

She nodded, fiercely and unbreakable. "Together."

When silence finally fell, we were still standing. The pools shimmered, the castle glowed with new breath, and the sea, our sea, was safe, for now.

But deep beneath, I could still feel the kraken, watching and waiting. The old gods and monsters weren't done with us yet, and neither was I.

Chapter Twenty-Nine: What's Locked Down Deep

-Maddy-

The water churned with the taste of prophecy. I floated alone, on the obsidian ridge that formed the barrier between the known sea and the magically sealed trench. My skin shimmered with the iridescence of power, not fully my own. Salt burned into fresh wounds, my breath steady despite the aching grief that curled like seaweed in my gut. Triton was gone, stolen, and King Trent too. The battle had cost them everything, yet the tides whispered of something older; something stirring beneath the waves.

A pulse hit my sternum like a war drum; it wasn't mine; it was the ocean floor beneath me shuddering.

"What in the name of Harmony?"

I barely had time to brace before the sea cracked open like a shell. Steam hissed upward, as if the planet itself exhaled after centuries of silence. Deep in the trench, ancient chains snapped. The sound wasn't metallic, it was cosmic. All across Harmony's seas, whales screamed in terror.

A murky whirlpool twisted beneath me, and from its heart, something massive stirred. Something imprisoned long before memory, bound in a forgotten war of the Gods. Why do I feel more scared of this than the damn aliens?

My heart raced as fragments of knowledge not my own unfurled in my mind. Not words, but sensations. They were of God's wrath and betrayal, and oceans turning black with sorrow. The kraken, the leviathan, no one alive remembered its true name.

It rose now, tentacles like mountains, eyes ancient as stars. Armor plating clung to its form like coral-grown ruins; its body lined with the sigils of a forgotten pantheon. Behind it came others, uncoiling from the black depths, sea serpents crowned in kelp. They were shadowed leviathans with mouths like whirlpools; beings once revered as Gods.

I felt my knees falter. They had not died; they had been sealed away and I had awoken them. The ocean trembled with chaos as the creatures roared their return. Surface storms whipped into cyclones; coral structures shattered beneath the pressure of their awakening. Sea dwellers across the ocean fled in terror. The kraken turned to me, not with rage, but with recognition.

"You carry her scent."

The kraken's voice boomed directly into my mind, its telepathy thunderous. A thousand currents stopped moving, awaiting my answer.

"Whose scent?" I demanded, though my voice cracked from fear and power.

"Harmony and the Great Mother," it hissed, tentacles fanning wide as the sea darkened.

My heart beat out of sync. I stepped forward on instinct, power surged in my fingertips, hot and crackling with divine salt.

"She's my Goddess. I fight for her, for her mother too." The sea grew still and the kraken leaned closer. "You are her, a severed splinter of her."

The water gods behind him murmured, a chorus of clicking language and sonar tones. I trembled, as something clicked into place deep in my chest; like a lock undone or a seal broken. My skin gleamed with markings of light, webbed in intricate runes. The power within me, once dormant, had bloomed with Harmony's blood and will.

My personal kraken moved silently behind me, a show of support in front of the bigger beast before me.

A scream of revelation tore from my lungs as memories that were not mine surged. The Mother Goddess weeping and forcing her kraken into the depths for its rebellion towards the Gods. The sea became a divine shackle to keep them hidden and safe. The Goddess Harmony herself sending them her reassurance and calming magic.

I had brought them back, broke that seal and opened the floodgates. The kraken bowed its head not in defeat, but in eternal allegiance.

"Daughter of the Sea Flame, bearer of Harmony's Light. You have freed us, and the Deep remembers."

The rest bowed, next came a chorus of thrones long forgotten. They were the Gods and monsters once feared across galaxies. They bent on knee, tentacle, fin, and claw.

I didn't feel like a queen, I felt more like a storm about to break.

"We will help you," the kraken intoned, "the old darkness stirs and Kane comes."

My hands clenched as I saw the dark God's face in her mind, the tyrant, ever craving power and chaos. "Thank you for your help."

The kraken studied me, then pulsed a signal. All around me, Gods began to move, not with chaos, but purpose this time. Leviathans swam toward the edge of the sea kingdom, circling the trenches and cliffs, rising like sentinels. Storm Gods conjured shields of whirlwinds. A Siren Queen with eyes like abyssal pearls, offered me a coral blade, woven from memory and magic.

"He will come for you," she whispered. "As he is coming for Harmony."

I took the blade. "Let him try."

Back in the underwater kingdom, panic raged. The sudden return of ancient monsters had sent the civilians into lockdown. Sea towers trembled, coral palaces sealed themselves, and soldiers prayed.

When they saw me, I was riding the kraken like a goddess of vengeance, my hair haloed in light, eyes lit with bioluminescent fury.

The sea didn't just obey me now; it worshipped me. The Sea Gods followed me, adding their power to the planet and the ocean, claiming Harmony's world as home.

The ancient Gods formed a ring around the city, pulsing protective energy into the reefs. A new power pulsed at the city's heart. Not of the old wards, not Triton or Trent, but something far deeper. Something primarily feminine and divine.

I touched down before the water dwelling kingdom, children gathering in awe.

"The Deep has returned," I declared, my voice layered with Harmony's resonance. "They remember who and what they are." The water vibrated with the promise of reckoning.

Far above in the distant reaches of space, something stirred. A mad God cloaked in darkness.

Kane turned his burning gaze toward the sea on Harmony's planet. He smiled, craving to consume its power.

Chapter Thirty: Cracks In The Crystal Sanctuary

-Survivors-

In the Crystal Sanctuary, the wind outside the mountain screamed like a dying God. Deep within its core, hidden in the ancient heart of the world, magic pulsed like a whisper. A thousand glowing veins of crystal lined the cavern walls, casting a warm shimmering glow over the faces of those gathered there. All of the surviving elves, nymphs, druids, dryads, sprites, and shifters stood by. A congregation of the old blood, those who were tied to Harmony. When the stars burned and the skies rained fire, they hid.

The room itself was sacred. The Crystal Healing Chamber. Forged in the first age of the planet's breath, when the Goddess Harmony walked openly among her children. It held her tears laced with divinity, the very gemstones they now clutched to in prayer.

Children were silent. Huddled in moss-lined alcoves with eyes wide and their bodies pressed against trembling mothers. Some were bandaged. Most were too tired to cry. A dryad named Seralee pressed her palm to the central crystal altar, voice hushed and trembling.

"Please," she whispered, "please, my Goddess. Don't forget us."

Others joined her one by one, placing fingers, foreheads, and whole bodies against the ancient quartz-like structure that rose in the middle of the chamber. It pulsed a slow, dim heartbeat. Once it had glowed bright enough to light the mountain from within. Now, it flickered like a dying ember.

"The stars are gone," muttered an old warlock, gripping his staff. "All magic is blocked. No one comes."

"She hears," Seralee said firmly, eyes wet. "She must."

A ripple of silence passed through the cavern as footsteps echoed down the stone corridor, soft and cautious like someone trying not to wake a corpse.

It was Elion, a young half-elf boy with blood on his tunic.

"They're getting closer," he gasped, stumbling into the room. "D rones... Kanenites drones are down in the caverns below us. They're breaching the mountain... breaking through the obsidian wards like they're wet bark."

Gasps. A woman sobbed. Someone shouted for the elders. A centaur warrior unslung her bow, hands shaking. "We can't fight them, not here. Not in the sacred chamber."

"We have no choice," muttered an older fae, wings clipped and face smeared with blood. "It's death or stasis."

"Better death," hissed someone.

The lights dimmed for a moment. A low mechanical hum echoed from deep below. Not natural or elemental. It was cold and synthetic. Drones, hundreds of them.

They came in swarms, forged from black metal with writhing limbs that hissed streams of laser beams. Each was the size of a wolf and twice as fast, flying and scanning, searching for prey. When they finally breached the healing cavern, they did not roar. They didn't need to.

They descended in perfect silence and the screaming began. The centaur released the first arrow, blessed by the good wood that the forest gave and tipped in silver, and took one out mid-air. It fell with a crunch, sparking and twitching. Two more replaced it, then ten and then many more.

The drones zipped between crystals and bodies alike, wrapping terrified beings in glowing blue stasis bubbles. They hovered above the ground, immobilizing limbs and freezing breath.

A druid summoned roots from the cavern floor to grab at one, dragging it down, screaming invocations. A drone blasted through his chest before the spell could take. Blood spattered the crystals, staining divine memory.

Elion tried to protect a group of children. His knife broke on the alien metal of a drone. He was slammed against the wall, a burst of blue energy sealing him inside a bubble before he could shout.

Seralee's scream was raw. Her hands lit with ancient fire, as she hurled bolts of it into the oncoming swarm. Three drones exploded into burning wreckage. A fourth one wrapped a serrated limb around her waist and hurled her against the altar.

She slid down it, blood smearing the divine quartz. "Harmony," she whispered, barely able to lift her head.

A dryad clutched a toddler running for the back tunnel but drones sealed it off with a mechanical gate. There was no escape. Only capture or slaughter. Some chose to fight. Some dropped to their knees and begged for the crystals to open, to release the ancient magic that was as old as the stars, buried deep inside.

"Goddess Harmony, please," a sprite sobbed, clutching a crystal shard so tightly it cut into her palms. "Take us. Hide us in the light."

The crystals pulsed a flicker, a heartbeat. But no miracle came. Only more drones. A few people dove off the platform into the dark belly of the mountain, dying defiantly rather than be captured.

The stasis bubbles filled the air like floating corpses. Rows of them, hovering silently above the shattered sanctuary.

A soldier drone turned toward the altar. One extended a buzzing limb and sliced into it, not to destroy but to extract the blessed crystals.

They were harvesting even this sacred room. The ground shook, not from them. From something else.

The oldest elf in the room, a woman named Thalenya, eyes blind but soul still vibrant, lifted her chin from where she'd been cradling a child. "She is here."

No one had time to respond before a pulse of silver light erupted from the cracked altar, throwing drones back like ash in a hurricane. The light swept through the chamber in a wide arc and for a breathless moment, the room was still.

Inside every stasis bubble, the light pulsed again, and those trapped opened their eyes, awakened once more. Still unable to move and now aware. Tears streamed down Elion's frozen face.

"She's not forgotten," Seralee whispered, lips stained with blood. "She knows."

Then the drones began to adapt.

They rebooted, now shielded, glowing a menacing shade of red. The ones who had been briefly fried reactivated with vengeance. They advanced again, now faster.

A scream echoed through the chamber as they descended upon the survivors.

Thalenya was the first to go, trying to stand, arms spread in peace. A drone pierced her chest and she crumpled without a word.

The centaur was next, captured mid-leap, yanked into a bubble that shimmered violently as her rage rippled through it.

Seralee gazed back toward the altar, wishing for the light one last time.

They took piece by piece, our hope, Gods, and crystals. In the silence that followed, only the hum of the drones remained.

The room was filled now with the pale blue light of stasis orbs. Some floated slowly toward the exit tunnels being herded by drones. Others hovered high, pulsing quietly like forgotten stars.

The altar cracked, splintering down the middle. One final surge of energy burst from it and it vanished. A signal, a prayer sent into the void. And somewhere far beyond, in the storm-choked veil of Harmony's planet, she heard it.

Chapter Thirty-One: Ash and Ocean

-The Dragoon Children-

-Dean-

You ever try to keep six terrified kids alive while the sky's falling and half the planet's on fire? No? Well, lucky you.

The ash made it hard to breathe. Not that I was complaining, choking on soot was better than hearing the drones overhead. They sounded like someone had mixed a swarm of hornets with a rusty chainsaw and turned the volume up to "fuck you up" level.

I crouched behind a shattered Wildwood tree, motioning the others to stay low. Sam was dragging the twins, Tia and Renn, both five and crying silently. Blaze had little Kai on her hip, blood streaking down one arm from something that looked more like a burn than a wound. No time to look.

We were only half a mile from the beach. If the Goddess was feeling generous—and let's be real, she had been allowing this to happen—let's see if we'd make it to the shore without being liquefied or captured.

"I think I see a path through the eastern ridge," I whispered to Sam.

He glanced down the slope, eyes narrowed. "Unless it's a trap."

"Everything's a trap now."

He cracked a grin. "Great, let's walk straight into it, maybe they'll give us tea and cookies."

"You're not funny," I muttered.

"Neither are you, Dean."

"Yeah, but I'm prettier."

-Blaze-

My arms were killing me, and Kai kept wriggling like a damn salamander. "Hold still or we're all gonna die," I hissed through gritted teeth.

He hiccupped, blinking up at me with wide golden eyes. "Blazey... are we gonna find Mommy?"

"Sure, kiddo. We'll find Mommy, Daddy, and a spaceship full of unicorns. Just keep your head down, yeah?"

He nodded solemnly, then buried his face in my shoulder.

The Wildwood trees were mostly burnt stumps now, twisted like bones. Occasionally we found one still standing, scorched but alive, glowing faintly with the old magic. Sam stopped once, pressing a hand to one, muttering a prayer to Harmony.

I didn't pray; I wasn't going to either. Not because I didn't believe in it. Because I did, and if Harmony was watching... she was probably crying.

We broke through the final bramble ridge just as the sun was dying behind a veil of blackened clouds. I longed for my colorful skies, clear of the ash and aliens. We resisted the urge to shift into our dragon form. It is easier to hide and keep the kids safe.

The beach shimmered like glass covered in wet ash and driftwood. Stumbling toward us was someone.

"Hold up," Dean said, hand on his blade. "We got company."

She was a tall water-dweller, her hair like kelp soaked in blood, stumbling through the shallows with one hand clutched to her ribs.

"I know her," Sam breathed. "She was one of the water-dwellers we sent to the Crystal Sanctuary—that's Elena, she survived."

The woman collapsed.

We sprinted.

Dean caught her head just before it hit the sand. "Hey, hey, Elena you're with us? Don't you dare die on us, ocean lady."

Her eyes fluttered. "Children... too many... too loud..."

"Yep. Welcome to our life," I muttered, lowering Kai beside her.

"Can you help us?" Sam asked, kneeling. "We need to get them to the kingdom, they're all that's left."

She coughed hard, blood bubbling from her lips. "I can... create a bubble, but it will cost me."

Dean looked at us. "We don't have a choice."

Sam carried her to the waves.

Then Elena closed her eyes, muttering in the ancient tongue of the deep. Water trembled around her, forming a circle, then a sphere. Oxygen pushed back the salt, and the children gasped as air filled their lungs again.

"You first," she said, voice fraying. "Hurry."

-Sam-

Being inside the oxygen bubble was like standing in a dream. Everything outside was blue and endless. Above us, the surface turned to shimmer and below, black water yawned open.

The water-dweller stood at the edge of her spell, blood mixing with magic at her feet. Her limbs trembled. I could see her skin turning sickly from the strain.

"She's not gonna make it," Blaze muttered, she held Elena's head in her lap.

"She knew that," I said.

"People don't just sacrifice themselves for strangers."

"They do," Dean said quietly, guiding one of the older kids toward the center.

"Our parents did, and so did the Dragoon Throne."

The descent was slow and painful. We floated in the bubble along the sea floor, kelp brushing past like ghost hands. We passed the broken statues of old kings, mermaid queens, dragons, and guardians of the deep, all decimated by war.

Then we saw it, a sea creature, an octopus that sliced through the water toward us. Long tentacles wrapped around the weak bubble; grabbing us, it took the bubble quickly into the deep. The underwater kingdom loomed ahead, still glowing and standing.

A ring of light like a halo, crystal and shell towers stretching out in spirals, pulsing with sacred magic.

-Blaze-

She dropped as soon as we reached the gates.

The water-dweller collapsed to her knees, the oxygen bubble flickering out like a candle. I grabbed her before she could faceplant into Blue.

"Whoa, whoa, easy there, shit she's bleeding out."

From the gates, three figures emerged. Maddy, Balthazar, and Gemma. The power coming off them hit me like a freight train. Maddy's eyes widened as she saw the kids and then the woman in my arms.

"Get her inside," Maddy barked.

"Gemma, triage now. Balthazar, help me with the children."

Dean handed off the youngest to Balthazar, muttering, "Careful. He bites."

"I do not!" Kai shouted. "That was one time!"

Gemma crouched beside the water-dweller, murmuring a healing chant. Light pooled beneath her hand but the woman was barely clinging to life.

"She gave everything for them," Dean said softly.

Maddy looked at us, really looked, and something softened in her war-hardened face.

"You're Tallon's kids."

"Yeah," Sam said. "The brood of chaos."

"Not to mention devastatingly gorgeous," I added, blowing on my sharp nails and whipped my hair back for effect. Just to ease the tension in the air now that we are safe.

"And humble," Dean finished.

Maddy let out a breath that could've been a laugh or a sob. "You're safe now, come inside."

-Dean-

They led us through the coral gate into the inner sanctum of the underwater kingdom. It was different than I remembered. The throne room was smaller, lit by wavering blue crystals. The dome above was shimmering, letting rays of broken crystal light pour in like a fractured blessing.

The kids were laid out on sea-silk beds. Healers bustled around them. Someone offered us kelp tea, which tasted like mossy sadness. I downed mine in one gulp, I was just grateful to have the ash washed out of my mouth.

"The kids can join the other children as soon as we heal them," Gemma said.

"Just a few scrapes, you all did a great job protecting them." Balthazar spoke proudly. Gotta love that Moose.

Sam leaned against the wall, looking like he was trying not to pass out.

Blaze sat next to Kai, who was asleep, drooling on her shoulder.

Maddy returned, her expression unreadable.

"She'll live," she said.

"Barely, her name is Elena. She said she saw the mountain breach. Said... the drones took hundreds. Some were vaporized on the spot."

I nodded, staring at the stained coral tiles.

"We tried to fight," I said.

"But we had the kids. We couldn't risk them."

"You did right," Maddy said. "They're alive. That's all that matters."

Blaze cracked her neck, always a tomboy. "So. When do we hit back?"

Maddy raised a brow. "You just got here."

Sam grinned. "Yeah, but we're already bored."

Gemma chuckled from the corner. "You Dragoon kids, all fire and blood."

"That's us," Dean said. "Fire, blood, and really bad timing."

-Sam-

Later that night, after the healers checked us and the kids were finally sleeping, I walked to the outer corridor and stared through the magical sea wall. The ocean beyond was full of motion, shadows of sea life and schools of fish. Glowing ruins and kelp forests twisted with wreckage and debris from above.

Dean joined me, tossing me a chunk of coral candy. I chewed on it without tasting it.

"We're not done," I said.

"Nope," he said.

Blaze slid beside us, arms crossed. "We've got enemies now worse than even the vampires from before."

"Uncle Fang and Aunt Brooke, Mom and Dad need rescue, if they still live... We've got our cousins to protect, the others to find and if we're lucky, a war to win."

Dean nodded. "They thought they could end us."

Sam looked back at the sleeping children behind the crystal wall. "But we're Dragoon."

"Dragoons don't die easy," Blaze added, smirking. Her sweet face lit up the dark.

The ocean rumbled around us with a sound like thunder, or prophecy.

We weren't safe; however, we weren't broken either, not yet.

"Blaze, I think you should stay here safe with the kids."

"The hell you say!" She shoved me hard into the dome wall.

Chapter Thirty-Two: Witches, A Worlock and Fury

-Maddy-

The air reeked of smoke and scorched moss. Each breath burned my throat, the taste of ash and old pine sap clinging to my tongue. I moved lightly across the forest floor, what was left of it, anyway. My boots sinking into layers of blackened needles and tangled roots.

Harmony's planet was bleeding. Every step I took, I felt it: the agony of the land, the way the trees themselves cried out in a chorus only I could hear, their voices rising like a hunting prayer for vengeance and mercy.

Smoke curled through the shattered canopy, drifting in ghostly tendrils. The once-lush forest was a graveyard now. Burned-out homes and splintered tree trunks jutted from the haze, and the worst part was the silence broken only by the faint, shuddering breaths of the dying. Bodies, some Kanenites, some not. They lay sprawled in grotesque tableau. The Kanenites had torn through here like a plague.

I pressed two fingers to my temple, drawing on the well of divine awareness that pulsed beneath my skin, a second heartbeat, Harmony's heartbeat, rushing through my veins. I reached for it, let it open me to everything: the pain, the hope, the faint flicker of magic that meant not everyone was lost.

Suddenly, a burst of power, earthy, floral, and fiercely male, tugged at my senses. A warlock and witches. Harmony's chosen family. If they mattered to the Goddess, they mattered to me. I closed my eyes, searching for the thread of their magic, and found it shining in the darkness like a beacon.

"Fabian," I whispered, the name a prayer carried on the wind. His voice echoed back to me, faint but alive. "I'm coming."

A memory of the Goddess Harmony flashed of Fabian and his daughters at the Festival of Blooming Moons, weaving light into the sky, his wife dancing with flames with a careless flick of her wrist. That warmth, that laughter, was a knife in my chest now, but it drove me forward. I quickened my pace, sliding down a slope slick with soot, coming to a crouch at the edge of a charred clearing.

The witches were under siege. Fabian stood at the center, his white hair singed, one arm pressed tight around his waist. His five daughters formed a protective ring, casting shields and sigils with trembling fingers. Alien foot soldiers advanced in staggered lines, black synth armor gleaming, movements too fast, precise and wrong for this place.

Helena hurled a spear of lightning from her palm, sending three Kanenites flying like broken dolls. But more came. Dozens more, pouring from the smoke.

The trees behind me whispered a warning. I felt more Kanenites closing in, reinforcements. I stepped forward, letting the divine presence fill me, flare out from my skin like fire in a drought. My eyes burned gold. Celestial tattoos shimmered along my arms, pulsing with Harmony's magic. I was the Goddess's fury made flesh.

A flick of my wrist and my dual blades slid free, shining with the sea-magic of Harmony. I charged.

"Fabian! Shields up!" I shouted, my voice ringing like a bell through the burning woods.

The witches sensed me. Theadora opened a gap in their formation, and I dove in, force and fury incarnate. My blades flashed arcs of gold and red, slicing through Kanenites armor with a satisfying shriek. Green-black blood spattered my face, hot and oily. A drone zipped toward me, I spun, cleaving it in half before it could scan.

Sybil screamed, one of the soldiers had broken through. Fabian turned, tried to throw a ward, but his magic faltered, his arm shaking. The Kanenite raised its rifle.

"No!" I hurled a coral dagger from my palm, the blade embedding between the alien's eyes. It dropped before it could fire.

"Go!" I barked. "Margery, lead them through the moonstone grove. I'll cover your path."

But Fabian didn't move. "We fight with you," he insisted, voice hoarse.

"You'll die with me if you stay," I snapped, anger and terror warring inside me. "That's not an option."

Cordelia, Fabian's mate, narrowed her eyes at me. "We don't leave people behind."

"Then fight smarter!" I growled. "Theadora, Sybil, left flank, use Harmony's magic. Fabian, bind them. Get behind me. Now!"

They moved, casting spell after spell through the air, violet and gold sigils dancing around my blades. I whirled, stabbed, in our battlefield was a storm made of fire and magic, of blood and survival.

Behind us, drones descended, netting beams ready to snatch the daughters away. Margery raised both hands, unleashing a tornado of witch-light that shredded the machines, raining twisted metal onto the ground.

Cordelia grabbed Helena, pushing her behind a fallen trunk. Her hand blazed with phoenix fire. "Not my daughters," she hissed, hurling the flame at the Kanenites. They ignited, screaming, burning like paper.

But the Kanenites were endless. A high-pitched wail split the air, a war-horn from above. A sleek black gunship dropped over the trees, spotlights flooding the battlefield. More foot soldiers rappelled down, black shapes against the fire.

"We have to move!" I yelled, grabbing Fabian's arm. "If we don't leave now, they'll take you. They want your daughters for harvest."

Fabian's face went ashen. He looked at Cordelia, then the girls, and nodded. "Retreat to the old vampire caverns!"

The witches converged, casting a shared spell that pulsed beneath our feet. The ground trembled, then ruptured, forming a glowing tunnel of silver energy. They jumped in, one after another. I was last to jump, my blade catching a Kanenite in the throat before I dove through. Magic sealed the way behind us, blocking pursuit.

We tumbled out onto a mossy ridge, the ocean's roar was in my ears, the air was cool and clean at last, we were safe for now.

I slumped against a cliff wall, panting, blood dripping down my arm. Fabian crouched beside me, pressing glowing hands to my wound. Warmth spread through me, the pain receding.

"You saved us," he whispered.

"You're family," I rasped. "I don't leave family behind."

Fabian pulled his wife and youngest daughter close. "We felt Harmony's power fading. We feared…"

"She's alive," I said, staring up at the bruised sky. "But the war isn't over."

Sybil sat down beside Margery, tears cutting tracks through the ash on her cheeks. "We lost the orchard. Everything's gone."

"Not everything," I said softly, voice breaking. "You still have each other and we still have this fight. I promise you; we'll make them pay."

I pushed myself up, summoning a sphere of magic, cool, shimmering air and water to escort them down to the Water Dwelling Kingdom.

"Let's get you to Gemma. She'll heal everyone up."

As we floated down, I felt the shift inside me, the demigod, the sea queen, the magic that was more than I could comprehend. These witches, these warriors, they were Harmony's family, and now, they were mine.

My old life on Earth felt like a fading dream. My brother's face blurred in my memory; he'd grieve for me. He'd think I'd drowned on the California coast. My family would pray for my soul, mourn me as lost.

Maybe they were right. This war was hell, and I was fighting it with everything I had. For Harmony. For this new family, for a world worth saving, even while it burned.

Chapter Thirty-Three: Kane's Water Portal.

-Maddy-

The sea was too quiet; an uncanny heavy quiet that presses against your skin, making the hair on your arms stand up. I hovered in the blue-green hush just beneath the dome, suspended in the gentle sway of the current. Every sense stretched thin. The only sounds were my own heartbeat, and the distant clicks of the dome's machinery. The faint, exhausted pulse of the guardian octopus drifting above the coral towers. Even the bioluminescent reef fish seemed to be hiding, their lights dimmed in fear.

Harmony's last stronghold, our oceanic sanctuary, felt like the eye of a hurricane; a momentary peace before the world split open again.

Billie was inside, safe for now, clutching Murial to her chest in the throne room, surrounded by terrified refugees. The guardian octopus floated nearby, her great tentacles drooping from the last battle. We were all holding our breath, waiting for the next horror to descend.

That's when I felt it; a tremor, but not of earth or water. Something deeper. A wrongness that vibrated through the marrow of the world, through the magic that had become my blood. My skin prickled and my heart stuttered.

The ocean above us darkened, strangled by a spreading shadow. A pulse rippled through the water. A silent scream that sent every creature fleeing, scales flashing silver as they dove for cover. I turned my gaze skyward, and my soul recoiled.

A rupture split the surface, jagged black and crimson, bleeding like a wound in the sky. Reality itself tore open, and out of it poured the Kanenites ships, their hulls gleaming with hungry red lights, all sharp angles and predatory lines. The portal spat them into our world, dozens at a time, trailing swarms of drones, razor-finned, blinking with malice.

"No... not now," I whispered, the words dissolving into stunned silence.

The first ships hit the water with a soundless impact, sending shockwaves through the dome. The drones dove straight for us, their eyes flashing, fins slicing through kelp and coral as they closed in.

"Everyone to defensive stations!" My voice rang out through the telepathic link that bound us all inside the dome. I felt the minds of my people snap to attention, fear sharpening into resolve.

Below me, the ocean gods stirred. The great Krakens, ancient, bio-luminescent titans, rose from the trenches, their bodies coiling in the darkness, eyes burning with sacred power. Leviathans slithered from their hidden grottos, scales lighting up the gloom with pulses of blue and green. Sea gods, old as the tides, raised their hands, conjuring walls of current and spears of ice.

"They're heading for the dome!" a voice cried out, panic and awe tangled together.

A flash of heat surged through me, rage, purpose, a wild, desperate hope. I pushed off the sea floor. My body shifting into battle form, gill-marks glowing; runes spiraling down my arms and coral armor hardening over muscle. The water around me shimmered with power.

Billie's voice pierced the chaos, raw and terrified. "Maddy! They're coming! The dome!"

I spun, scanning for her through the dome's crystalline walls. She stood in the throne room clutching Murial, her face pale but determined. Murial's tiny hands glowed with infant magic, her cries muffled by the barrier.

"Guardian! Get Murial to sanctuary in the Krakens tunnels!" I sent the command with every ounce of will I had.

The octopus blinked, understanding flickering in her massive eyes. She reached for Billie and Murial, but it was too late.

A beam of sickly silver light sliced through the dome, not of a blast, but a theft. It snaked through the water, wrapping around Murial, and in a blink, she vanished, ripped from Billie's arms.

"NO!" Billie's scream tore through the water, a sound of such agony; it nearly broke me.

"KANE!" I roared, my voice vibrating the water around me, echoing through every current.

I dove, following the trace of the light, senses locked onto the magic like a predator. Rage blazed in my veins, fueling a power I'd never touched before. Every cell in my body screamed for retribution.

Above, the Kanenites escape ship twisted, vanishing into the swarm. "You're not getting away with her," I snarled, voice low and deadly.

Beside me, a Sea God in the form of a monstrous Leviathan surged upward, his scales crackling with power. "We will flank the vessel. You strike."

"Go!" I commanded, and we moved as one, thundering through the water, slicing through darkness and debris.

The ship dove, trying to lose us in the blackness of the deep. I felt Kane's magic, it was sour and corrupt, a poison in the water. It clawed at my mind, trying to slow me, but Harmony's power rose up, burning it away.

I closed my hand, summoning a spear of pure light. I drew Harmony's essence to a focused, single deadly point. I aimed, heart pounding. "Murial, hold on." I hurled the spear.

It struck the ship mid-spine. The hull shuddered, systems shorting out in a burst of sparks and black smoke. The vessel reeled, and from its belly a smaller pod jettisoned; Murial's prison.

I surged forward, the Guardian's tentacle wrapping around me, flinging me into the wreckage. Alien metal tore at my skin, but I didn't care. I ripped through the plating, hands bleeding and breath burning.

There she was. Murial, inside a stasis pod, her tiny body glowing with magic and fear. I cradled her, pressing my forehead to the bubble. My power rushed into the pod, nullifying the field and shattering the lock.

"I've got you, baby," I breathed, tears mixing with seawater. "I've got you."

Murial blinked, her magic flickering and then settled, her cries fading to soft hiccups. Her little body in its mermaid form, her tail swishing as she snuggled closer to my heart. Relief crashed over me, fierce and wild. I pressed her to my chest, wrapping her in every protection I could muster.

Above, the battle still raged, ships firing and Sea Gods roaring, the dome trembling with every impact. I had her, I had my daughter.

-KANE-

Far above, suspended in a rift between realities, Kane watched the unfolding chaos with eyes like burning coals. His gaze pierced the veil between worlds, drinking in every detail; the trembling dome, and the swirling armies. His focus on the stubborn resilience of Harmony's defenders. His jaw clenched, muscles bunching so tight the air around him warped, shimmering with barely contained power.

He had expected carnage. He had demanded annihilation. Instead, he saw hope flicker where only despair should have reigned. Maddy, Harmony's chosen one, that insolent whelp still lived. The dome still stood, battered but unbroken; the sea itself refused to yield. The tides rising in defiance, cradling the wounded, shielding the weak. The ocean dared to answer Maddy's rage with its own.

"Incompetent imbeciles!" Kane's voice thundered through the void, there was a soundless quake that made the fabric of reality tremble. "She should be drowning! The dome should be in ruins! My will is LAW!"

He slammed his fist into the ether, the rift around him rippled, bleeding shadows and flame. Madness flickered in his eyes, old and bottomless, the kind that comes from centuries of unchecked power and festering hate. He remembered worlds he had shattered, and the civilizations he had ground to dust beneath his heel. Yet, here on this insignificant purple planet, he was thwarted again and again by mortals and demigods. Harboring the stubborn pulsing hope of Harmony.

Below, the sea lifted the injured and guided the survivors to safety. It spat in the face of his destruction. Every act of defiance was a needle under his skin, a fresh insult to his pride. His lips peeled back in a snarl, teeth bared in a predator's grimace.

"Fine," he growled, voice a guttural promise of ruin. "If the universe will not break for me; I will break it myself."

He spread his arms wide, the rift yawning open behind him like the maw of a beast. Shadows writhed at his feet, whispering madness, and feeding on his rage. A blade of black flame coalesced in his hand, growing longer and hungrier; pulsing with the hatred of a thousand dead worlds. The weapon screamed with the voices of the lost and damned, and conquered. It longed for blood, for obliteration. Seeking total annihilation.

Kane's mind fractured and re-formed, his wrath burning away reason, leaving only the hunger for destruction. He saw Harmony's sanctuary below, a fragile jewel, pulsing with life and hope. His vision tunneled, narrowing to a single point of obliteration.

He raised the blade, the void itself bending toward its edge, and pointed it at the heart of Harmony's last refuge.

"I am coming, Harmony," he whispered, his voice a caress and a curse. "I will drown your hope, burn your sanctuary, and grind your champions to ash. I am the end, I am the storm. I AM WRATH!"

The rift screamed as the blade of black flame began its descent; with a promise of decimation, it was a herald of the God's unending madness.

Chapter Thirty-Four: Andromeda's Freedom

-Andromeda-

The stars churned in blood. The Kanenites General Varnok stood hunched over the control dais, his exoskeletal jaw twitching as the feed from the outer perimeter screamed warning after warning. Red lights stuttered across the command deck of the Ravager, illuminating the chitinous features of the Kanenites war commanders. Each of them bore wounds from previous battles, proud scars of a race bred for war and harvesting.

Andromeda was on the Galactic Enforcer ship. Commander Andromeda, High Strategist of the Kanenites, the one-armed fury, who had personally driven tens of thousands of planets into submission.

Her mind was a weapon. Her will, a virus. She was too valuable to lose. The Galactic Enforcement ship held her prisoner, kept her for intel and as a bargaining chip against the Kanenites.

"Open the commlinks to the fleet," Varnok hissed, his mandibles clicking. "Initiate Operation Reclamation." It had been high priority to rescue the Commander if her signal was ever detected.

The stars outside shifted. Dozens of Kanenites warships uncloaked, each shaped like a spear tipped with gnashing fangs. Their hulls were plated in organic metal, pulsating with a fearful presentation. These were not just ships. These were living things, bred in the deepest bio-wombs of the outer voids, half mechanical and half monster.

Their target, the Galactic Enforcer ship, that held their prisoners; just for tactical intel. This one held prisoner Commander Andromeda. In a past battle she was captured, the Enforcer had that abomination, and it had attacked her. Candy, they called it. The domesticated Cheetaht, turned combat beast. A creature so fierce, it had ripped through an entire battalion before anyone understood its power. It had taken her arm. It wanted to devour Andromeda, its hatred palpable. Now she was in our reach.

The ships attacked, stealing Andromeda and rescuing her. Varnok would receive many accolades for this mission.

As soon as Commander Andromeda entered the captain's deck she took over. "Move out of my way, you moron, what took you so long to rescue me?"

Andromeda searched the star maps seeking the lifeforce she wanted to take her revenge on. "Got it, I am coming for you Flame and your little beast too."

Inside the ship of Flame, Flame sat poised in the captain's throne, her red hair braided tight against her head like a crown of fire. Darah stood beside her, one hand on the navigation matrix, eyes gleaming with anticipation. Terrek cracked his neck with a lazy, dangerous smile, already suited in command armor. His twin horns gleamed under the bridge lights.

A holographic window opened in front of them. "Kanenites fleet incoming," came the smooth voice from engineering. "Thirty warships, uncloaking, they're coming in hot." "Get 'em babe," Darah said grimly. "Open comms," Flame said.

The void screamed with tension as the lines opened. Andromeda's face filled the screen, a jagged, metallic prosthetic replacing her left arm; her eyes glowing like molten lead. Her beauty was as severe as it was terrifying, piglike ears twitching when she spoke; the silence that followed was absolute.

"You vermin. You scorch-lings. You dare imprison me."

Flame leaned forward. "So, you managed to escape?" "I knew I should have let Candy eat her." Darah stomped her foot and huffed.

"I will gut that giggling horror of a pet of yours," Andromeda snarled. "And then I will roast your ship from the inside out. Your planet Harmony will fall next. I will burn every tree and crack every moonstone. I will drown your oceans in the bones of your children. Then I will get Laverian, and Gia..."

Terrek rolled his eyes. "Same speech as last time. You really need a new writer."

Candy, seated on a cushioned throne behind Flame, hissed. Then he bared his rows of dagger teeth, jumping down he went to Darah, pointing his tail like a scorpion towards the viewing screen. The feed cut; the battle began.

The Kanenites fleet surged forward in a fan formation, while launching laser cannons and warheads. The ship of Flame dipped and weaved through them, shields absorbing the first volley with shimmering resistance.

"Release the drone space fighters," Darah commanded.

Dozens of Laverian war drones detached from the Enforcer fleets, surrounding the mother ship in a kaleidoscope of mirrored light. As the enemy warships fired again, the mirrors deflected and refracted the energy beams, scattering the attack.

Kanenites piloted by Andromeda bit through the void, targeting Harmony's orbiting drone defense fighters. The purple planet spun below, oblivious to the chaos above. But Harmony would not remain untouched.

Andromeda, aboard her newly docked Kanenites warship, stood in her private command deck, one arm plugged into the neural spire of the ship. She became the fleet. Her mind linked with every ship captain, her anger infecting every command.

"Burn Harmony," she growled. "Harvest right down to their roots, take it all from the deepest seas to the fucking clouds."

Andromeda's fighter ships rained down like locusts, tearing into the trees, extracting life-energy, turning beauty into fuel.

Back in space, Terrek's jaw clenched. "They're hitting the planet in another wave. We need to draw her focus." "Target Andromeda's ship first," Flame said, eyes burning. "We cut off the head, the body dies."

Candy roared in agreement, leaping onto his bed. Terrek manned the weapons console, triggering more advanced laser cannons.

Flame charged, the ship's plasma railguns opened fire, piercing through the hull of Andromeda's ship. Sparks and gore exploded in the dark. Kanenites ships moved to intercept, forming a living wall around Andromeda's ship.

Flame snarled. "You want war? I am war!" "Brace for impact!" Flame shouted.

The Laverian ship flew into the hull, biting into the shield. Alarms shrieked, the decks shook. Candy leapt from his bed and latched onto the first Kanenites it ran into. Flame released an atmospheric shield that contained both ships. They wasted no time breaching the Kanenites ship, and with fury, tearing its passengers apart.

The Kanenites shrieked and thrashed, trying to dislodge the demonic Candy furball.

Flame activated the ship's merging tech. The ships lit up like the sun, solar energy flaring from its hull in blinding arcs. The living Kanenites ship molded and blended together with Flame's. She used her advanced tech that was created by the Glacier space engineers. She overran the Kanenites authority, and now was the captain of a new Galactic Enforcer ship.

Andromeda screamed with rage as her command was lost.

"You think I need beasts to kill you? Watch me." She activated her new arm, her prosthetic glowed red, opening like a petal. From inside, a god killer-class cannon emerged.

She fired, but was robbed of her fury. Her arm was built by the living ship and now would not grant her authorization to use any of its tech.

The creature was upon Andromeda once more, latching onto her shoulder and biting down.

Andromeda howled, using her body she launched herself, slamming the creature into the wall.

Candy flew backward in a trail of Andromeda's blood pouring everywhere like abstract art.

Candy used his whole body and was on her like a panther attack, her head in his maw. His tail struck Andromeda in her ribs.

Her screams bounced off the walls as she melted into sloppy gore on the floor. Cleaning bots rolled around the mess, taking every trace that was once Andromeda away.

The ship spoke through open comms. Flame, her voice hoarse but victorious. "You picked the wrong planet to harvest, you unworthy bitch."

Silence reigned.

The Kanenites fleets, dispersed now that their mother ship had become a new Galactic ship. In orbit, the drones searched for enemies.

On Harmony, the world was in ruin. On the bridge of the Eclipse, Flame collapsed into her seat, breathing hard.

"We win?" Terrek asked.

"Yeah," Flame rasped. "We won... this round."

Chapter Thirty-Five: The Baby

The ocean trembled with power, of warning and promise; a living force that seemed to pulse in time with my own frantic heart. I collapsed to my knees on the shoreline, the sand scraping my skin, and seawater soaking my dress and tangling my hair. I screamed until my voice was nothing but a hoarse rasp, my cries lost to the endless indifferent sky.

My baby girl, my daughter, Murial. Stolen, ripped from my arms by a God's cruel magic. The ache was unbearable, a hollowing that made my bones feel carved open, arms empty and useless. I clawed at the surf, my hands raw, pleading with the sea, Harmony, or any divine force that would listen. All I wanted was to hold her, hear her cry and to feel her warmth.

The water boiled with raw power, ancient and furious. The tide recoiled, then surged forward. The sea cracked open like the sky in a storm, and from its depths something rose. At first, I saw only light, shifting and alive. Then I saw her; Maddy battered and bloodied, but radiant with magic, and not alone.

She waded through the surf, water streaming from her wounds, her face a mask of exhaustion and triumph. In her arms, she cradled something precious and fragile. Even before I saw what she held, I knew. My soul exhaled, and my heart, which had felt frozen and dead, stuttered back to life.

Behind Maddy, the ocean itself seemed to rise. Towering from the deep came the Sea Gods; three shimmering entities forged from divine power, the Leviathan. They moved with the fluid grace of the tide. Their forms shifting between the shapes of men, women, and something wholly other. Their faces both beautiful and terrible, eyes deep as the abyss.

With them rising like a nightmare from the trenches, came the Kraken. Its body was a mountain of muscle and shadow, tentacles trailing phosphorescent fire. Its eyes burned like suns beneath the sea, ancient and knowing. The guardian octopus, a descendant, smaller but still massive, floated at its side, her purple speckled arms trembling with exhaustion and pride.

I stumbled forward, the surf lapping at my thighs, barely able to breathe. Maddy met me in the shallows, her knees buckling as she knelt in the foam. In her arms was Murial, and she was alive.

Cradled against Maddy's bloodied chest, Murial glowed with sea-born magic. Her gills fluttered, delicate and perfect. Her tiny hands clenched and unclenched, as if grasping the threads of fate itself. She blinked up at me, with eyes the color of a deep blue stormy sea flecked with silver.

"Billie," Maddy gasped, her voice breaking, the Kraken looming protectively behind her. "She's here, she is safe. The Sea Gods... the Kraken... they came to help, we weren't alone."

I collapsed beside her, water swirling around us, my arms reaching before I could think. Murial was warm, solid and impossibly real. The moment she curled her fingers around mine, the world stitched itself back together. My heart swelled until I thought it would burst.

"You're okay," I sobbed, pressing my lips to her brow. "You're okay, my baby girl."

Maddy's voice trembled with awe and relief. "They protected us, Billie. The Sea Gods fought beside me. The Kraken tore through the Kanenites machines. The Guardian shielded us. I...I couldn't have saved her without them."

I clung to Murial, my heart too swollen for words. I looked up through tears at the celestial figures still hovering in the waves. The nearest of the Sea Gods inclined its head, and a voice rippled through my mind, deep as the trenches, ancient as the moon.

She is more than you know, protect her. The tide of fate will rise around her, for now... rest.

Murial cooed a soft, musical sound, and I kissed her forehead, my voice shaking. "Murial," I whispered.

Maddy leaned in, her hand trembling as she brushed Murial's cheek. "I love you, my sweet pea." "Murial. It means sea-bright in the old tongue. She's... our light." Maddy smiled, exhaustion etched deep in her face. "It's perfect." Behind us, the Kraken let out a deep resonant sound, part growl and part hum. The sound was a benediction from the oldest guardian of the deep.

I pressed my forehead to Maddy's, our tears mingling. "I couldn't have done this without you. Without the Gods, and my Grand Guardian, I could not have done it." My voice broke, and she took my hand, squeezing hard.

"We're family," I said fiercely. "That's what we do, we fight for each other. We come back for each other always."

We huddled together, Murial between us, waves rocking us gently as if the whole world was giving us this moment of peace. The Sea Gods lingered, their eyes full of sorrow and wisdom. The Kraken hovered, a living shadow watching over us.

But then Maddy's expression faltered, her gaze distant and troubled. "There's more," she whispered.

My breath caught. "What is it?"

"Triton," she said, his name striking like lightning. "He's still missing."

My gut twisted. I had almost let myself forget, just for a moment, the other hole in my heart. "Then we go get him," I said fiercely. "We don't stop, not until our family is whole again."

"We will," Maddy swore, her voice raw with exhaustion and hope. "I swear it. But first..." She swayed, her body shaking, blood mixing with seawater at her side.

"You need to rest," I said, brushing her hair back, my thumb trembling against her cheek. "You saved our daughter. You fought with Gods at your side. You don't have to fight more tonight."

She smiled, a faint, crooked thing. "You don't have to carry this alone anymore."

"I know," she whispered. "And neither do you."

The Sea Gods began to sink back into the ocean, their forms dissolving into moonlight and foam. The Kraken gave a final thunderous rumble, a sound that shook the bones of the world; then vanished in a whirl of ink and shadow, returning to the deep to dream of battles yet to come.

I looked down at Murial, our miracle. Whatever her human father had started, whatever seed he had planted was now transformed. Harmony's magic had claimed her, making her something new and divine. A child of Gods, born of war and hope.

I looked at Maddy, my love. The thought of Triton, the missing piece of my soul still out there in the dark.

"We'll bring him home," I promised, voice steady now, strong. "We'll be whole again."

Murial opened her mouth and let out a piercing cry full of life and fury. We both laughed, tears streaming down our faces, the sound echoing over the waves.

"I think she agrees," Maddy said, her eyes shining.

I kissed Murial's brow, pressing her close. "Then let the tides rise. Let the stars burn. We are not afraid."

From the depths below, we had risen. Gods, monsters, or the wrath of the universe could ever take us down again.

As the moon rose over the battered sea I knew, this war was not over. But for this heartbeat, we were together and for tonight that was enough.

Chapter Thirty- Six:
No Rest For The Wicked

-Maddy-

No rest for the wicked, fuck my life. One moment Murial was safe in Billie's arms, the next there was another assault directly from Kane's power. Our kingdom fell just like that. The water-dwellers' power was used to create air bubbles for the land dwellers. We ascended to the beach.

I dragged myself out of the surf, the shallows stained red with blood. A mix of black, red, and green, like an eighty's lava lamp. My limbs screamed with every movement. Something had torn the flesh across my ribs again. Every breath hissed as my gills turned to lungs. But I was breathing, barely.

Around me, the beach was littered with the shattered remains of what had once been our last refuge. People crawled from the sea like the newly reborn, coughing up water, pulling others with them. Mothers screamed for children. Warriors held broken weapons like lifelines. The sky was a funeral veil of smoke and ash. Harmony's kingdom had fallen. Not even the Sea Gods could save us. I had been overly confident with them guarding us.

Behind me, the ocean swelled. The Sea Gods, or what remained of them, carried the unconscious and the dying to shore. The Guardian, her once-gleaming violet body now a bruised black, dragged herself onto the sand with the last of her strength. A dozen children clung to her massive tentacles, and not one of them cried.

Even grief required strength we didn't have. I turned my head and spotted Billie. She was on her knees, Murial cradled in her arms, surrounded by a makeshift circle of survivors. She was sobbing silently, rocking our daughter with a rhythm that seemed more prayer than comfort.

I tried to call out, but the words didn't come. Just a hoarse croak. My hands dug into the wet sand. I pulled myself forward, dragging my half-broken body one painful inch at a time. I felt it, the subtle tug of familiar magic. Billie turned.

"Maddy!"

She was beside me in seconds, helping me sit, helping me breathe.

"You're here. You're alive." "Barely," I rasped. My head lolled. "Is she okay?"

Billie nodded. Murial blinked up at me from the crook of her mother's arm, her eyes still glowing faintly with sea-light. Somehow, in all that ruin, she looked untouched.

"The Sea Gods protected her, then Gemma wrapped her in a ward while we escaped." "Good," I whispered. "Good."

A scream pierced the haze. One of the survivors stumbled from the surf, his arms wrapped around a lifeless body. A teenager, her eyes wide and unseeing.

"We lost too many," Billie said softly, voice shaking. "So many."

I nodded, tears slipping silently down my cheeks. I looked behind us; the ocean was rolling in defeat now. The surface shimmered unnaturally. Was this another attack? Or just the remnants of Kane's power still poisoning the water?

"We need a headcount," I said, forcing myself to stand.

Billie grabbed my arm. "You need to rest. You're hurt." "Later. We need to know who made it."

Together, we limped across the beach.

The sand was a battlefield of debris, broken bodies, and scattered magical artifacts. The Kanenites ships had withdrawn, for now, but the damage was done. The dome was gone. The Water Dwelling Kingdom was lost, but not all of us.

Blue stumbled toward us, face streaked with blood, one arm cradling a child who had lost her parents. She dropped to her knees beside us, voice hollow.

"The tunnels collapsed in two places. We only managed to get half the people out before the pressure took the rest."

Billie held Murial tighter. Blue looked down at her. Her lips trembled.

"She's a miracle." "She's a target," I said. "Kane took her once. He'll try again."

The Guardian stirred, letting out a low, keening sound. Her tentacles curled around a huddle of orphans as if to shield them from the air itself.

"She needs sea water and rest," I said. "They all need to recover." "We need shelter, and food," Blue said. "We'll find it," Billie said firmly. "We have to."

I looked out at the sea, scanning the horizon. The sky was still dark. No sun had broken through the clouds yet.

But above, far above, I thought I saw something glint. A ship, no, ships. I narrowed my eyes.

"Triton," I whispered. "Please let that be Triton."

Maybe, just maybe, we had reinforcements, as Ember promised.

"Get the signal flares," I barked.

Blue didn't hesitate. She called to a pair of surviving mages, and within seconds a stream of blue fire shot into the sky.

We waited. The ships grew closer. Then, finally, a crackle of magic lit the sky. A voice, clear and commanding.

"This is Empress Flame of the Laverian Galactic Enforcer Fleet. Stand fast. We are here."

A sob escaped me.

"We're not alone anymore," Billie whispered.

The ships descended in formation, sleek and silver and armed with energy beams that shimmered in violet arcs. Drones descended with food packs, med kits, and mobile wards. Healers poured out. Warriors spread to the edges of the beach, forming a defensive line.

Flame herself landed in a flash of red armor, her predator eyes scanning the crowd. She locked eyes with me.

"You held the line," she said. "Barely." She nodded. "But you held it."

I collapsed back into Billie's arms, we managed to survive, but not sure how. Tomorrow, we will fight again. This time, we wouldn't be alone.

Chapter Thirty-Seven: To Keep Billie and the Baby Safe

-Billie-

After Flame's ship landed, Maddy insisted that Murial and I stow away somewhere safe, with Flame and her crew on a freaking spaceship.

"Babe, I need to help and possibly fight again," Maddy said, her hands framing my face, eyes wild with worry and determination. "I need to know you are protected. Please stay safe with Flame and her family on this ship."

The beach around us was chaos with shouts and injured bodies being carried. The roar of the sea was loud, distant Kanenites engines screamed above. The sky was bruised purple and black, streaked with smoke. I wanted to grab her and drag her onto the ship with me, lock the door, and never let her go.

"If you insist," I said, my throat tight, "but I wish you would just come with us. Haven't you done enough? We have reinforcements now."

Maddy leaned in and kissed me softly, the taste of salt and smoke on her lips. Then she kissed Murial's forehead, lingering there for a heartbeat like she was imprinting herself into our daughter's soul.

"It breaks me every time I leave you both," she whispered. "But this war is not over yet, and I fight for our future, for the life Murial deserves. I have to go back and help."

I saw the torment in her eyes, the way her shoulders shook just a little. She was torn in pieces, a warrior and mother, mate and queen. I swallowed my fear and nodded.

"I love you, Maddy. Stay safe and come back to us." "Nothing will keep me from coming back," Maddy said, voice low and fierce. "I will hold you to that. Go. Save this planet. I love you, Madds."

She gave me one last look, like she was memorizing my face, then turned and ran toward the sea. Her body shifted as she dove into the waves, disappearing beneath the surface. My heart felt like it went with her.

The beach was too much with the blood, shouting, and the smell of burnt flesh and salt. I turned away, clutching Murial to my chest, and followed one of the Laverian enforcers up the ramp into Flame's ship.

"Please, take us to Flame," I said, my voice shaking but steady enough.

The enforcer, a tall figure in sleek armor with glowing sigils along the chest, touched a device at his ear. "Copy. Escorting a civilian and infant. Name?"

"I'm Billie, and this is my daughter, Murial. I am one of the Sea Queens."

His eyes widened behind his visor. He repeated my words into the comm, and the air around us seemed to shift with a new kind of respect.

"Please follow me, Sea Queen."

Inside, the ship hummed with life. The air smelled fresh with some kind of floral cleanser. Lights pulsed softly along the corridor edges, guiding our path. I tried to take everything in, seamless walls, the low thrum of engines and the way the floor vibrated under my boots. Murial slept against my chest. Her tiny breaths warm through the fabric of the sling.

We stopped before a smooth, featureless metallic wall. The enforcer scanned his palm, and a viewing screen shimmered into existence.

"Sir, I was told to bring you a visitor. Please open the door," he said.

The seamless wall parted with a soft hiss, becoming a doorway. Inside was a small bunk in a room containing built-in storage and a tiny washroom; everything compact and efficient. As we stepped through, I heard a voice that froze my blood and then sent it roaring through my veins.

"I'm sorry, but I must leave the ship. I have to find my mates..."

Triton's voice.

He stood in the small restroom, buttoning his shirt, his hair damp like he'd just showered. He turned, and our eyes met.

"You're alive," I whispered, the words barely air. "You're here."

The world narrowed to him. The ship, the war, fear—all of it was blurred by his presence. Triton crossed the space between us in three long strides, his hands coming up to cup my cheeks. His lips crashed into mine, desperate and shaking. He kissed me like I was his lifeline, like if he let go, he'd drown.

Murial squirmed and cooed between us, a small protesting sound, and we broke apart, panting. Triton's gaze dropped to the bundle in my arms.

He froze.

"My Goddess," he breathed. "You are so perfect... my beautiful child."

He sank to his knees, his hands hovering over Murial like he was afraid to touch her, afraid she'd vanish if he did. His shoulders shook as he bowed his head, tears dripping onto the floor.

"I feared I would never see my mates again," he choked out. "And here you are... and now I have my daughter too. I am so sorry I missed her birth. I wasn't here to fight for you, for Maddy and our baby."

Triton wrapped his arms around my waist, pressing his forehead against my stomach, his body trembling with sobs. I patted his dreadlocks, my own tears falling onto his head.

"Babe, you're alive. You're back with us. That's what matters," I said, my voice thick. "Stand and hold your daughter. Her name is Murial."

He drew in a shuddering breath, composing himself. When he stood, his eyes were red but blazing with something fierce and tender. I shifted Murial carefully and held her out to him.

He took her like she was made of glass, hands steady but reverent. He cradled her in the crook of his arm, his thumb brushing her cheek. Murial's tiny fingers flexed, then wrapped around his finger, and something in his face broke open.

"She is so tiny," he whispered, awe-struck. He examined her toes, and the soft curve of her ear. Murial yawned, her little mouth opening wide, and Triton let out a sound that was half laugh, half sob.

"Congratulations," I said, my heart overflowing. "You're a daddy now."

He swallowed hard. "Hi, Murial," he said softly. "I am your Daddy, and I will never let any harm come to you. Ever. I swear it on the Sea, my soul and every breath I have left."

He sat on the narrow bunk, and I sat beside him, our shoulders touching. For a few precious moments, the war faded. There was only the three of us, the soft hum of the ship, the steady rhythm of Murial's breathing.

"Where's Maddy?" Triton asked eventually, reality creeping back in.

"She's trying to save as many as she can," I said, my chest tightening. "We took a bad hit from the Kanenites. The Water-dweller kingdom has been destroyed."

His jaw clenched, eyes hardening with grief and fury. "Destroyed," he repeated, like the word itself was an insult.

He stood, kissed Murial's forehead again, and gently handed her back to me. She sighed and settled against my chest, already drifting back to sleep.

"You put her to sleep," I said, a small, shaky smile tugging at my lips.

"Billie," Triton said, his voice low and steady now. "I love you both so much. I want to stay here, hold her, and never let go. But I need to go help our people. I need to keep Maddy safe, I must leave the ship. It's time for me to return to my duty, to my home and our world."

My heart clenched, but I understood. This was who he was, a protector, warrior, and king. Just like Maddy.

"I know," I said quietly. "Just... come back to us. Both of you."

He cupped my face again, kissed me softer this time, like a promise. "I will."

We left the bunk room together, Triton walking beside me like he couldn't quite bear to step away yet. He led me through the corridors to the command center.

The captain's command center was a dome of glass and metal, filled with holographic displays and glowing controls. Stars stretched out beyond the viewing ports; below, Harmony's wounded planet turned slowly, scary but still beautiful. We were on the beach but still Flame monitored space.

Flame stood at the center in her battle form, scaled, tall, her red eyes like molten fire. Power radiated off her in waves. If she hadn't been on our side, I might have pissed myself in fear.

"Flame," Triton said, voice ringing with authority and gratitude. "I owe you, my life. My whole planet owes you for fighting to save us. I must ask you to protect my mate, Billie, and our child, Murial; while I go to help my other mate, Maddy, and my people. This war is not over, but I refuse to let those Kanenites win."

Flame's gaze shifted to me and Murial. Her monstrous features softened just a fraction. "It is an honor to have you aboard," she said, her voice deep and resonant. "Rest assured, you are safe with me."

"I've got them," a warm voice chimed in.

We turned to see Darah approaching, a woman with kind eyes, blonde hair pulled back, and a familiar easy smile. She looked like she could've stepped out of a Texas diner, not a galactic warship.

"Are you hungry, Billie?" Darah asked. "Mom needs to eat well to feed that beautiful baby. Come with me, I'll get you anything you're craving."

The accent hit me like a hug. Southern, from Earth, a far way home. My stomach growled loudly enough to answer for me.

"Triton, go find Maddy," Flame ordered over her shoulder.

Triton kissed me once more, then pressed his lips to Murial's head. "I'll come back," he whispered. Then he turned and ran, his footsteps fading as he left the ship.

"These men we mated to are so valiant, aren't they?" Darah said with a little laugh as she guided me down the corridor. "Even though my wife is also something to reckon with."

I knew exactly what she meant, my two mates, strong and protective, were everything I wanted and needed.

She wasn't wrong, I was starving. We entered a dining area with sleek metal tables, soft lighting and a food dispenser that smelled like spices and fresh bread. It was strangely cozy for a warship.

"Please, let me hold your baby while you eat," Darah said.

I hesitated for half a second, then nodded. Something about her felt safe. Murial barely stirred as I transferred her into Darah's arms. Darah held her like she'd done it a thousand times, swaying gently, humming under her breath.

I loaded a tray with whatever looked edible, some kind of protein stew, flatbread, and a drink that tasted faintly of citrus and mint. The first bite nearly made me cry. I hadn't realized how empty I was until that moment.

As I ate, Darah and I talked. She told me about Flame, about their home world, about how they'd answered Harmony's call. I told her about the Sea, Maddy and the moment Murial was born in the sacred pools. We laughed and cried a little; somewhere between bites and stories, we became friends.

Murial slept peacefully in Darah's arms, her little chest rising and falling, her fingers twitching in dreams. For the first time in what felt like forever, I felt... safe, not completely, not permanently. But it is safe enough to breathe. Safe enough to hope.

For this moment, I let myself believe that Maddy and Triton would come back. That our family would be whole. That this war, somehow, would end.

Chapter Thirty-Eight:
The Wrath of Angels

-Azreal & Alice-

The God Realms trembled; not with footsteps or the clash of armies, but with something far older and more dreadful. A ripple of divine tension snapped through the ether, like a chord drawn too tight, vibrating through the universes and celestial realms. Even the eternal light that filtered through the ether started flickering as if uncertain.

The Gods paused in their celestial sanctuaries, turning their immortal faces toward the highest spire of the Celestial Seat. There, in a sanctum wreathed in white fire and violet storms, the Mother Goddess dwelled; she who breathed galaxies into life and buried dead suns beneath her tears. She had been silent, until now.

In the stillness of her sanctum, the Mother Goddess lifted her hand. The gesture was small, but it rippled outward, a soundless command that moved through time and space. Traveling through the marrow of creation itself. The air thickened, charged and expectant, as she summoned him.

Azrael, the Avenging Angel, stepped from the Void, obsidian wings folded behind him like blades sheathed in shadow. His armor pulsed with a thousand living sigils, each one binding from wars long forgotten and each a memory of judgment. His eyes were starlight burning with purpose, merciless and cold. Beside him, barefoot, hair a wild tangle of ebony curls and lightning, walked Alice. The first of her kind, a female Avenging Angel, his mate, his equal.

Once, Alice had been human, gentle, full of laughter and light. But that was a different life. Now, when the Mother Goddess called, she called for reckoning, not mercy.

Azrael knelt, his wings sweeping the floor with a sound like thunder over bones. "You summoned us, Mother."

Alice did not kneel, not even before the one who owned her fate. Her eyes met the Goddess's, steady and bright.

The Mother's gaze, ancient and burning, swept over them. "Your daughter is hunted," Alice spoke, her voice a creation of vengeance, echoing across the spires. Alice doesn't play when it comes to a child under threat, no matter what their age. Harmony was family and that is all she needed to know.

Azrael bowed his head, but Alice stepped forward, wings stirring the air. The faintest brush of her feathers shattered a comet streaking too close to the sanctum's edge. "Is it the God Kane?" she asked, her voice sharp as lightning.

The Mother's face hardened, becoming as cold and implacable as obsidian cooling in lava. "Yes. But you are not to kill him. The law remains. You may remind him, remind him what it is to fear. Remind him to leave my daughter alone."

Azrael lifted his head, a flicker of curiosity in his starlit gaze. "And if he does not listen?"

"Then," the Mother Goddess whispered, and the air itself trembled, "Make him remember why even Gods must bow to the light."

Alice's lips curled in a smile, dangerous and bright. "Understood."

Without another word, the angels vanished, leaving behind a sanctum stripped of warmth, echoing only with the hum of wrath.

Kane stood atop his throne of ash and void, laughter echoing across a realm built from the bones of forgotten gods. He conjured miniature stars, snuffing them out with a careless pinch. His fire-white hair flickered in the gloom. His armor was forged from the ribcages of pantheons, each plate inscribed with the names of those he'd unmade. Around him, lesser Gods cowered, their eyes darting between the shifting shadows and the storm brewing on the horizon of eternity.

He felt it, a tremor in the fabric of divinity, a ripple that made even the oldest Gods shudder. The Mother moved. Harmony's power was rising, threatening the ancient order and him. Kane sneered, his lips curling with disdain.

"A little Goddess," he spat. "Still suckling star milk from her mother's teat. She dares think herself divine, and strong enough to defeat me?"

The air shivered as a boom cracked through the realm, splitting the sky above his spire like an egg torn open by a dragon's talons. Kane rose from his throne, eyes narrowing as two burning forms tore through the rift. Azrael and Alice, the Avenging Angels, landed like meteors. The obsidian floor beneath them melted to molten glass, the air screaming with their arrival.

Azrael's wings unfurled, casting a shadow that swallowed the light. "Get out," he commanded, voice cold as the Void. "This is not your fight."

None argued. The dark Gods fled, vanishing like mist before sunrise.

Kane's smirk faltered for just a heartbeat, but arrogance reasserted itself. "They send angels now, Heaven's tired dogs to come to bark at my gates?"

Alice stepped forward, her blade a jagged thing shaped from sorrow and vengeance. "Do not speak." Kane only laughed even as Azrael moved closer and every step was a promise of violence.

"You think to intimidate me, Avenger?" Kane snarled, flinging a spear of black lightning at Azrael's chest. Azrael didn't flinch as the bolt shattered against his armor, sparks hissing in defeat.

"I do more than intimidate, asshole," Azrael replied, his voice the sound of fate closing in.

The sky broke open again, not with light, but with war. Azrael lunged, wings slicing through reality itself. Kane met him with a roar, their blows colliding in echoes that made lesser realms quake. Alice was already moving, her dance of destruction slicing through Kane's spells like wind through silk. She struck low, forcing him back, while Azrael drove him up into the clouds. They fought like myths reborn; as Kane bled ichor, Alice bled light and Azrael didn't bleed at all.

Azrael moved like destiny, each strike tearing away not just Kane's flesh, but his pride, power, and certainty.

"You think you're untouchable," Azrael snarled, seizing Kane by the throat. "You thought Harmony would be easy prey and that her pain made her weak."

Kane gasped, divine energy flaring in protest. "She is weak!"

Alice struck him from behind, and Kane crashed down like a falling titan, the ground shattering beneath him. She knelt beside him, her blade at his throat. "Then why," she whispered, her voice a storm, "are you so afraid of her?"

Kane coughed blood that sizzled on the stone. Where it landed, monsters grew, writhing shadows that hissed and clawed at the air.

Azrael crouched, his eyes cold as a dying star. "This is mercy. The next time we come you will beg us to unmake you."

Alice straightened, wiping blood from her blade. "Let's go, love. I want to kiss Destiny goodnight before we're called to war again."

They didn't wait for a response, and left Kane broken and sprawled on his throne's shattered steps. With armor cracked and eyes wide with disbelief, he felt something he hadn't felt in eons, fear.

The High Assembly of the Gods convened in silence. They had all felt it, Kane had been bested by angels. Not by Gods or Titans, just Angels.

Kane stood alone, staring into the mirror pool of destiny. His wounds had healed, but something deeper remained cracked; his pride, certainty, and the belief that Harmony was just another pawn.

"She is not a pawn," he whispered, voice raw. "She's the storm itself." His fists were clenched. "I will not fall to Angels, or Gods, especially not to the daughters of fate."

From the shadows, something ancient stirred. Something older than Gods, even older than fear. Kane's lips curled into a bloodied smile. He spat, and from his blood monsters grew, creatures of nightmares born from his pain and hate.

If Gods could not win this war; perhaps monsters would.

Still, the tremor of fear still haunted him. When the Mother's voice echoed in his mind, Kane trembled.

"Enough hiding," he growled, forcing himself to his feet. "Let them come, let them all come. I am Kane, breaker of worlds!" Lost in his madness, Kane searched for Harmony.

The shadows writhed around him, monsters hissing, their claws scraping stone. He raised his blade of black flame, summoning storms of darkness, and hurled himself through the Void, straight toward Harmony's sanctuary. Kane was gone, swallowed by his own madness and monsters and fear. Harmony, triumphant, stood as the new force in the cosmos. No longer a pawn, but the player, the storm that would reshape the worlds. No longer a secret but the ascension of the most powerful. Her destroyer is held back only by her love, and the beings that she calls family.

With her world in shambles, she was barely able to contain her rage, Gods and all the celestial beings trembled in her wake.

Chapter Thirty-Nine: Fuck Around & Find Out

-Harmony-

Harmony stood on the threshold of becoming; it wasn't a place, not exactly. It was more a divine boundary, an edge of existence so thin it hummed with primordial power. A liminal space of silence and stars where Gods came to either break or ascend. Harmony was splintering.

Her skin shimmered with golden cracks, light pouring through the fissures like molten stardust. Her eyes were no longer wholly her own and burned with the ancient fire of creation, judgment, and endings. Her breath stirred storms in a thousand realms. Her heartbeat synced with the last pulses of dying stars. Every second she stood still was a second the universe stayed intact. She was holding on by a thin thread. The universes depended on her keeping her powers in check.

Yet... Soft fingers touched her spine, calloused, warm and familiar, Hecat her mate.

The only one who dared come near when the sky above her trembled and time bent around her footsteps. He had crossed the boundary into her divine storm, unafraid of the chaos she radiated.

"Harmony," he whispered, voice a tether to the life she'd once loved. "Come back to me." She didn't move, couldn't move. The prayers were too loud.

They crashed through her skull like tsunamis, raw, frantic and endless. Millions of voices crying for her.

"Save us, Goddess." "Stop them, please, our children are dying." "I beg of you, Harmony, we have no one else." "They've burned our forests, our seas, our homes." "Help." "Help." "HELP."

Each voice twisted inside her like a blade. These were her people, planet, and seas being slaughtered and erased. All the Gods above watched in silence, weighing whether to leash her again, or destroy her before she became something they couldn't contain.

"No," she whispered aloud, her voice shaking the edges of galaxies. "Not again."

Hecat stepped closer, circling to face her. His eyes glowing blue were threaded with ancient lightning and softened with grief.

"You're unraveling," he said, touching her cheek. "They're forcing you into your true form too soon."

Harmony's lips curled in pain. "What choice do I have, Hecat? Every scream was tearing at my soul, and the pleas carve scars into my being. They are mine to protect and I've failed them."

"You haven't failed. You've held back and waited, giving yourself time to contain your power, and to trust and love."

"But that time is ending." Her voice fractured into static and flame. "They're burning, Hecat."

She collapsed against him, her golden hair swirling like nebulae behind her, tangled with strands of midnight and moonlight. He caught her easily, pulling her into his chest, arms anchoring her as she trembled.

"You don't have to do this alone," he murmured, pressing a kiss to her forehead. "You have me and you will always have me."

Tears escaped her eyes that were molten, silver bright as each drop seared new stars into the cosmos as they fell.

The weight inside her chest was unbearable. A divine heart wasn't meant to carry these many cries, this much sorrow and doom.

"Do they think I want this war?" Harmony whispered into his skin. "That I crave destruction?"

"They think you're dangerous because you're powerful," Hecat replied. "You are powerful, mate, but power isn't the enemy; fear is."

The wind around them changed, as the veil thinned. Harmony felt it, the other Gods watched in fear, whispering and plotting.

They were afraid not of the Kanenites, or even of the Great Creator discovering divine realms plotting.

They were afraid of me, afraid of what would happen if I, the Goddess of Peace, finally broke the suppression spells my parents had sealed my power with. I was no longer a secret; I was feared.

They were all afraid of what I'd become. "Should I destroy them all?" She asked quietly. There was a dark power tinting her veins with the urge to show them all.

"No," Hecat said, brushing his fingers down her back. "Because that's not who you are. Fuck what other Gods fear. My love, you control your own destiny."

Harmony lifted her head, eyes flashing with gold flame. "What if I don't know who I am anymore?" Her voice was no longer ethereal; it changed into darker deep power.

"You are Harmony," he said, cupping her face. "You are the breath between storms and silence between screams; you are the Goddess they pray to when all else fails because they know you will not fail them."

The prayers surged again.

Children.

Mothers.

Fathers.

Dragons and Sea-dwellers, all the magical beings she created crying out.

Even the wind whispered her name. "Harmony," among them, one voice cut through the noise.

Her daughter Maddy. She was bleeding again, still fighting as she was screaming into the salt-dark, begging her people not to die.

Billie was beside her, clinging to Murial.

A whole kingdom buried beneath the ocean, holding on by coral threads collapsed in ruin.

Harmony clenched her fists and the air around her ignited.

Hecat stepped back as Harmony's body lifted from the cosmic floor, her golden skin turning to white flame, hair a solar flare of living divinity. Wings woven from aurora and shadow, unfurled from her back stretching wide.

The universe trembled, the heavens bent low; Gods trembled in fear.

Harmony was now fully the God of the Void and Destroyer of all.

"Let them come," she challenged, voice suddenly layered with echoes of thunder and volcanoes. "Let them strike, let them try."

She saw them, Kane and his ilk gathered in secret God halls, whispering strategies to contain her. Trying to bind her power before it surged beyond comprehension. But they were too late; she had already changed. Somewhere deep inside the throne of realms, the Great Creator stirred, his voice rolling like an avalanche across the divine plane.

"ENOUGH."

Gods dropped to their knees. Even Kane flinched as the Creator's shadow fell over him.

"YOU WILL NOT TOUCH HER." "YOU WILL NOT CONTAIN HER." "YOU WILL REMEMBER WHO SHE IS AND WHY YOU SHOULD FEAR HER."

The Gods trembled. But Harmony stood taller, brighter and whole. She turned toward the mortal realm, her eyes burning through layers of stars and time. Seeking the planet that bore her name, Harmony. Once a gentle world of oceans and wind-kissed peaks.

Now scarred and bleeding but ever brave. She reached out her hand, and the veil between worlds shattered.

Down she fell, not as a Goddess descending... as a reckoning.

Chapter Forty: Battle Weary, & Damn Near Hopeless

-Maddy-

Blood streaked the edges of my vision. My muscles burned from relentless battle; my triton arm shaking as I slashed through another Kanenite drone. The underwater kingdom, once shimmering with serenity, had become a war-torn battlefield, rubble under the waves.

I had no time to think, no space to breathe. The energy of Murial's cry echoed faintly in my heart. Somewhere, Billie had taken their baby to the refuge of Flame's spaceship.

I remained in the fray, my body an iron shield against the darkness descending on the only home I had.

A sonic boom cracked through the salt-rich waters. A ripple of something ancient and wrong tore through the battlefield. I turned just in time to see a cluster of Kanenites soldiers unleash a seismic charge that split the coral ridge in half. A dozen sea warriors were caught in the blast, their screams muffled by churning bubbles and shrapnel.

"Maddy!" someone screamed through my head. Blue panicked. "Fall back, dammit! They're closing in..."

I couldn't move, a hulking Kanenites war mutation three times my size surged forward. I tried to lift my triton, but the weight of too many dead hung on my shoulders. My vision dimmed and the world held its breath.

A heartbeat, then two.

The ocean screamed with light. A column of pure divine flame pierced the sky above the water, visible even through leagues of sea. The light bled into the depths, igniting ancient runes etched into coral bones, melting alien tech like wax. The air crackled with thunder not meant for mortal ears.

I sank to my fins as the pulse of that presence thundered through my soul. The Goddess had arrived, my new mother Harmony.

The air hummed with celestial rage and transcendent sorrow, a sound that didn't come from a throat but from the bones of the planet itself. Even the Kanenites warships stuttered in their programming, their AI freezing for a single second, as something greater than logic shattered their understanding of the battlefield. In a burst of golden-green flame, she manifested. Not descended or arrived, but manifested.

One foot rested upon the seafloor as if it had been sculpted for her. Her hair shimmered with shifting galaxies, constellations twining through each silken lock. Her body, though divine, shimmered with a rawness that bled emotion, grief, fury, and love.

I sobbed at the sight, my battered hand gripping a coral pillar as the water grew warmer around me.

The Kanenites reacted, if it could be called a reaction. They lunged, fired, and charged with the ferocity of machines made to slaughter.

Harmony did not move. She merely looked at them as they burned.

Fire did not spark from her fingertips, it erupted from the ocean floor. White-hot and screaming with purity, it surged in writhing tendrils, devouring the Kanenites where they stood, boiling their armor from the inside out. Their screams echoed through a thousand frequencies, now silenced by divine fury.

"Maddy," Harmony said gently, her voice a symphony. "You've fought long enough."

I tried to answer and stand. Harmony moved to me in the blink of an eye, kneeling beside my half-conscious body. Her fingertips brushed my brow, and every aching bone and battle scar was kissed by a healing warmth so pure it brought me to tears.

"You're safe now," the Goddess whispered. "Let me rage on." The sea turned green above them.

The Kanenites, sensing annihilation, deployed every ship they had. The great war cruisers, those shaped like glass knives and bearing annihilation weapons, soared into attack formations. The AI chanted combat codes in unison, a cold choir of logic-based war strategy. Harmony did not flinch.

She rose with the current, her form glowing with layered sigils, the symbols of the ancient pantheon; once sealed and now broken open by the sheer volume of prayers bombarding her spirit. Her people needed her and her daughter cried out in fear. As her world bled, she became the storm.

The planet Harmony itself had a renewed pulse of magical power, welcoming the Goddess in reverence.

She stretched her hands outward, and the waters trembled. Above, the skies split in half, revealing the impossible vastness of her celestial body. Time bent and Magic resurrected. Thousands of praying voices filled her ears, and with every word whispered into the void, Harmony absorbed more strength.

The Kanenites launched their cannons, firing a beam of antimatter meant to erase anything in its path, intent on world destruction.

Harmony caught it with one hand.

The beam shattered against her palm like glass against a mountain. Her eyes blazed with colors that had no name. She whispered one word.

"Return." She flung the antimatter back into the sky.

The Kanenites cruiser exploded in a crescendo of light and ash.

Above the ocean, the mortals watching from burned battlements gasped, as the divine manifestation of their Goddess tore the heavens in two.

I was cradled by two warrior water-dwellers now; we watched with tears in our eyes as Harmony hovered. With the will of a Goddess, the kingdom was remade with divine will. Our once shattered Sea kingdom now stood with a gleaming new dome. Fish and sea creatures gathered around me like subjects bowing before their sovereign. The bloodied survivors rose slowly; some weeping, some laughing, all of them looking upward in reverent disbelief.

From every corner of the ocean, the fighters paused. The Sea Gods swam to Harmony in support, circling under her in reverence.

From every ruined citadel, all the battle-scarred souls, and in every hidden cavern, hope ignited. In the floating Kanenites mothership far above orbit, the Kanenites watched in cold fury. The Commander's hands trembled as he observed the Goddess on every screen.

"Impossible," his tech officer stammered. "It's a Goddess in a mortal realm." "Can it be contained?" the Captain snarled. "Analyze our options."

Harmony had returned and she targeted them. With a thought, Kane and his Kanenites were unmade. A ripple of aftermath rolled through the universes and all celestials. Harmony broke no rules; she was the rule maker now.

Below, Harmony descended gently toward the dome and I rushed forward, barely able to believe my limbs still functioned.

"You came," I whispered.

Harmony smiled. "I am here now and I won't leave you again."

We embraced, and that embrace soothed a hundred wounds in both my body and spirit.

"Where's Billie?" Harmony asked. "Hiding the baby with Flame." "Bring her to me. I want to hold my granddaughter."

In the next moment, Billie came running with Murial cradling against her chest. The baby, as if sensing something divine, let out a small giggle.

Harmony held her granddaughter with hands that glowed like starlight. "She will be the dawn," she whispered. "Born of battle and of love."

Above them, the skies lit anew. Harmony turned toward the horizon and smiled, handing Murial to Billie. Her focus on repairing her planet and bringing peace.

Chapter Forty-One: A Goddess & Her Revenge.

-Harmony-

She was no longer merely just a Goddess; she was the storm, the song of stars, the fury of creation itself. Her form blazed with light and shadow, hair a torrent of galaxies, eyes burning with the birth and death of worlds. Every step she took cracked reality, the ground beneath her feet blossoming with new life and wilting to ash in the same breath.

The split open sky was a wound pouring in starlight and midnight. Kane's armies, monsters, Gods, and shadows gathered on the horizon. Their forms flickering with terror. The ocean rose as mountains bowed, and even the sun seemed to have dimmed. Harmony had entered her world in her true form.

She spoke, and her voice was wild with thunder and the hush of the Void. "All that is Kane's shall be no more."

She raised her hand and with a gesture the sea surged, swallowing Kane's monsters, dissolving them into foam and memory. The world burned with holy fire, purging the taint of his corruption. The very air shimmered with her rage that was pure and absolute.

Kane appeared before her, battered but defiant, his eyes wild with hatred and terror. He summoned storms of black flame, hurling them at her with a scream that split the heavens.

When Harmony caught fire in her palm, it fizzled and died.

"You cannot win," Kane spat, voice trembling. "You are too merciful, too weak."

She advanced, every step unraveling the world around them. "I am not mercy, nor will I be for you."

She reached for him, and the cosmos bent to her will. Kane screamed as her power wrapped around him, unmaking him molecule by molecule until he was a memory. His form flickered and his essence howled, as a thousand voices of conquered Gods rose in a final desperate wail.

With a thought, Harmony reached further into the bones of Kane's pantheon, into every twisted soul bound to his name. She unmade them all. They were erased, not merely killed but unspun from the fabric of existence. The Void swallowed their names and deeds, their very echoes.

The world shuddered and the sea rumbled as the sky bled light.

Harmony stood alone, her power a storm threatening to unravel everything, matter, time and hope. The ground cracked, air thickened and stars themselves flickered, as if fearing her next breath.

But in the eye of her hurricane, voices called.

Maddy reached for her. "Harmony! You're not alone! Come back to us please!" Hecat, ancient and wise.

Her mother's voice trembling with love and fear. "Daughter, remember who you are, remember what you love."

Her parents, their hands joined, their faces shining with tears. "We are here, you are not only power, you are our heart, but you are also hope, and ours."

The voices threaded through the storm of her mind, weaving a net of memory and love. Images flashed of Murial in her arms, her first cry, Maddy's smile and the warmth of family, laughter of friends, and the beauty of creation. Each memory anchored her, pulled her back from the brink.

Harmony's rage faltered. The light in her eyes softened, the storm within her chest eased. She fell to her knees, the world sighing in relief. The cracks in reality began to mend, the air cleared and the stars shone brighter.

Maddy ran to her, arms wrapped tight around her trembling form. "We need you not as a destroyer, but as our Harmony, our mother. You are our hope."

Hecat knelt on her other side, his hands gentle. "Let the rage go and love hold you."

Harmony wept tears of starlight and rain. The world drank in her sorrow; where her tears fell wounds healed and forests regrew, the oceans calmed.

She gathered her family close, her power folding inward, contained by love. The sky cleared, the sun rose, and the world began to heal.

Kane and his pantheon were gone now, unmade, and forgotten, no longer a shadow on creation.

Harmony, once storm and fury, became again the heart of her world. Her power, infinite and terrible, was now a shield, and a promise; a song of hope for all who would come after.

As the dawn broke, Maddy whispered, "You saved us, you saved everything."

Harmony smiled through her tears with family holding her close. "No. We saved each other."

Her creation for the first time in ages was finally at peace.

Chapter Forty-Two: In The Aftermath

-Maddy-

As the smoke thinned and the ash finally began to settle, the battlefield went silent.

Survivors emerged from the ruins like ghosts waking from a nightmare. The Dragoon remnants found one another; first, Kayla, Talen, Brooke, and Fang. All of them collapsing into messy, tearful embraces with their families. Laughter and sobs tangled together, raw and disbelieving.

Gemma and Balthazar stood with the Water-dweller allies, armor scorched, their faces streaked with soot and salt. Around them, the shattered remains of once great structures jutted from the earth. But now their eyes were lifted and grateful, the war was over and they were alive; that was enough for now.

I stood a little apart from the crowd, heart pounding, my eyes fixed on the sky where Flame's ship was due to descend. Every time a shadow flickered overhead, my breath caught.

Billie and Murial, please be safe... I prayed.

I scanned the crowd again, searching for familiar faces. Talen was here with Brooke and Fang, and Gemma was with her Balthazar. Water-dwellers, Laverians, and all the survivors from two worlds stood there.

But still, there was no sign of Triton.

My chest tightened, I turned in a slow circle, eyes stinging, searching for that one face; that one presence that always felt like home and storm all at once.

"Where are you?"

Behind me, footsteps approached heavily, sure and unhurried. Before I could turn, strong arms wrapped around me from behind, pulling me back against a solid chest that radiated warmth and strength.

"You are a hard one to track down," a deep voice rumbled against my ear.

Triton. The sound of his voice sank into my soul like a tide finally returning to shore. My knees nearly gave out. I grabbed his forearms, my fingers digging into his skin just to make sure he was real.

"Triton," I breathed, turning in his arms.

He was battered, hair wind-tossed with a jagged cut along his jaw. His eyes were dark, locked on me like I was the only thing in the world that mattered. For a heartbeat, we just stared at each other, the noise of the crowd fading into a distant hum.

I launched myself at him and he caught me easily, lifting me off the ground as I wrapped my legs around his waist and arms around his neck. He buried his face in my shoulder, inhaling like he'd been drowning and finally found air.

"I thought I lost you," I whispered, voice breaking.

"Never," Triton murmured against my skin. "I told you, nothing would keep me from coming back."

I pulled back just enough to see his face. "Billie? Murial? Have you seen them yet?"

A slow, fierce smile curved his lips. "They are safe on Flame's ship, they're coming."

Relief hit me so hard it hurt. I sagged against him, laughing and crying at the same time.

Around us the survivors continued to reunite, Kayla hugging Talen so hard he wheezed, Brooke and Fang arguing and crying in the same breath. Gemma was leaning into Balthazar's side as Water-dwellers clasped forearms with Dragoons and Laverians. The world was still mostly in ruins, but in the midst of the wreckage life was stitching itself back together.

I pressed my forehead to Triton's, my voice barely a whisper. "We made it."

He cupped my face in his hands, his thumbs brushing away the soot and tears. "We did, and we're not done yet. We need to help rebuild and heal together."

I nodded, swallowing hard. "Together."

Above us, Flame's ship broke through the clouds, engines humming as it descended toward the battered shore once more.

I tightened my grip on Triton's hand.

"Let's go get our family," I said.

For the first time since the war began, hope didn't feel like a risk; it felt more like a promise.

Chapter Forty-Three: Family United

-Billie-

The Seaside house had never been this quiet. Not the heavy, waiting kind of quiet from before a storm; the thin, trembling kind that comes right before someone decides whether they're going to run, or stay.

Triton stood in the middle of the sitting room, shoulders squared, jaw tight. Harmony's light poured in through the high windows, catching the warm brown of his skin, the tight coils of his hair, the faint shimmer of power that always seemed to hum just under his surface.

The door opened with a soft hiss.

Amelia stepped in first. Triton's mother, with her pale pink-hued skin and light pink hair braided back from her face, her eyes startling green as opposed to Triton's brown. Her hand flew to her mouth, her knees almost buckled when she saw him standing there alive and whole.

"Tr–Triton?" Her voice cracked on his name.

Trent filled the doorway behind her. Taller, broad-shouldered, skin the color of cream left too long in the sun, hair going silver at the temples. His gaze swept the room once, wary, and then found Triton. Everything in him softened at the sight.

For a heartbeat, no one moved. Maddy's fingers tightened around mine, both of us holding our breath like if we exhaled too hard the moment might shatter. Then Triton took one step forward.

"Hi, Mom," he said.

It wasn't the smooth, confident voice I'd gotten used to. It was rough, scraped raw, the voice of a boy who just missed his mom.

Amelia made a sound that was half sob, half laugh, and then she was running.

She hit him hard enough that I almost flinched, but Triton caught her, arms wrapping around her like he'd been built for this exact impact. Her hands were everywhere, cupping his face, clutching his shoulders and smoothing over his hair like she had to relearn every inch of him by touch.

"My baby," she whispered into his chest. "My baby, my baby, my baby."

Triton's eyes squeezed shut. His throat worked, for a second, I thought he might pull away, might shove all that emotion back down where he kept everything else.

Instead, he folded, burying his face in his mother's hair.

"I'm here," he said, voice breaking. "I'm here, Mom. I'm home."

Trent moved slower, like each step cost him something. He stopped just in front of them, his hand hovering in the air, not quite touching.

"Triton," he said quietly.

There was so much packed into those two syllables that my chest ached with regret, pride, fear, and love so fierce it looked like it hurt him.

Triton lifted his head, eyes wet, and met his father's gaze.

"Hey, Dad."

For a long second, they just looked at each other. Trent's jaw clenched. His eyes shone. Then he did something I hadn't expected from the man who always seemed carved out of stone in Triton's stories. He stepped in and pulled his son into his arms.

It was awkward at first, too tight, stiff like Trent had forgotten how to hug someone that tall and grown. Then Triton's hand fisted in the back of his father's shirt. Trent's shoulders shook once hard, and the stiffness melted.

"I thought we'd lost you," Amelia said, I thought I'd lost you both. "I thought..."

"You didn't," Triton cut in, "I'm here."

Maddy let out a breath that sounded suspiciously like a sniffle. I glanced over at her.

Her eyes were shining, her usual sharp edges softened. She had my hand in a death grip, her thumb stroking absently over my knuckles like she needed the contact to stay grounded.

"Look at them," she whispered. "He finally got them back."

I swallowed around the lump in my throat. I'd never had this. Not really. The idea of parents who ran toward you instead of away felt like something out of a storybook.

Amelia finally pulled back enough to see Triton's face again. Her fingers framed his cheeks, thumbs brushing away tears that had escaped despite his best efforts.

"You're beautiful," she said fiercely. "You always were." She broke off, shaking her head like she could fling away the memories.

Trent cleared his throat and seemed to notice, for the first time, that they weren't alone.

His gaze shifted past Triton and landed on me.

For a heartbeat, my stomach dropped. I'd been in enough rooms where I was the only one who looked like me; to recognize the way people's eyes sometimes snagged on my dark skin, on the tight curls I'd twisted into a puff on top of my head. Knew the way I simply didn't match the people standing beside me.

Trent's eyes did catch. So did Amelia's, when she followed his line of sight.

Heat crawled up my neck. I became hyper-aware of the contrast: Triton's parents, both pale, both with light eyes and hair in different shades of light and pink. Triton, deep brown and radiant, like polished mahogany catching the light.

I'd wondered, the first time I saw his family, but I'd never asked. It felt rude, so human and falling to my earth life standards.

But now standing here, watching Amelia's fingers still on Triton's cheek, watching Trent's eyes flick from Triton to me and back again, the question came up anyway.

How?

How did two people who looked like that have a son who looked like Triton?

On Earth, I knew what that meant. Questions and assumptions. The whispers I'd lived with.

My chest tightened. Did they see him as theirs? Did they see me as other?

Maddy must have felt the shift in me, because she squeezed my hand, hard enough to pull me back into my body.

"Hey," she murmured, leaning in so only I could hear. "You okay?"

I forced a shaky smile. "Yeah. Just... thinking."

Amelia blinked, as if waking from a trance, and then her whole face lit up when she really saw me.

"Oh!" She stepped around Triton, wiping her eyes with the back of her hand. "Hi, Billie."

I straightened automatically. "Yes, ma'am."

She laughed, a wet and broken sound. "Oh, don't 'ma'am' me. Come here."

Before I could overthink it, she wrapped me in a hug that smelled like citrus and something warm and familiar I couldn't name. It was the kind of hug that didn't ask permission, the kind that assumed you belonged.

I froze for half a second, then let myself lean in.

"We've been waiting for the chance to finally get to know you two, properly."

My throat burned. "I am just happy we all are home," I managed.

When she let me go, Trent stepped forward, offering his hand first, like he knew I might need space.

"It's good to finally meet you, Billie," Trent said.

His grip was firm, steady. His eyes were kind.

Some of the tightness in my chest eased. But the question still sat there, heavy and insistent.

I glanced between them, Trent, Amelia, Triton, and then down at my own hand still wrapped in Maddy's. Harmony's light spilled over all of us, soft and shimmering, making our edges blur and glow.

"Can I..." I hesitated, then forced myself to push through. "Can I ask something? And if it's rude, just pretend I didn't say anything."

Trent's brows lifted. Amelia tilted her head.

"Of course," Amelia said gently. "You can ask us anything."

I looked at Triton. "It's about you and them."

His lips quirked, but there was no mockery in it. "Figured this might come up eventually."

He stepped back so he was between his parents and me, a bridge.

"You're wondering how two very white people," he said dryly, "ended up with a very not-white son."

I winced. "I mean... yeah. On Earth, that's... complicated."

Amelia's expression softened with understanding. "On Earth, people see race," she said quietly. "Lines, labels and neat little boxes."

Trent nodded toward the window, toward the glowing canopy and the faint, ever-present hum of Harmony's magic.

"This world doesn't care what color your parents are," he said. "Or what anyone thinks you should look like. Harmony has... its own rules."

Maddy shifted closer, her voice warm at my ear. "There's no race here," she said. "Not the way you're thinking. Just species, it's the magic that determines your features. It's what the planet makes you."

Amelia's gaze went to Triton, her eyes shining with something like awe.

"The magic here," she said, "it sees what you are. Who you're meant to be and that's how you're born. Not as a copy of your parents. You are born as yourself."

Triton shrugged one shoulder, but there was a quiet pride in it. "The planet decided I needed to be exactly who I am. To do what I'm supposed to do. My skin, hair and magic, all of it."

"Born as you're meant to be. Not as a compromise between two sets of DNA. Not as a problem for other people to solve with stares and questions. Just... right."

"So, it doesn't matter," I said slowly, "that you don't... match."

Amelia's hand found Triton's again, fingers lacing through his like she was afraid to let go.

"It matters to people who still think in Earth terms," she said. "But to Harmony? To us?" She shook her head. "He's our son. The planet just made sure he arrived exactly as he was meant to be."

Trent's gaze met mine, steady and sure. "Harmony doesn't make mistakes with souls," he said. "Only humans make mistakes with labels."

Something in me loosened, a knot I hadn't even realized I'd carried from world to world. I looked at Triton, at the way he fit so perfectly between his parents even if their colors didn't match, at the way Harmony's light seemed to claim all of us equally.

Maddy bumped my shoulder lightly. "Kind of beautiful, right?" she murmured. "You don't have to explain why you look the way you do. You just... are."

My eyes stung. I blinked fast and laughed, the sound was watery.

"Yeah," I said. "It is. I am just happy we don't have to worry about the three of us, or for Murial, to grow up here, with all the magic and love. Where diversity is welcomed and individuality is celebrated."

Trent clapped a hand on Triton's shoulder, then glanced at Maddy and me, taking us both in.

"Family looks different here," he said. "But here, Family means more than you could ever imagine. Maddy and I had many heartbreaks because of family. Here, we are so grateful to all of you for welcoming us into your family."

Amelia smiled through her tears, reaching out to tug Maddy and me closer, folding us into the circle with Triton.

"You two need never worry, you both are our daughters now and forever."

Harmony's magic hummed under our feet, through the walls, in the air between us. It wrapped around us like a second embrace, warm and sure, as if the planet itself approved. For the first time in a long time, I didn't feel like I was standing on the outside of someone else's picture. I was in it, exactly as I was meant to be.

Chapter Forty-Four: The Goddess in the Garden

-Harmony-

Years had passed, for them, anyway. For me, time had become a soft, elastic thing. Five years of their lives, birthdays, scraped knees, quiet dinners and new cities rising from rubble. It was only a few stretched out heartbeats in the God realm.

If I'd wanted, I could have unspooled those years like thread. I could have turned back the clock before the first Kanenites set foot on my world; before the first scream and the first drop of blood hit the soil. And before that wretched vampire ever entered my world. I could have saved Laverian from ever being harvested. I could have made it so my planet never knew pain, but I didn't.

I watched it instead, watched them grieve and cling to each other. I watched them rebuild and become something stronger than they'd been before the war. Bonded and alive.

Five years for them. Only a few seconds, to unmake Kane. I let the seconds stand. The world healed slowly, like a wounded animal learning to walk again. Every scar became a reminder of survival, of battles being fought and miracles won. The great planetary oceans shimmered clearer now than ever before; as if they too, had decided to start over. The skies of my world no longer bore the soot and blood of war but stretched wide with soft clouds and warm suns. Cities had grown from the rubble made of stone, living vines, and crystal humming with magic and peace.

This was my planet, my heart, and I had almost ended it. In the heart of this reborn world, in a meadow kissed by both ocean mist and mountain wind, a garden bloomed. My garden.

I stepped barefoot across soft grass and glowing petals. My golden skin drank in the warmth of the twin suns and the rainbow-streaked sky. My long white hair fell loosely down my back, streaked now with silver, not of age, but of memory. A reminder of the Destroyer that had once risen inside me like a black sun.

I had no throne here, trumpets sounding off or kneeling crowds. I would never accept that now, just earth, sky and breath.

The world recognized me anyway. Where my feet touched soil, flowers bent in reverent bloom. Trees whispered my name through their leaves. Hummingbirds with glittering wings buzzed around me, their tiny hearts beating joy into the wind. The magic of the planet responded to my presence like a beloved child seeing its mother return after a long absence.

I felt it all, every root, tide and heartbeat.

I walked through the garden toward a modest home tucked into the curve of the hillside. My grand hall had been rebuilt there by loving, once mortal hands, my Maddy and Billie, Kayla and Brooke, guiding the people as they restored it. Its beams were carved from driftwood, its walls laced with climbing roses and runes, wide windows thrown open to the creek that met the seas. My Darah in a universe away, always ready to help.

I could have done it with a thought, in truth, I did. With a single decision, every scar my world bore was remade, not erased, but transformed. Forests rose taller and stronger, their canopies thick and lush. The Dragoon Kingdom's castle stood again, higher and more magnificent than before, its stones singing with warding spells and ancestral pride. The water dwelling kingdom expanded, its crystal domes gleaming beneath the waves, corridors alive with color and laughter.

The world was restored, but I refused to make it perfect. Perfection is sterile, it leaves no room for choice. So I rebuilt, but I left the echoes. There was a crack in a wall here, there was scorched stone in a courtyard there. Memorial gardens where battlefields once lay. Stories etched into the bones of the world so they would never forget what they survived.

The dead... I could not leave them as absence alone. I reached into the Weave and called some of them back, not as they had been, but as something new. Phoenixes, my own kind of angels, souls reborn in wings of fire and light, their eyes bright with memory and purpose. The children who had been adopted and imprinted stayed with their families; I would never rip them from the love they'd found. Their reborn parents in Phoenix forms became guardians instead, woven into those families like living blessings.

They watched over their own, I watched over all of them.

From inside the grand hall, a high-pitched giggle rang out, bright and wild. The sound cut through every ancient, heavy thing inside me like sunlight through fog.

That, I thought, is more divine than anything I ever created.

"Grandmaaaaaa!"

The shout came a heartbeat before a blur of motion barreled out the door and collided with my legs.

Murial.

Five years old now. Wild hair held in a puff tail, she was sharp-eyed, with stubby little wings that hadn't quite grown in yet. She smelled like sea-salt, sugar, and mischief. She wrapped her arms around my leg and squeezed as if she could anchor me to the world by sheer will.

She looked up at me with wide, glowing dark eyes and grinned. "You smell like sparkles," she announced.

I laughed, the sound bubbling up before I could stop it. "That's because I am sparkles, little moonbeam."

Her nose wrinkled in fierce disagreement. "You're not a sparkle. You're Grandma. Do you wanna play mud dragons?"

My heart bloomed, I had been called many things, Goddess, Destroyer and Mother of Worlds. But "Grandma" might have been the holiest title of all.

To this child, fierce, funny, and unstoppable little being, I was not the one who unmade Gods.

I was the woman who made magical tea and helped her chase butterflies in a garden.

"I would be honored to play mud dragons," I said solemnly.

From the porch, Billie leaned on the railing, her curly dark hair tied back in a messy bun. Her eyes shone with a smile that turned slowly into tears.

"She doesn't know who you really are," Maddy murmured, walking up beside her. Her hand brushed the small of my back in a gesture that was more grounding than any cosmic tether.

I glanced up at them, then back down at the little girl clinging to me. "She knows exactly who I am," I said.

Later that afternoon, when Murial finally surrendered to sleep beneath the willow tree draped in sea-pearls, I sat at the garden table with my daughters and my son-in-law. The air smelled of salt, flowers, and steeping tea.

Billie passed me a cup of sea rose tea, her fingers warm against mine. Maddy rested her head on Triton's shoulder, his hand laced with hers, his other hand absently stroking Billie's arm. Their spirits were older now, weathered by battle and love, but stronger like roots that had learned to dig deeper after the storm.

"You came back," Maddy whispered.

I nodded, staring into the swirling surface of my tea. I could see stars in it if I looked closely enough. "I promised I would," I said. "But I needed a few moments. After... everything. Time works differently in the God realms."

"The stars dimmed without you," Triton said softly.

I met his eyes and saw no fear there, only faith and family. "Yet you shone," I told him. "All of you. You rebuilt what Kane nearly destroyed. I watched it all. I watched her grow up." My gaze slid to the willow tree, to the small sleeping shape beneath it. "You gave me a thousand reasons to come home."

Billie blew on her tea and grinned. "It's weird," she said. "I thought when you came back, the skies would crack and choirs would sing."

"Choirs did sing," I said, smirking. "You just weren't listening."

"Too busy wrangling a baby Goddess who thinks sharks are puppies."

Maddy snorted. "She gets that from you."

"I know," Triton replied, far too proud.

I looked out over my garden, world, and family. The Destroyer inside me was quiet, but I could still feel her, a coiled shadow at the edge of my light. A reminder of what I was capable of and what I had done.

"I didn't think I could be this again," I admitted. "Not after what I became. I stood on the edge of all things and almost ended it all. Still... you called me back."

Maddy reached across the table and took my hand. Her grip was firm, human and real. "You never stopped being our Goddess," she said. "More than that, family and our mother."

"I'm still scared," I whispered. "Every prayer and ripple of pain... I still feel it. It still echoes. The world needs healing."

"You gave it the most important thing," Triton said. "A future."

"And a grandma who can summon constellations to entertain a five-year-old," Billie added, trying not to smile but failing. "That's some bonus level shit right there."

I burst out laughing.

The sound startled a flock of birds into flight. Magic rippled through the garden, the flowers glowing brighter and the air warmed. My laughter felt raw and pure, it felt like mine.

That night, after the stars climbed the sky and the sun sank beneath the horizon, I walked alone to the beach.

The Sea whispered to me, ancient and infinite, carrying memories of every life it had ever cradled. The sand was cool beneath my feet, waves reached for my ankles like old friends.

I raised my arms and sang.

Not the song of destruction or the terrible beautiful chord that had unmade Kane.

This was an older song. Softer, a melody only Gods remembered, of restoration, of weaving the last tattered threads of suffering into new hope. My voice carried across the water, through the forests, over the mountains and down into the deepest caverns of the world.

My song stitched the final wounds of the planet.

The hearts of the weary lightened. Nightmares loosened their grip. Old fears faded to echoes. The world exhaled with me. But more than anything, the song grounded me. As a mother, a grandmother and protector.

When I returned to the house, the lamps were low and warm. Inside, I found Murial awake again, sprawled on the floor between Billie and Maddy, drawing winged ponies with fire breath on a scrap of parchment. Crayons were scattered like fallen stars.

Murial looked up, her eyes heavy with sleep. "Grandma," she mumbled. "Can you read the sparkle story again?"

I knelt beside her. "The one about the star who didn't know where she belonged?"

She nodded, her curls bouncing.

"That's my favorite one too," I said.

I scooped her up and held her close. Her small body fit perfectly against my chest, her heartbeat a steady, mortal rhythm beneath my hand. I could feel galaxies turning and the universes humming, prayers rising all around us. In that moment, the only thing that mattered was the little girl in my arms.

The most powerful Goddess in all creations sat on a simple floor, in a simple house, in a garden on a once broken world; wrapping herself in the quiet joy of love, laughter, and belonging.

Not for power, or thrones, not to wage wars, I was everything I always wanted to be, and I was with my family. Outside, in the meadow, a newly created horse with wings pawed at the ground, its feathers catching starlight. She tossed her head, sensing the little Goddess who would meet her in the morning.

I smiled, pressing a kiss on Murial's hair. Let the cosmos spin around the other Gods. I was home, and that's all that mattered now.

Chapter Forty-Five: Ashes and Saltwater

The Dragoon Throne, -Kayla-

The sea shimmered under a colorful sky. It was no longer stained with smoke or bruised like all of us. For the first time in what felt like years, the horizon wasn't on fire. Home...my home, the word hurt.

I stood at the cliff's edge with my toes curling over the familiar rock. My dress torn, my body bloodied and stiff as it slowly healed. My breath burned and muscles ached. I could feel each cut and bruise; where my magic had knitted flesh together too fast, leaving me raw and tender.

This was the same cliff where I'd stood, years ago when I first arrived at the castle. Daring the waves to reach me. The same wind that used to carry the scent of salt and wildflowers now tasted like ash and iron. I'd dreamed of coming back here a thousand times during the war; but never like this. Never with so many ghosts standing just behind my shoulder.

Beside me, Talen limped, one wing dragging half-shredded, but still held high in defiance. His wings were matted with blood and soot, but he refused to lower it. Typical, even broken, he had to look like a black dragon carved from legend.

Brooke's braid was coming undone, strands of hair sticking to her face, her spear clutched in blistered hands. She looked like she'd been carved out of the same stone we stood on, cracked, but unyielding. Fang, ever silent, carried the weight of our grief on his back like a second skin. He didn't say a word, but the set of his shoulders told me everything. We were all holding ourselves together by threads.

Below us, in the sea, deep in the depths, the once-thriving water-dwelling kingdom was a graveyard. Coral towers that used to glow with life now lay toppled. Glasslike spires were shattered into jagged shards that caught the crystalline light and threw it back in cruel flashes.

I remembered the first time I'd seen it, how the colors had stolen my breath, how the laughter of the water-dwellers had echoed through the domes like music. It had been a sanctuary then; a promise that not everything in this world was cruel.

Now, looking down, it felt like I was staring at the bones of a dream.

"They're down there," Brooke whispered, her voice raw and frayed. "I know they are. I felt Harmony's presence just before the last quake. I think she repaired the dome over the kingdom itself. I heard Rina in my head a bit ago."

Harmony. The name twisted something deep in my chest. She was a thread that tied all of this together, past, future, and impossible chances. If she was still down there, still fighting, still fixing what she could... then maybe we weren't as lost as we felt.

I nodded, jaw tight. "Well, that's a good start to rebuilding everything."

The words felt too small for what we'd lost, but I needed to say them and needed to believe them. If I didn't, the grief would swallow me whole.

"Agreed."

But before we descended, I stepped away from the cliff, drawn toward the broken remains of what had once been our courtyard. Stones were scattered in jagged chunks, beams splintered and blackened. I picked my way through the rubble, heart pounding for reasons that had nothing to do with battle.

Something pale caught my eye beneath a fallen support beam, The Good Wood.

I knelt, fingers trembling as I brushed away ash and dust. A curved piece of smoothed timber emerged, then another, joined by a cracked spindle. My breath hitched. "No." It was my cradle, or what was left of one of my cradles.

The sides were split, one leg snapped clean through, the gentle rocking base crushed under stone. But I knew instantly by the grain of the wood, the faint swirl of carved wolves and dragons along the rim, the way the headboard arched like a wing. Talen and Fang had made them for me when I had my babies all those years ago.

He'd gone into the old wildwood forest himself, years ago, when my first clutch had begun to stir. He'd chosen trees that only grew on the wildwood trees the elders said were blessed by the first Dragoons. He'd run his hands over the bark, listening, as the trees had donated limbs, they call it the good wood, it sings a soft lullaby to soothe the babies.

Then they spent the night carving them, building by hand refusing to let me see until it was perfect, they surprised me.

I remembered the look on Talen's face when he'd finally shown me, proud, nervous and hopeful. I remembered laying my babies in it for the first time, their tiny bodies curled in on themselves, wings no bigger than my hand. I remembered the soft creak of it rocking in the quiet hours of the night, listening to the soothing lullabies; when the world outside our walls had felt so far away.

Now, my fingers traced a deep scorch mark along the rim, the carvings blackened and split. A splinter bit into my skin, sharp and unforgiving, I welcomed the sting.

My vision blurred, the courtyard around me dissolved into shapes and shadows, all I could see was that cradle, broken and alone in the ruins of our home, it no longer sang.

This was what the war had done, not just toppled castles and shattered domes. It had reached into the most tender, sacred corners of our lives and crushed them under its heel.

Behind me, I heard Talen's uneven steps. I felt his presence at my back, heavy and quiet. He didn't say anything, but when his shadow fell over the cradle, I knew he recognized it too.

"I'm sorry," I whispered, though I wasn't sure who I was apologizing to, our babies who had long since grown. Or the younger version of myself who'd believed we were untouchable. My mate had carved this with his own hands, believing it would always be safe here.

My throat burned, I swallowed hard, forcing the grief down deep until it settled like a stone in my chest. I couldn't fix this, not with all the magic in the world.

But I could remember. I brushed my thumb over one unbroken wolf, then gently set the piece of the cradle back where I'd found it, like laying a body to rest. When I stood, my legs shook, I turned back toward the cliff anyway.

"We should have Rina take us down to check on the water dwelling kingdom. Maybe we can help." Brooke's voice shook on the last word.

Help...I wasn't sure we had anything left to give. My magic felt thin, frayed at the edges. The ocean, which had once embraced us like a second home, now felt heavy and resistant, as if it were mourning its own. I used to dive into these waters without thinking, laughing as the currents wrapped around me like welcoming arms. Now, as Rina's power gathered around us, I felt the sea's sorrow pressing in, cold and relentless.

Rina was waiting, eyes shining with unshed tears. Brooke watched me with a look that said she understood more than I wanted her to. Fang dipped his head, a silent acknowledgment of the grave I'd just walked away from.

"Let's go," I said, my voice rough but steady. "They're waiting."

The water closed over our heads, and for a heartbeat, panic clawed at my throat. Not because I couldn't breathe, I trusted Rina's magic for that, but because I was terrified of what we'd find, or of what we wouldn't.

Shattered domes, broken statues, empty streets where there should have been music and light. Every ruined corner was a memory turned on its head. I saw the place where we'd once shared a feast with the water dwellers, now choked with debris. The training arena where I'd sparred with their warriors, now split open like a wound.

Tears slipped free, I didn't bother to wipe them away. For a moment, all of us just held on to each other, bloodied, broken, but still breathing. The water dwelling kingdom stood whole again, its dome intact. Somehow, impossibly, Harmony had done it. The outer world was wrecked, but the heart of this place still beat.

"By the stars," Rina whispered, tears welling as she rushed forward to the entry dock.

Hope was a fragile thing, sharp as glass, it hurt to hold it. I watched Rina's shoulders shake with relief, I realized I'd rather bleed from hope than go numb from despair.

"I don't know how we start again," Brooke said hoarsely, staring past us toward the broken sea outside the dome. "The cost... was everything."

She wasn't wrong. The price we'd paid was written on every scar, every empty space where someone should have been standing beside us. On every broken cradle left behind in the rubble.

"Almost," I said softly, the word scraping my throat on the way out. "But we still breathe, and we need to rebuild now."

I didn't know how, I didn't know where we'd find the strength, magic, or will. Standing there, surrounded by the remnants of what we'd fought for, I knew one thing with absolute certainty; giving up would make every sacrifice meaningless, and I refused to let that happen.

After checking on the dome, Rina took us back to the surface. The ascend felt longer than it should have, like the ocean didn't want to let us go. When we finally broke through, the air hit my lungs like fire and ice all at once.

Above us, Flame's fleet from the galactic enforcers circled in protective formation, banners flying in quiet solidarity. Once, the sight of warships would have made my stomach knot. Now, they looked like guardians standing watch over a wounded world. I appreciated them for this.

Our Dragoon throne was still alive among our people as I watched them remove debris and start to rebuild already, as the first foundation stones were laid for the new castle we stood together, Talen, Brooke,

Fang, Richmond, Stan and I, with all of our children. A Dragoon family, battered but unbroken.

The ground beneath my feet was familiar, but it didn't feel like the same home I'd left. Maybe it never would again. Maybe home wasn't a place anymore, it was our people, their stubborn refusal to stay down, this shared promise that we would not let the darkness be the final word.

We mourned the dead, we honored the living. Names were spoken like prayers, spells, and anchors to keep us from drifting too far into the numbness. I felt each one settle in my chest, heavy and holy, in the shadow of all we'd lost we made a silent vow; we'd rise again.

I wrapped my arms around myself, feeling the wind tug at my dress, the sting of salt in my cuts, the ache in my bones. This was my home, scarred, changed and haunted, but still mine.

We'd rise again, I promised the sea, the sky, and the broken stones. With the memory of a wooden cradle that would never rock again, we'd make damn sure we'd never fall again.

Chapter Forty-Six: Bound by Love

-Maddy-

Weeks had passed since the war's end. And for the first time in what felt like forever, the world was starting to breathe again.

The scars were still there, in the cracked stone and scorched earth. The faint echo of grief was in the air. But life was returning and children laughed where there had once been battle cries. New homes rose where craters had been. The Sea sang softer now, no longer a roar of rage but a lullaby of calm.

The place they chose for us looked like something out of one of my dreams.

A secluded glade sat healing.

In the middle of all the rebuilding, we did something wild, we planned a celebration. Not a strategy meeting, or a war council. A wedding, our wedding.

The Ceremony

Cradled between forest and sea, where ancient trees arched high overhead, branches weaving into a natural cathedral. Luminescent blossoms clung to bark and leaves, glowing softly as dusk settled. Pearlescent blues, soft golds, and rose pink light painted everyone in a gentle magical glow. Fireflies drifted lazily through the air, drawn to the Magic humming around us.

A small stream wound along the edge of the clearing, its waters singing over smooth stones, carrying petals and reflecting starlight. Beyond the trees, I could hear the ocean breathing against the shore, steady and familiar, like a heartbeat.

Our people gathered, Dragoons, Water-Dwellers, Laverians, witches, guardians, even a few Gods watching from just beyond the veil. They weren't lined up in ranks, there was no armor or weapons. Just friends, family, and survivors. There was us.

I stood beneath an arch woven from coral, moonstone, and flowering vines. The scent of salt and blossoms wrapping around me. My gown was seafoam silk, soft and cool against my skin. The fabric moving like water when I breathed. Tiny crystals caught the fading light, sparkling like droplets on a wave. A circlet of silver and shell rested on my brow. I felt like the sea had dressed me herself. On my right stood Billie.

She was a radiant calm, grounded and beautiful. Her dress shimmered like the ocean at sunrise, all shifting blues and silvers. Along the hem and bodice, delicate scales had been embroidered, honoring the mermaid's blood now singing in her veins. Pearls and coral glinted in her dark hair, and her eyes... gods, her eyes. They held that soft, fierce joy that always made me feel like I'd done something right just by existing.

On my left stood Triton looking like a king who'd finally been allowed to relax. His ceremonial robes were deep blue trimmed with silver, echoing tides and moonlight. His dark eyes were fixed on me and Billie like we were the only things in the universe. There was pride and awe, and something so tender it made my chest ache.

The officiant stepped forward, robed in white and teal, holding a braided cord of blue, green, and silver, the colors of Sea, life, and starlight. The colors of us.

"Do you come here freely and without reservation to enter into this union?" He asked, voice gentle but clear.

My heart pounded, but my voice was steady when I answered with them.

"We do."

We joined hands, my fingers laced with Billie's and Triton's, forming an unbroken circle. The officiant wrapped the cord around our joined hands, binding us together with soft careful movements.

"Then speak your vows," he said.

I went first.

"I pledge to stand by you, in calm and storm," I said, looking from Billie to Triton. "To be your anchor when the world tilts, and your sail when you're ready to chase new horizons. I will fight for you, laugh with you, and choose you, every day, in every life."

My voice shook at the end, but I didn't care. It was the truth.

Billie's turn. Her smile trembled, but her voice didn't.

"I vow to share my song and my silence," she said. "To be your solace when the world is loud, and your spark when the night feels too long. I will hold your fears, dreams and scars, and love all of you, without condition."

Triton swallowed hard, his thumb brushing over our knuckles.

"I promise to protect and cherish you," he said, voice low and reverent. "To be your strength when you are tired, and your sanctuary when you are afraid. I will stand at your side in war and in peace, in sorrow and in joy, and I will never stop choosing this family we've created together."

The officiant tied the final knot, the cord snug but gentle around our hands.

"May this binding be a testament to your unity," he said, "a symbol of your intertwined destinies. Not three paths but one, braided, strong, and unbreakable."

They smiled, eyes bright. "By the power vested in me by the Seas, the stars, and the Gods who are smart enough not to interfere, I pronounce you bound in love and fate. You may seal your vows."

I didn't hesitate.

I turned to Billie first, cupping her face in my free hand, and kissed her slow and reverent, tasting salt and tears and home. Then I turned to Triton, and he met me halfway, his hand rising to cradle my cheek as our lips met. When we broke apart, our foreheads rested together, sharing one breath, one heartbeat.

Billie tugged Triton down by his collar and kissed him too, laughing through her tears.

The clearing erupted in cheers and whistles. Someone whooped loud enough to startle the fireflies. The stream seemed to sing louder. The blossoms glowed brighter.

For the first time in a long time, the celebration wasn't just for surviving. It was for living.

It was for us, it was everything I ever dreamed of, it was perfect.

The Honeymoon

Flame and the Laverians gifted us a honeymoon that felt like a fantasy.

A private island hidden in a cradle of turquoise water, shielded by wards and watched over by gentle Sea guardians. The sand was soft and white, the palms swayed lazily in the breeze. The ocean glowed faintly at night with bioluminescent light, turning the shoreline into a ribbon of stars.

Our villa was tucked among palm trees and flowering shrubs, all white stone and open terraces. Inside, everything was soft linens, carved wood, and wide windows that opened directly onto the sea. The air smelled like salt, citrus, and something sweet I couldn't name.

But inside the master cabana, the mood shifted from serene to electric.

Silken scarves and soft ropes hung from the canopy bed, draped like constellations. A carved chest in the corner held feathers, blindfolds, and cuffs; little promises of mischief and trust. Candles flickered in wall sconces, casting golden light over plush rugs and scattered pillows.

The fire crackled softly in the hearth, its warmth mingling with the night breeze drifting through the open windows. Moonlight spilled across the floor, painting everything in silver.

Billie lay stretched across the bed in a deep blue silk robe, the fabric pooling around her thighs like liquid midnight. Her hair spilled across the pillows like ink. That smirk, her "I already know I'm going to win" smirk, curved her lips.

I stood by the open window, barefoot and wearing a sheer slip of silver gauze that clung to my body and caught the moonlight. The ocean wind toyed with the hem, teasing it around my legs. I felt strong and seen. I was wanted. The Sea Queen in her element, but this time not on a battlefield, just in a room with the two people I loved most.

Triton leaned in the doorway, watching us. His shirt hung open, showing the lines of his chest and stomach, still marked with faint scars. His long dreadlocks were damp from a swim, curling at the ends. His eyes were dark and hungry, but soft. He looked like a storm barely held in check.

I lifted my hand, palm out.

"Not yet," I said, my voice low.

He arched a brow. "Are you giving orders now, my Queen?"

I turned slowly, letting the silver fabric whisper against my skin. "I've earned the right, haven't I?"

Billie laughed, warm and husky. "She did just marry us both. Let her have her moment of ruling."

Triton pushed off the doorway and stalked closer, the air thickening with every step. "Then let her rule properly."

I stepped toward him with the ease of tidewater, cool and sure. My fingers found the tie at my waist, and I let the slip fall to the floor in a soft sigh. I stood naked in the moonlight, scars, strength and softness all on display. I met his gaze and didn't look away.

"Kneel," I said.

His breath hitched. For a second, I saw the challenge in his eyes, the King, warrior and protector. Then it melted into something else; devotion, trust and love. He lowered himself to his knees in front of me, not because I forced him, but because he chose to.

Behind me, Billie propped herself up on one elbow, eyes dark with heat and affection.

"Gods, you two are dangerous together," she said. "Am I going to have to compete for attention tonight?"

I glanced over my shoulder, lips curving. "Not to compete, rather to participate, a full ravenous night of embracing each other."

I crossed the room to the bed, sliding my fingers into Billie's hair, cupping the back of her neck. I pulled her forward and kissed her, slow and deep. She tasted like wine, laughter and safety. She sighed into my mouth, hands gripping my hips.

I eased her back against the pillows and swung a leg over, straddling her.

"You're mine tonight," I whispered against her lips.

"And every night," she breathed, already a little undone.

Behind us, Triton made a low sound in his chest. I snapped my fingers once, the sound sharp in the quiet.

"Now you may worship," I said, looking back at him.

He rose with eyes blazing and joined us.

What happened after wasn't just heat; it was healing.

I pulled the basket of the Laverian toy box closer, and I took out the black silky eye mask.

"Billie, will you let Triton and I blindfold and bind you tonight?"

"Yes, PLEASE!" Billie begged.

I placed the mask on her eyes, trying to make it snug. I kissed her deeply, then I handed Triton a furry cuff and I gestured to the bed frame. I took her right hand and with the second furry cuff I bound her to my side of the bedpost.

"Billie, you are being such a good girl, I think you need a treat." Billie laid before us like a holy offering, she arched in need making her breast perky and inviting. Her anticipation had her very aroused, I have never wanted a woman more.

"Please..." She moaned.

I picked out a large feather and took my time, mapping out her body with a soft feathery tickle. Her skin pebbled in gooseflesh and I leaned down to kiss her neck.

"I think she deserves our lips all over her body from head to toe, what do you think, Triton?"

"Oh, definitely she deserves our lips all over her." Triton leaned down to kiss her neck, as he whispered in her ear. "Baby, you taste so delicious I can't wait to taste the nectar between your thighs."

I sucked on her nipples, "Harder, please Maddy bite me please."

So my Billie wants a bit of rough play, I released her nipple with a wet pop. Billie moaned. I pulled a set of nipple clamps from the basket. I rubbed the end of it around her dark, pert nipples. "Do you want to try these clamps?" I asked then kissed her.

"Mmmm" she moaned in my mouth shaking her head yes vigorously.

"Are you sure?" I asked teasing her breast.

Triton was reverently kissing her everywhere, he skipped her apex and worked down her leg.

"Yes." Billie moaned.

I added a clamp to her right breast. "Fuck, yes!" Billie arched more, spreading her legs wide.

I placed another clamp on her other nipple. "That's my girl."

I said as my own arousal spiked seeing Billie so turned on. "Triton, I think you should please her with that talented tongue of yours."

They both moaned in response. "Gladly." Triton said in a deep sultry voice.

He moved between her legs and started eating Billie out. The sight of them laying on the red silky sheets, with Billie bound, blindfolded, naked and spread before us, was so sexy. Triton between her legs, his muscles prominent, his strength and her softness. Together, they are perfect, I was unbelievably happy to have them.

"He feels so good, licking and sucking in all the right places, doesn't he?" I asked in her ear.

"Oh, God yes."

"Cum all over his face, I want to kiss your juices from his lips."

With that she let loose, her orgasm pulsed through her whole body.

"Yes, just like that babe, you're so perfect." Triton praised.

I kissed Billie's trembling lips and then I moved to the end of the bed, cupped Triton's face in my hands and pulled him in for a thorough kiss, tasting her.

Triton moved off the bed and I took his place, kissing Billie's thighs. As her panting calmed, I started to gently lick her core. Working her slowly back up to a peak. I felt Triton from behind me. He worked his finger inside me for a short bit, when I drenched his finger, he put his huge cock into me and fucked me with his vibrating cock, working circles around my clit with his right index finger. Billie exploded with another orgasm, Triton and I came together right after, this consummation of our marriage was more than I ever imagined.

"I love you both so much." I said panting and blissfully happy.

For the rest of our honeymoon, we explored each other slowly, reverently, with laughter and whispered questions. We tested boundaries and honored them. We used cuffs and silk and playful commands, but every moment was wrapped in trust. Every touch said; you're safe now, loved and home.

"Starlight," I reminded them at one point, breathless, our agreed safe word hanging between us like a promise.

Triton kissed my wrist. "You good?" he asked quietly.

I nodded, smiling. "More than good."

We took turns leading and yielding. Triton's strength became gentleness. Billie's softness sharpened into a delicious edge. My own need for control softened into something tender and protective, even as I gave orders and they gladly obeyed.

It wasn't just sex, it was a ritual, a reclaiming.

Our bodies had been weapons and shields for so long. That night, they were just... ours. To enjoy, cherish and love each other.

Hours later, we lay tangled together in the middle of the bed, sheets twisted around our legs, skin warm and flushed. The fire had burned low, embers glowing softly. The ocean whispered beyond the windows. The moon was fading, making room for dawn.

Billie was half sprawled across my chest, one arm draped over Triton's stomach. Murial was safe and sleeping with trusted caretakers for the night, and for once, my mind wasn't racing with worry. I was just lost in love and peace... contentment.

Billie chuckled, her voice thick with sleep. "So... how do we top that tomorrow?"

Triton laughed softly, tightening his arm around us both. "We don't, we just repeat it, maybe slower."

I smiled, my fingers tracing idle patterns on their skin. "You two think you've seen all of me," I murmured. "Just wait."

Outside, the stars dimmed as dawn painted the sky in shades of purple and rose. Light spilled into the cabana, soft and warm, touching our faces like a blessing.

"We've faced battles and darkness," Triton said quietly, his voice almost reverent. "But this... this is our light."

I nodded, my heart so full it almost hurt. "Together, we've found our sanctuary."

Billie lifted her head just enough to look at us both. "Bound not just by cords," she said softly, "but by choice, by our love."

I kissed her and then Triton, slow and unhurried, sealing the words between us.

Outside, the ocean rolled in and out, steady and eternal. Inside, three hearts beat in sync, wrapped in silk, sunlight, and something stronger than any war.

Our world had nearly ended and now we were building a new one, starting right here. In this bed and on this island, with love.

For the first time, the future didn't feel like a battlefield; it felt like happily ever after.

Chapter Forty-Seven: Rising From The Rubble

-Maddy-

The new Dragoon palace was no longer made of opulence; rather built from stone, soul, and salt. Rebuilt on a high bluff overlooking the ocean, it was a fusion of elemental pride. Marble streaked with iridescent quartz carved from the sacred cliffs, and the windows reforged from shattered remnants of war. They glittered like constellations in the two moons' light. Every brick whispered of loss and hope. It wasn't perfect; however, it was alive, that was a start.

I stood barefoot in the garden courtyard, my hands buried in the soil. New life rose from the ashes, green tendrils sprouting where once there had only been ruin and ash. My magic pulsed quietly, coaxing life forward in time with my heartbeat. Wind played with my blonde hair as if the world was breathing again.

Billie emerged behind me, holding our baby wrapped in soft sea-silk woven by handmaidens of the sacred birthing pools. Her skin shimmered faintly in the moonlight, with eyes deep and endless; she watched me like the sea watches the shore.

"She won't stop staring at you," Billie said, her voice filled with warmth.

I turned, wiping my hands on my tunic. "She's already smarter than both her mothers."

Billie grinned, stepping closer. The baby reached a tiny hand toward my hair and tugged gently.

"See? She knows who's in charge," Billie teased.

Before I could answer, a warm voice cut through the peace. "Looks like the royal family's getting soft."

Triton approached, carrying crates of seed and supplies. He set them down and dropped a kiss to my temple, and then gave Billie a look that promised mischief later.

"You're late," I said.

"I was charming the rebuilders, someone has to make sure the new defenses aren't made of twigs and optimism."

They shared a laugh that was short, real, and healing.

But the moment shifted as footsteps approached. Four figures came from the path beyond the gardens, Kayla, Brooke, Talen, and Fang. Their Dragoon armor was gone, replaced by simple tunics and cloaks. Yet they carried the same gravitas; carrying ferocity that was held in check by grief.

Kayla led them, her eyes darker than before, heavier but not empty.

I straightened and walked toward them. "We are glad to see you."

Kayla nodded. "We lost too much not to help rebuild our castle."

Brooke stepped forward and pulled me into a fierce hug. "We owe you, for protecting our fathers, children and people. Most of all, our future."

I looked at each of them. The weight they carried was visible in their posture, the silence heavy.

"You owe me nothing, you saved my Triton and our people too. If you need sanctuary, you can always join us at the Water-Dwelling kingdom while you rebuild."

Fang looked down, his voice barely above a whisper. "We didn't think we'd make it out. We thought we'd be sold as Kanenites slaves. Our fathers…"

"Are safe," I said gently. "Stan is healing and already joking again. Richmond sleeps most days but wakes with strength eager to learn how to walk with one leg. Give him time," I said.

Kayla exhaled a slow breath. "We're not used to asking for help."

Billie stepped forward, placing a gentle hand on Kayla's shoulder. "Then don't think of it as help. Think of it as family supporting family."

Talen, the quietest of the group, nodded. "Family… I thought we were going to lose it all."

Triton shifted the baby into his arms. "It's loud, exhausting and worth every second."

Their laughter cracked the solemn silence. Later that evening, lanterns flickered across the courtyard. The soft glow of storm glass lit pathways lined with flowering plants that hadn't bloomed in a decade. Music drifted from what was rebuilt so far in the Dragoon palace. Dancers moved barefoot across stone floors polished with saltwater and prayers.

Billie sang a melody from Earth, her voice shimmering with enchantment. It spoke of ocean depths, deep mourning and rebirth. It held the ache of battles fought, the children born in sacred waters and futures forged in fire and salt. At least the folks of this planet thought so. We earthlings giggled at the old Johnny Depp pirate movie. Billie sure loved her movie soundtracks.

Triton danced with me, our banter echoing like waves crashing playfully against rocks. Kayla watched us from a carved bench, her expression softer than it had been since the war's end.

Ember and Brooke sat beside one another, watching Billie sway with the baby in her arms as she sang. Fang's hand reached out and found Brooke's. No one spoke; there was no need.

Chapter Forty-Eight: The Destroyer of Gods

-Harmony-

Every God, minor and major, felt it. A presence more ancient than time itself surged outward from me, like a tidal wave of raw elemental force. My wings, once made of light and hope, unfurled with arcs of black fire and silver fury. The music of the universe shifted; my Harmony now laced with a deeper, far older chord. Something the Gods had never known. Something none of them had dared speak of.

I hadn't even known it was in me. My parents had kept me hidden and muted my powers. The Destroyer was there all along, waiting.

"I... AM... HARMONY!" I declared, to all the Gods that trembled on their knees now that I had unmade Kane. He didn't die, no God truly dies. He had ceased to be.

I pulled his thread from the tapestry, unknotted it and fed it back into the Weave. It would be rewoven into something else. The silence afterward was terrifying.

Even the Gods bowed their heads, trembling in fear. I turned back to the mirror. I no longer shimmered with gentle light. Now I burned. My reflection had changed; I was not just the balance. No longer Harmony, I had become the consequence.

A whisper echoed across the pantheon, carried on the breath of terrified immortals. "She has become the Destroyer of Gods."

None dared speak against it, they knew if I could unmake Kane; I could unmake any of them.

A dark craving rose in me, sharp and intoxicating. I wanted more. More Gods to tear apart and realms to swallow. The power sang in my veins, a siren song of annihilation. It would be so easy to let go. To stop pretending I was anything but the storm at the end of all things. I almost did, almost surrendered to the darkness I had become.

Then my parents appeared before me, two of the most powerful Gods in existence. The Great Mother Goddess, radiant and fierce. The Great Creator, vast and steady as the first dawn. And with them my mate, Hecat, his eyes full of fear not of me, but for me.

They moved as one, they didn't attack, they embraced me.

Arms around my burning form, hands on my shoulders and face, with wings that cradled me gently. Their essences wrapped around mine, not as chains, but as anchors. They didn't force me down; they reminded me I had somewhere to land.

I could have thrown them off and devoured them. Somewhere deep inside, the Destroyer wanted to.

But somewhere deeper, I knew I loved them and I let that part of me decide.

The craving shuddered. The Void inside me screamed, furious at being denied. But it receded, inch by agonizing inch. Once again, my love for my family calmed my darkness.

Devotion rose to meet it, voices calling not to a weapon, but to a mother and savior to Harmony.

"I want to be her again," I whispered, my voice breaking. "But I don't remember how."

"You don't have to," Hecat said, stepping closer, his hand brushing mine. "Let us remind you."

He poured his essence into my fingers. Warmth and love, the feel of our first kiss. The ocean wind that had carried my laughter. Murial's name whispered like a lullaby that hadn't yet been sung but already existed in our hearts.

The Mother Goddess took my other hand. "You nursed life in your womb, not war," she murmured. "You touched stars into being with a laugh. You braided galaxies from nothing but dreams."

The Great Creator touched my forehead. His power was vast, but his touch was gentle. "And you are loved," he said. "Endlessly and fiercely."

My knees buckled, I fell and Hecat caught me as if I were made of fragile glass, holding me to his chest.

My light sputtered, then burst in a rush of golden warmth. Across the heavens, the wound in the sky began to heal. On my planet, the eclipse broke into radiant dawn. In the celestial plane, the other Gods wept as their knees hit the ground. Not from fear this time, but reverence.

The Destroyer was still there, coiled deep within me, but quiet.

In her place, at the surface, stood Harmony whole and healed; with endless power but no longer ruled by it.

Tears streaked my cheeks. I clung to Hecat, shaking. "I remember now," I sobbed. "I remember love."

He kissed my hair, his voice a low promise against my ear. "Then we're safe."

My Mother Goddess knelt beside us, pressing her hand over my heart. "The war is done," she said softly. "Now you must rest."

"No," I answered, and my voice was no longer just sound, it was a melody of creation, threaded with every life I'd ever touched. "Now I will heal the planet, my people and myself."

The Great Creator smiled with a depth only a being older than time could hold. "That's my girl," he said, pride warming his tone.

The cosmos exhaled, and I watched as the moons climbed high and the stars emerged like curious spirits.

Then I stepped through the Veil and appeared before everyone.

I no longer walked with the crushing weight of the divine. I returned to simply being Harmony. Power still rippled beneath my skin, but it was calm now, like a great sea sleeping after a storm.

I joined them in silence, gazing around at the new world we'd nearly lost.

"You've done the impossible," I whispered to Maddy.

"No," Maddy said, smiling softly. "We did, all of us." I nodded.

"Then let this be a new era, one of unity and light. I am finally home again." I did not vanish.

Magic returned to the people, not as punishment, but as promise.

Over the coming weeks, the world was rebuilt. Terrek and his wives, Darah and Flame, returned to the Hecate universe, but left galactic enforcers and glacial aliens to build an outer atmosphere space port. The Kanenites were no more. The great alliance was forged not in diplomacy chambers, but in gardens and courtyards and at the bed-sides of the wounded.

The handfasting vows of Maddy, Billie, and Triton became legend. Spoken beneath a sky of violet fireflies, their words bound heart to soul and soul to starlight. Their love, chaotic and eternal, became the keystone upon which peace was laid.

Not all wounds healed clean, nor every scar faded. But they were worn like armor, proof of survival and love.

In time, the baby we named Murial would take her first steps in those same gardens. Her laughter would echo in the temple halls. Her magic, born of water, fire, and defiance; infused with Demigod power unlike anything the worlds had ever seen.

The Dragoon throne stood beside my people. The stars once silent, now sang.

A new age had begun, it was perfect and radiant...and ours.

Chapter Forty-Nine: Gods

-Grandma & Grandpa-

It was midmorning on Harmony's world, and a slow golden mist drifted over the garden like spilled sunlight. The flowers buzzed softly, whispering to one another. The tongue of old magic, and the house by the sea glowed gently with joy.

Inside, a very ancient, very powerful being tiptoed.

Hecat, Eternal Architect of Stars, God of Time and the Great Creator of All Living Worlds in the Hecat universe, had a mermaid-print apron tied around his waist and was balancing two mugs of warm cocoa while wearing socks that said "#1 Grandpa".

"Careful now…" he muttered, brows furrowed as he floated the mugs into the next room with a flick of his fingers. "Don't spill, don't wake her… oh damn, she's got the teacup again."

From the center of a nest of blankets and plushies, little Murial, six years old, sat. She was part water-dweller, wholly stardust as she was a little Goddess, and holding a chipped porcelain cup clutched in both hands.

"I'm serving cosmic tea," she announced grandly, pretending to pour from an invisible kettle. "It tastes like moonlight and secrets."

Hecat chuckled. "Of course it does, my little moonstone."

"Don't forget to slurp," she added, very seriously. "That's the law."

"Slurp it is," Harmony's voice said from behind him.

She floated down the staircase barefoot, wearing a soft robe that shimmered like starlight through diamonds. Her golden silver-white hair was pulled up in a lazy twist. Stardust still clung to her skin from the night before.

Hecat turned to her with open adoration, pressing a warm mug into her hands.

"Morning, wife of my soul," he said, kissing her temple. "The child Goddess has demanded tea and slurping rituals."

"She's clearly in charge here," Harmony replied, dropping to the floor with the grace of a falling feather. "We must obey."

Murial beamed as she handed Harmony a teacup. "Now we're having a tea party of legends."

Hecat sipped the fake tea with an exaggerated slurp, earning a satisfied nod from Murial.

Harmony raised her cup. "To mud dragons and mermaids."

Murial lifted hers. "And to kissing!"

Hecat choked.

Harmony grinned. "And who have you been watching to learn about kissing?"

Murial pointed toward the window, where Maddy, Billie, and Triton were waving goodbye and climbing aboard the claws of Ember's dragon form.

"They smooch a lot," Murial said wisely. "Especially when they think no one's looking."

"Well, they are in love," Hecat said. "Today's their special day. Their wedding anniversary."

Maddy adjusted her hold on Triton's arm, water sparkling beneath them as they skimmed over the sea. They flew toward a crescent-shaped cove, where a secret waterfall spilled down to a cliff of glowing stone, hiding a retreat carved eons ago by skilled carpenters.

"Thanks for the lift, Ember." Triton bellowed.

"Anytime, have fun!" Her answer boomed in our heads.

The waterfall loomed ahead, and they disappeared through its curtain into warm steamy mist, laughter trailing behind them.

"Can you believe we've been together this long?" Billie murmured, leaning back into Triton's arms as they settled into the bed.

"I can," Triton said, kissing the top of her head. "Because I remember every second of it."

"Still smooth," Maddy grinned, leaning in for a kiss.

"Happy anniversary, my loves," Billie whispered, tangling her fingers with theirs.

Back in the garden, Hecat and Harmony had been thoroughly defeated by a game called Hide and Roar; which consisted of Murial vanishing behind magical bushes and leaping out at random intervals with a battle cry.

Hecat had fallen dramatically to the ground at least four times.

"I've been slain!" he declared, flailing his arms.

Murial stood over him proudly. "You'll live. I'll heal you with a lollipop."

Harmony, sitting nearby and conjuring floating star-shaped bubbles for Murial to chase, watched her husband with a soft smile. These were the moments that kept her grounded, more than the worship of galaxies or the reverence of pantheons.

"I still remember the first time I held her," Harmony whispered. "She was so tiny, just a flicker of power, but so bright. I touched her in Billie's womb and made her family. I didn't think I could love again, not after the darkness. But here we are."

Hecat rose and sat beside her, brushing his thumb along her cheek.

"You gave the universes so much," he said. "You deserved something back. This? This is the universe saying thank you."

They watched Murial try to teach a confused bird how to juggle.

"I think she's going to accidentally rewrite reality someday," Harmony murmured.

"She already has," Hecat said, eyes misty. "You just haven't noticed."

That evening, after a dinner of magically summoned pancakes and an interpretive dance about jellyfish (performed by Murial), the trio settled on the porch.

Murial fell asleep curled on Harmony's lap, drooling slightly on her gown. Harmony didn't mind. She cradled her gently, her fingers brushing back sea-blue curls.

"She's dreaming," she said softly.

Hecat looked up from his carved pipe, smile warm. "Of what?"

"Of flying whales," Harmony replied. "Of cupcakes that sing cake sprinkle."

Hecat chuckled. "She gets that from you."

Silence wrapped around them as the stars blinked into view. Constellations slowly rearranging themselves in reverence to welcome the Goddess...the creator Murial.

But here on this porch, in this simple life, none of that mattered. What mattered was the little hand curled in Harmony's. The safety of the world they'd saved. The love they could finally rest in.

"I don't need to be the Goddess of Gods tonight," Harmony whispered.

Hecat kissed her hand. "You never did. You only needed to be you."

Above them, the stars sang a lullaby. Not to a deity or to a destroyer. To a grandmother cradling the future, and the God who loved her. As new life sparked in Maddy's womb. "We are having another grandbaby." Hecat chuckled. "It had to be another girl, didn't it."

"Well, I have to keep you on your toes, don't I." Harmony smiled.

Together at last in peace.

The End.

Meanwhile, in the
Temple of Origins...

-The All-knowing Mother-

The Mother Goddess stood alone in the vault beneath the first stars, eyes closed, her hands soaked in shimmering light. Around her, runes burned into the marble sky, spelling an ancient truth the Gods had long forgotten.

Love alone would not be enough this time. This enemy, a monster bred from Kane's hatred, was not born of war. It was born of survival and drops of his blood. A twisted survival, that the Void had allowed to create balance. It would wait until Harmony was peaceful. Until she was vulnerable. Until she had something precious to lose again.

The Mother began to shape the warriors from divine essence, something powerful enough to combat the monsters that grew. The fury of her angels, from the blades of Azrael and the fire of Alice. From the broken hearts of mortals and the cries of children. The great Mother broke all celestial treaties and ancient oaths.

She formed them not in the image of the Gods, but in the image of justice, of righteous destruction. The Nephilim. Her final creation. From her most powerful angels. Avengers made flesh. They are not made to rule, or heal, not made to adhere to the Gods like the avenging angels.

They are made to end what Gods could not.

Seven of them rose from the blood from Kane, monsters of pure evil, born when Azrael himself spilled the blood of a greater God. Unheard of, for an angel. Only Nephilim, born of her avenging angels, could stand against those vile celestial monsters now.

Each one forged from the Mother's pain. Each one is unshakably loyal to the Mother of All.

Because if that darkness rose to its full strength... If the monster slithered forth into the stars and among the Gods... It would not find a Goddess waiting to reason, it would wake the Destroyer in Harmony.

In the deepest places... those blood-born things opened their eyes. Seven white fires blazed in the dark, drawing closer, it hissed.

"Not yet." The Mother whispered, drawing their attention. When they rise, it would challenge even the Great Creator.

The Mother's Nephilim would be there. They won't be heroes or saints, they will be endings for that evil. Should they fail, all might be doomed.

Azrael stood at the edge of the altar, eyes closed, wings furled tight like a blade sheathed. His mate, Alice, knelt in prayer, not to any God. To the Great Mother, their child had been the beginning of the Nephilim.

Now, the runes on the temple walls pulsed with an ancient rhythm, older than time itself. The call had come, a low growl echoed across the multiverse, so deep it cracked moons and sent celestial beasts fleeing. Something beneath the layers, something made of hatred and God-ichor, was awake.

The monsters born from Kane's blood were no longer sleeping. The Mother had been busy making true mates for the strongest of avenging angels so she could create a league of Nephilim to battle the seven monsters.

Somewhere, Harmony woke in a sweat.

She felt it, a tug beneath her ribs, the shiver in the stars and the echo of a scream yet to happen.

On her planet, little Murial sat still on the saddle of her Pegasus along the shore. Her tiny wings buzzed. Her eyes glowed. She clutched her stuffed dragon tighter. She didn't know what was coming. But she knew this:

"Grandma's gonna need help."

Enjoy a sneak peek into the Avenging Angel Series

-Azreal-

S itting in this Seattle biker bar, I observe all the patrons, if that's what you call them. Most of these humans are generally dicks, real assholes. Personally, I'd eliminate them all; they're just wasting good oxygen.

I am hardwired to seek out evil, so hate, anger, and dicks annoyingly ping my radar. All of that infects this bar. It is very aggravating here.

The Creator made me for one purpose: to be one of his avenging angels. So, here I sit, almost human-like, designed to blend in and understand these beings. I have desires, opinions, and thoughts, but I'm bound to my creator's will.

"Don't get me wrong, I love the old God. He is my father, in a sense of being my creator, but he has his own vision for these humans. He loves them and focuses on them mostly. I don't understand it myself. However, he's the big boss, and no one would dare defy him."

Well, there's one guy I know. I chuckle thinking about Lucifer, he always speaks his mind. I will never understand how he does and gets away with it.

I have my own thoughts, but they remain just thoughts, I'm ever the obedient avenging angel. I am here for one punk of a man, a glitch in the system. He's irredeemably broken and evil from birth. In my opinion, my father takes way too long to mark someone irredeemable.

Like most of the assholes in this bar, they feed off each other, festering in their evil, growing like a fetus in the womb. Once they go too far, God finally marks them.

In my experience, assholes like these inevitably meet their doom. Again, I am not in charge.

I stare at the man's aura I am waiting for. His beacon is about to give me a green light.

The server, a beautiful Hispanic woman, is unique and empathetic. I sense her light pulsing with fear and frustration. She doesn't belong here.

She sees evil around her, like me. Chaos gravitates toward her. If I had free will, I'd help mute her empathic visions. I could easily be her friend; we both generally hate people.

She walks past my target, who grabs her ass. He's been fantasizing about all the vile things he wants to do to her. Not tonight. I fist my hands in anticipation. She drops her tray of drinks on him, and I smile, getting off the bar stool to get him.

His mark flares as he stands, dropping his chair. A trance freezes her; I see his vision clearly, this psycho harming an innocent woman.

Fuck! I am frozen, forced to watch. This shit pisses me off— I marked this asshole; he's mine. Nothing should restrain me.

I watch her fearlessly confront him, see him raise a fist. I strain to resist the power holding me back.

"Why?" I scream at my maker in my head, startling us both. I've never done that before. Something's changing. I feel my chains loosening. My will soon to be uncaged.

I feel the weight of God's attention, want to sink to my knees, but I am frozen.

"She belongs to Harmony. Mind your business, Azrael." Every fiber of my being sizzles with pain. I just got spanked.

Anger seethes, but I don't care for my father's attention, much less his anger. Though stern, I sensed amusement from him. I can't fathom his genuine anger.

It's bad enough dealing with death and the chore of eradicating irredeemable evil.

I've heard of Harmony, a mystery in the realm of the Gods. Lilith mentioned wanting to visit her, then changed the subject when she saw me. Now, the Creator says this woman belongs to Harmony.

Who is Harmony that my father would give her a human? My mind races. No one in the God realms dares to near the humans, much less claim one. I focus on the woman.

My probing usually reveals when I or my brothers will arrive at someone's death, hers is hidden from me. Another anomaly I've never experienced.

I watch helplessly as the bouncer grabs the lady by the arm and drags her away. "Kayla! Stop fighting the customers," he booms.

The owner, Mike, offers a towel to the asshole who almost punched his server.

"Here, man. Next round's on me," Mike says. What a pussy for not protecting his employees.

"You ought to train them waitresses up better. They should know their place," the asshole yells.

"I got it. She's fired. Sorry, man. She's a klutz," Mike says, grabbing her purse and heading out back.

The flaring blackness marking him is my cue. It's stifling, the compulsion to act, being frozen makes me fume. As he settles back, drinking his free booze, my chain snaps. I am moving.

He grabs a pint of beer off another server's tray, as she rushes to serve the customers and continue business as usual.

"Hey, that's not for you! Derrek, deal with this dude!" she hollers.

I ignore her and Derek, step closer to my target. I raise the pint and smash it on the asshat's head. The glass shatters with a satisfying crunch.

The big tattooed man falls to the floor, clutching his bleeding head as his buddies jump me.

"Our president is down!" a biker shouts, proudly displaying a Sergeant at Arms patch on the chest of his leather vest. Like the weasel at my feet, this knock-off biker gang thinks they're hot shit.

They're atrocious, shitty human beings. I smile, and the tough guy in front of me pisses his pants as my angelic power seeps through my eyes. I show him his fate; he falls to his knees weeping.

"Derrek, get your ass in here and deal with this mess!" Mike calls from the back.

They call him "Ripper" what a joke. He struggles to stand; I kick him back down to the beer-stained floor. His jaw shatters into a gruesome mangled mess.

His pals swarmed me like angry ants. I throw the guy on my back, one-handed over tables to the bar, shattering the bottles and the grimy mirror.

They freeze at my supernatural strength. My dark wings unfurl, the human illusion gone.

These humans fall to their knees, seeing a vision of what they'll become if they feed their inner evil.

I am their nightmare, the thing in the dark. Their final destination, heaven or purgatory. Justice is mine, and my brothers', for we are the avenging angels.

The irredeemable are mine to punish, and mine to annihilate. I lift Ripper; too mutilated to beg, I feel his internal plea.

My body bursts into flames, black wings ablaze, my monstrous fiery skull opens wide. I grow, swallowing Morris, who called himself Ripper.

I am a gateway, a portal to purgatory or heaven. This guy goes to my special place. A prison of misery to let him suffer ten times worse than his victims. His soul is consumed by unending suffering.

He is stuck in his head, feeling what he did from his victim's perspective. I increase his fear and pain so he can truly feel the justice I seek. As his soul turns to mush, I unmake him by taking his soul into my burning hands and disintegrating it.

Morris the Ripper is no longer anything. There is no reincarnation, no heaven, no purgatory; he is now unmade into nothingness. It took me only a moment to dish out this justice.

From Morris's perspective, he was suffering endlessly in a timeless loop. Time is a human concept. It is simply of no relevance to me or my kind.

Humans think Lucifer is trapped in hell, and he takes evil souls. Lucifer is content with his domain in the underworld and prefers solitude.

I am death, and one of God's avenging angels. My hell is what humans should fear.

I left my irredeemable prison to check on the souls in purgatory. Some were leaving, having learned their lesson and chosen a new life in reincarnation. I wished them well and sent them on to their next life. Others remain trapped in their loop, unwilling to accept accountability and move on.

I felt that all too familiar itch in my wings and the compulsion to hunt another marked soul. The monotonous duty repeated itself, as this was my purpose and my eternal existence.

Like
Share
Follow
Author Tanya Steverding
Thank you!
PLEASE Review
goodreads
amazon
https://linktr.ee
/tanyasteverding
JOIN ME LIVE
monthly GIVEAWAY!
Blind date with a book!
& Author, Interviews with
a sip & paint class

www.ingramcontent.com/pod-product-compliance
Lightning Source LLC
Chambersburg PA
CBHW030748310726
48969CB00005B/1349